Praise for MERCY

"*Mercy* is compulsively readable, a triumph of
York's storytelling prowess. It would be an impressive
novel from an established author; from a debut novelist,
it is a small miracle, graceful and unflinching, violent and
beautiful, heartfelt and haunting. . . . While it has much
in common with Ann-Marie MacDonald's *Fall on Your
Knees* and Gail Anderson-Dargatz's *The Cure for Death
by Lightning . . . Mercy* is by far the strongest of the
three novels, riskier, more challenging and,
ultimately, more rewarding."
The Vancouver Sun

"Lean and poetic . . . potently seductive."
Now (Toronto)

"York is emotionally unflinching, and her writing is
sharp-edged and intense. She can depict both beauty and
rot with equal felicity. . . . The novel ultimately ascends to a
level of Gothic melodrama that thousands of *Fall on Your
Knees* fans will no doubt adore. . . . Rewarding . . .
a blinding flash of light, a flare gun in a
darkening universe of lost souls."
The Globe and Mail

"The first novel by Winnipeg writer Alissa York is
stunning in its emotive power and emotional resonance.
York's prose is taut and finely honed; her themes and the
characters and settings that propel them are far-reaching
and profound. It's sensual, full of yearning and longing
for the heat of love. . . . York has wrought a wonderful,
thrilling, complex, immensely satisfying tale. . . . York's
novel is beauty in words, and *Mercy* be upon us."
The Hamilton Spectator

MERCY

✝

A Novel

ALISSA YORK

VINTAGE CANADA

VINTAGE CANADA EDITION, 2003

Copyright © 2003 Alissa York

All rights reserved under International and Pan-American Copyright Conventions. No part of this book may be reproduced in any form or by any electronic or mechanical means, including information storage and retrieval systems, without permission in writing from the publisher, except by a reviewer, who may quote brief passages in a review. Published in Canada by Vintage Canada, a division of Random House of Canada Limited, Toronto. Originally published in 2003 by Random House Canada, a division of Random House of Canada Limited. Distributed in Canada by Random House of Canada Limited. Vintage Canada and colophon are registered trademarks of Random House of Canada Limited.

www.randomhouse.ca

National Library of Canada Cataloguing in Publication

York, Alissa
        Mercy / Alissa York.

ISBN 0-679-31217-X

I. Title.

PS8597.O46M47 2003a   C813'.54   C2003-902074-6
PR9199.3.Y523M47 2003a

Text design by CS Richardson

Cover design by CS Richardson

Printed and bound in Canada

10   9   8   7   6   5   4   3   2   I

for my mother, Ann,
and as always
for Clive

what I wouldn't give for arms to hold you.
we are creatures of such like desires.

Christine Fellows, "bird as prophet"

‡

The moon is my mother. She is not sweet like Mary.
Her blue garments unloose small bats and owls.

Sylvia Plath, "The Moon and the Yew Tree"

THEN

‡

(June 1948 – June 1949)

I

BEEF: A GOOD BLEED

Six o'clock. Thomas Rose steps out from behind his counter and crosses to the shop window, finding Train Street long with light, deserted for the supper hour. In the opposing storefront he can see Hy Warner bending to sweep the last feathery mound of hair into his dustpan. Thomas lifts his hand as Hy straightens, anticipating the barber's evening wave. It's a small thing—the kind of thing Thomas was dying for when he landed in Mercy, Manitoba, determined to call it home.

He might not have made the best impression that day— a sweetish stench wafting before him down the corridors of the town hall—but he had an honest face, hard-working hands and, most importantly, the down payment in cash. Besides, the purchase seemed meant to be. The butcher shop's previous owner was called Ross, so Thomas didn't have to lay out for a whole new sign. Just change the second *s* to an *e* and it was Rose's Fine Meats. To celebrate, he had the sign painter crack open a small can of red and add a garish, overblown rose.

Upon finding that the place had no killing room, he immediately set about converting the garage. He had a sink plumbed in, sunk a drain in the concrete floor, screwed in hooks, rigged up a couple of block-and-tackle hoists. Two tables, a hog vat, a V-shaped box for lambs. It seemed the late Charlie Ross had taken on only butcher-ready carcasses and wholesale cuts. Thomas didn't judge him for it, either. He knew better than anyone, slaughtering was a whole other thing.

It's four years now since he built it, and the killing room has long since paid off. It'll keep on paying, too, just so long as there are those who haven't the stomach to slaughter their own. Take the heifer he's got tied up in there now, hauled in that morning by Ida Stone. Poor woman—husband long dead, stuck raising her drunk daughter's kids.

"They've gotten attached to the animal," Ida confided across the cow's back. "Especially the boy. You know how the city makes them. I'd keep her for a pet if I could, but a woman in my position doesn't have a whole lot of choice."

"Never you mind, Mrs. Stone," Thomas assured her. "She'll come back to you in brown paper parcels. They'll never be the wiser."

He's a great comfort to the women of the town. They linger gossiping in his shop, find themselves buying finer cuts than they're used to, asking for cooking tips, how long and how hot, even what side dish to serve. He listens to them, really listens. He doesn't have to try, either—growing up, he was his mother's only friend.

He's entertaining, too, another skill he honed at home, reaching down into Sarah Rose's dark. Sometimes he impresses the housewives of Mercy with his hands, surprisingly agile for their size. Without warning he'll take the tip of his knife to a steak fillet and carve a snowflake or a butterfly or a bird.

4

He opens the screen door to pull the glass one shut, flips the sign to read *Sorry We're Closed*. So what if he puts on a bit of a show. It's good for business, and it doesn't hurt to hear a woman's laugh now and then, feel the warmth of a female smile. He pauses, grinning to himself. After tomorrow he'll have all the female warmth he needs.

He opens the killing-room door, and the cow lifts her head and lows softly. Thomas is good with animals, always has been. She's calm, a little curious even, despite the strange surroundings, the rope at her ankles, the sledge-hammer in his hand.

He could've had his pick in that town. The hiccup in his heart kept him out of the war, but otherwise he's in his prime, not exactly handsome, but not bad either, beefy, a build plenty of women like. His sandy brush cut harbours little grey. He owns his own business and the apartment above, and if he takes a drink now and then, it's never more than two.

He's had offers. The Price girl hanging over his display case, all but spilling out the top of her dress. Or Pauline Trask—those long, lashy stares while she complains about her husband going out on the rails for nights at a time. Rachel Kane has cooled off now she's married, but Thomas can still remember the day she broke down in his shop, crying about her fiancé blown to bits overseas. She bawled until he offered a shoulder, then snuggled in close, moving her small, wet mouth against his neck.

But there's only ever been Mathilda. She was the first person he spoke to upon arriving in Mercy on foot, grey with road dust and reeking of pork. When he asked her for directions, she pointed without a single word. No one would call Mathilda pretty. Sloe-eyed and slender, with loose red hair, she made a far deeper impression than that. She was too young for marrying, so he waited. Four long years he waited, until the day she turned nineteen. Meantime, he heard all about her from behind his counter.

Transplanted to Mercy at the tender age of nine, she was niece to the Catholic church housekeeper, the wild-oat progeny of a wayward brother long gone. Mathilda had her father's looks, though most agreed they sat better on a boy—Jimmy Nickels always having been one to tie a girl's stomach up in knots. God only knows what the mother was. She was either dead or no mother at all, for the child had been shut up in an orphanage since infancy.

And just how did the housekeeper get wind of her abandoned niece? Some said Jimmy wrote a letter—one of very few indeed—in which he hinted at a Winnipeg girl he'd got in trouble and left behind. No return address but postmarked Yellowknife, or Vancouver, or Chicago, Illinois. Others claimed it was one of the sisters at the orphanage who wrote, a new one perhaps, who made an extra effort to track relations down. In any case, Vera Nickels boarded the westbound train alone and stepped off the eastbound two days later with her chin in the air and a slip of a girl in tow. It was anyone's guess under what sordid circumstances Mathilda had been conceived. "You know those Catholics," Louise Harlen said once, after making sure there were none in the shop.

Thomas moves in close to the heifer and pats her hot flank. "Mmmmm," he murmurs in her flicking ear, "mmm, mmmm."

6

He steps out in front of her and she lowers her head, closing her eyes for a scratch. As if through a scope, two cross-hairs appear, extending from the base of each horn to the opposite eye. Thomas hoists the sledge, strikes short and sure in the crook of the invisible cross. The cow sags, crashing to her side at his feet.

From the beginning Mathilda put him in mind of a doe. Not the way most people think of them, passive and maternal, nibbling leaves. Thomas knew their insides. His old man took a yearly trip back to the bush he came from, hunting over the limit, out of season, regardless of sex—the owner of a slaughterhouse killing on his own time. The deer he hauled home were radiant beneath their hides, scanty scented fat over muscle meat rich and red. As graceful on the cutting table as they were among the trees. The loveliest carcasses Thomas had ever seen.

He picks up his sticking knife and turns his back to the stunned cow, stretching its neck out long by bracing his boot heels against foreleg and jaw. Bending and reaching back between his legs, he starts at its breast-bone, cutting a foot-long slit up the throat, deep enough so the windpipe shows. He lifts the blade out and re-enters where he began. Tip pointed to the shoulder-tops, he cuts down hard toward the head. Severed vessels spurt. Thomas spins round and stoops to grab the beast's tail, placing one boot firmly on its side. Begins pumping, weight on the foot, then release and pull up hard on the tail. Over and over, make a heart of the body to hasten the bleed.

It's after midnight when Father August Day passes the wooden *Welcome to Mercy* sign three hours later than planned.

It had all added up on the map, but once he turned off the trunk road, a mile was no longer simply a mile. Coyotes rose up from the fields and darted madly between his wheels. Deer looked round on the long columns of their necks, flashed their eyes and stepped delicately onto the road. North of Mercy, where the trees closed in, he passed through a cloud of bats. He was unused to driving anywhere, let alone in the wilderness dark. Many would've ploughed on through, flattening whatever was destined to die, but August braked and braked, eventually slowing to a crawl.

It's a good-sized town—about double his hometown of Fairview. As the road carries him south into Mercy's heart, he mentally contrasts the two, taking comfort in every discrepancy he finds. To either side the sleeping houses look solid, more dependable than even the finest of Fairview's wind-beaten homes. So much more sensible to nestle a settlement among trees than to raise it exposed on the plain.

Hedged residences give way to shops—*Harlen's Pharmacy, Conklin Grocery, Taggart and Sons Dry Goods*—August committing each new name to memory as he rolls slowly past. Idling at the centre of town, he glances up at the crossed signs—*Fourth Avenue, Train Street*—and thinks briefly of Fairview's pitiful main drag.

To his left, Train Street recedes in a line of storefronts, including the office of the *Mercy Herald* and a skinny barbershop complete with candy-stick pole. At the limit of his vision, a poorly lit brick station surrounded by freight cars at rest on a yard. August looks right. Some four or five blocks down, the street comes to an abrupt end, culminating in an imposing silhouette. He feels his heart kick. Takes the turn without signalling, pressing his foot to the gas.

In his waking mind he's saddened by the unexpected death of Father Rock, the pastor he was to assist. His dreams are a different story. In the land of no volition August steps blithely into the dead man's gleaming shoes. He's young to be taking on a parish—newly ordained, still growth-spurt thin at twenty-six—but the bishop saw past all that. He noticed August's scholarly stoop, his old man's mouth and stony eyes. At the news of Father Rock's passing, he shocked the diocese by directing August to simply "carry on as planned." One year as an administrator and, if all went well, Mercy would be his.

August kills the engine and unfolds his lanky frame from the Plymouth's front seat. He stares up into the blunt face of the church, its heavy peaked doors pointing to the central window—a rose motif, glimmering warmly, centred on the Madonna and Child. The Church of St. Mary Immaculate. Within these very stone walls he will give voice to the Gospel, administer the seven sacraments, celebrate the grace of God. He lets out a long, satisfied sigh. *Alter Christus.* Finally, another Christ.

Beside the church, set back as though in modesty, the rectory's cut from more of the same speckled stone. Its door opens slowly to reveal a small woman, shapeless in a dark housedress, her hair raked up high into a grizzled bun.

"Father Day, I suppose?" Her voice carries sharply over the darkened yard, its tone belying his title, pronouncing him too green, too insubstantial to bear its weight. She has him at a disadvantage—he can't make out her face, knows his own to be flooded with coloured light.

"Correct," he answers, returning his eyes to the church.

"You're late."

He steels himself. Stoops down for his cases, takes the flagstone path in loping strides. Up close he meets a face perhaps once oddly fetching, now thoroughly pinched and drained. She's a good foot shorter than him, and she won't look up.

"I'm Vera Nickels," she tells his chest, "housekeeper these forty years."

He nods.

"There's a wedding tomorrow, in case you didn't know."

"I have been informed."

"It's my own niece getting married."

"Yes."

"The poor girl's tossing and turning upstairs."

He says nothing. Several seconds of stalemate elapse before she reaches inside to snap on the light. "Well, Father. Come in if you're coming."

HIS EYES

Mathilda's mind moves sluggishly, her thoughts stumbling as though drugged. *Wedding day.* She can't think how it happened, except that the butcher had asked.

It certainly wasn't the lure of family. In all her years at

St. Joseph's, Mathilda never once joined the others in their favourite game. *My perfect home*, they called it, spinning candy houses and lovesick parents out of air. She pitied them. What good were parents? Of her father she knew nothing at the time, of her mother only what little the Sister Superior had seen fit to divulge. She had been a dancer. She had given birth south of the city, at a house for unwed mothers run by the St. Norbert Sisters of Misericorde. Shortly thereafter she had died.

Many would have imagined a delicate woman on tiptoe, swathed in chiffon, lifted heavenward in a series of mournful pirouettes. Mathilda allowed herself no such luxury. To her the word *dancer* conjured up a painted face, a series of grotesque gyrations and vulgar, revealing kicks. While dancers gestured obscenely, she adopted the nun's trick of keeping her hands hidden and clasped. While they hammered the floor with their heels, she cultivated the soundless convent glide.

Let the other children dream of relations. When Mathilda projected a picture of herself into the future, it was inevitably a formal portrait of sorts, wherein she sat utterly composed and alone.

The change, such as it was, came in the form of a single crab-handed page, its folds so sharp they looked to have been ironed. She was wedged between two baskets of mending, darning a worn elbow, when Sister L'Espérance dropped the letter in her lap. "Aunt?" Mathilda turned the word over cautiously in her mouth. "I have an aunt?"

It's nearly time. She knows this by the increased intensity with which her Aunt Vera yanks stray threads from the veil. Mathilda glances at herself in the mirror. With her rusty hair drawn back in a knot, she's even more pie-faced and speckled than usual. She has no illusions, thinks herself neither pretty nor plain. Never having watched herself walk, she has no notion of her potential power over men.

Vera's tugging harder now, muttering in her ear, "—half of them lost in the war, and this one with his own business, and clean and well-mannered into the bargain." She pauses for air. "Not a Catholic, true, but he can scarcely help the heathen he was born to."

"No, Aunt."

"For pity's sake, Mathilda, *smile*. Were you waiting for wine and roses? Butterflies in your belly at the sight of him?" Vera heaves out a sigh. "He converted for you, girl. That shows consideration, and in the end a little consideration is worth more than all the blessed butterflies in the world."

Mathilda stares mutely into the glass. A vein dances in Vera's temple. "Now you listen to me." Her fingertips fasten into Mathilda's arms. "You're the bastard niece of the church skivvy, you haven't a penny to your name and you're no great beauty besides, but this one, *this one* came begging for your hand." She continues through clenched teeth. "You ought to be laughing. You ought to be rolling in the aisles at your luck, so the least you could manage is a smile!" Suddenly aware of her grasp, she flinches and lets go, covering her face with her hands.

Mathilda turns in her chair. "It's all right, Aunt Vera. Really. I'm all right."

She lays a careful hand on the older woman's hip. Her aunt is rail thin beneath her one good dress. It's a sombre shade of blue, otherwise indistinguishable from its rack-mates, every one of them spinster black.

Vera wipes her cheeks viciously. "Look at me, stupid old trout—"

"No," Mathilda murmurs. "It's just all the fuss on top of everything that's happened. Father Rock and all—"

Vera's face splits like a wound.

"Oh, Aunt." Mathilda stands and folds the hard little woman in her arms. Vera shudders against her, bawling a wet streak down the satiny shoulder of Mathilda's dress. That's when the organ sounds, so that's how the bride approaches the aisle, soggy-shouldered, following her sobbing aunt.

The church is roughly one-quarter full—not bad for a Tuesday wedding, especially one where the groom has no family and the bride has no friends. Peter Jablonsky shuffles forward to meet them, decrepit in his ill-fitting Knights of Columbus blazer. He grabs Mathilda's arm and steers her, patting her hand and muttering, preparing to give her away. She takes in Thomas's thick, twisting neck and trusting grin, then drops her eyes. Her shoes are two white, pointy-nosed rats, peeking out singly and retreating beneath her dress.

She looks up when she reaches the altar. Not to the new priest, not even to the groom, whose eyes seek hers, but beyond, to the crucifix, Christ's enormous wooden form. He's painted beautifully, his skin the exact colour of cloud.

The priest's voice draws her down. It's throaty, a little hoarse even, as though he's addressing her alone. She shifts her gaze to its source, the Adam's apple sharp in his throat, scoring his long neck from the inside.

Under a dark overhang of hair, his eyes are black. No, Mathilda corrects herself, grey. She peers at him. They're both, charcoal with black ripples, a series of concentric bands. The butcher dissolves at her side. For the moment she forgets everything about him—the stubborn blood beneath his nails, his helpless smile, his name.

When it comes time for Mathilda to speak, her jaw moves woodenly in the monotone of the entranced. The new Father may be young, but his eyes are ancient. Ringed with time like a fossilized tree.

During the reception Vera ricochets about the church basement like a thing possessed, piling plates high, filling coffee cups and wineglasses before they can empty by half.

Two weeks earlier, Mathilda was the one who ran around. Every ambulatory Catholic in the parish was there—the faithful and the fallen. They all ate sandwiches and little cakes, a few even tied one on in memory of Father Rock. Father Beaubien had done a passable job of the service. He stayed long enough to lift a few glasses before doddering back to St. Antoine.

There was no comforting Vera. She sat rigid as a corpse all afternoon, staring clean through any kind soul who tried. As soon as she could get away with it, Mathilda escorted her aunt back to the rectory, where Father Rock's dogs were locked up in the kitchen, howling.

"Shut up, all of you!" Vera rushed at them. "Shut up! SHUT UP!!" She hauled open the back screen door. "He's gone, do you hear me?! He's gone! NOW GET!" The dogs got the message in the form of a broom at their backsides. They squeezed through the door, yelping across the yard to disperse among the trees.

The moment Vera came back to herself, she wept and ground her teeth. "How could I?" she wailed. "How could I do it?"

"They'll come home," Mathilda told her. "Soon as they're hungry, you'll see."

But they didn't. Not a single, solitary dog.

Thomas's body gives off an inordinate amount of heat. Stifling beneath the sheets, Mathilda can't help but roll away from his reaching hands.

"What—?" He falters. "Mathilda, honey, don't be scared."

"I'm not," she mumbles. "It's—it's a bad time."

"A bad time?" He smothers her shoulder with his hand. "Honey, it's our wedding night."

"I know that," she snaps. "It's just not a good time." She sighs heavily. *"You know."*

"Know what?"

"It's my time, Thomas. My monthlies."

"Oh!" His hand springs back guiltily. "I'm sorry, I never even thought—"

"It's all right," she cuts him off. "Goodnight."

"Oh. Yes. Goodnight, sweetie." He drops a careful peck on her cheek.

Mathilda hugs herself. It's the first full-blown lie between them. Her period ended two days ago, Aunt Vera having quizzed her mercilessly before setting the date.

She inches further away from him, aligning herself with the edge of the bed. Her *husband.* For the first time ever she contemplates the stark reality, the physical implication of the word. She has some idea of the mechanics involved. At St. Joseph's the older boys stuck rigid fingers into

15

loosely formed fists, rubbing hard and rolling their eyes, laughing when she turned and ran.

As for passion, she's witnessed it only once in her life. Her aunt had let her keep the window seat all the way from Winnipeg, though she'd scolded when Mathilda left a nose print on the glass. As they slowed to a halt at Mercy station, Mathilda was careful to hold her face close to but not touching the pane. A freight train stood motionless on the next set of tracks. Framed between two cars—one golden with flower spots of rust, the other watery blue—two people were jammed up in a tangle against a corrugated shed. The man was slender inside his dark coveralls, his black hair oiled and combed, his gloved hand kneading the woman's breast. She was taller than him, broad-shouldered, sturdy-legged. Her pale braid kicked as they twisted their two faces into one.

Thomas sighs in his sleep, sending a blast of hot breath across Mathilda's cheek. She might as well be bleeding. She feels tender and sick all the same.

2

THE BOG

Shambling through the bog, Castor can feel it—the whole seething mess—not so much around him as inside. It inhabits him, from the tops of its knobby trees, down deep through the peat to the lake that lies dying below. The green stink of its slow, sodden growth. He hates it.

Then suddenly, achingly, he loves it. His beautiful bog, all puffy-lipped orchids, flying squirrels and feasting shrews. In winter, a hidden city of trails under snow. In summer, a chorus of wings.

Either way he ends up thirsty, lumbering back to his glinting cave.

"Ain't I a big baby," he says to no one. "Just stick me on a bottle and I quiet right down."

Sometimes he sees things.

Sometimes he just drinks, muttering sweet nonsense until he passes out blissfully cold.

Thomas stands alone in his shop. Half an hour until opening—plenty of time to finish up with his knives.

He's been alone since the day began. True, Mathilda left everything ready for him, laid out his clothing, his breakfast, called out to wake him as she left for the church. He shouldn't find fault. After all, she's only doing her duty by her aunt. As for her other duties— He stops himself. She can't help it if it's her time. His mother's washed-out face flashes before him, the old man's brute hands on her shoulders, shoving her before him into their room. *Never.* Not him, not Thomas. He'd do anything rather than force her.

He runs a hand down the belly of his apron. Snowy white, the starch just right. He smiles. Can't fault her on laundry either.

He casts an eye over the tools of his trade—the boning knife with its slender blade, the simple butcher knife, the cleaver on its silver side. His gaze comes to rest on the favourite. Limber and strong, it's the most well-balanced, most versatile, the butcher's best friend. His skinning knife, curved like a six-inch smile.

Thomas's hands become strangely formal, the left reaching precisely for the steel, the right retreating to smooth the white tail of his coat. He takes up the skinning knife, feels it tilt in his fist as he lays its heel behind the tip of the steel. He holds the pose a moment, then relaxes his wrist, inhales sharply and lets fly, drawing the blade swiftly downward until its tip meets the hilt of the steel. Lift to the near side and begin again, a single stroke from heel to tip.

Behind the steel, before the steel, pressure unerring, steady and light. It's hypnotic—the angle just so, the edge bevelling, coming up true. He closes his eyes as the steel begins softly to sing.

FLECTAMUS GENUA
(let us kneel)

Like many lonely children, August took notice of the natural world. And because he felt himself somehow earthbound, he paid particular attention to birds.

For a time there was a bounty on crows. Older boys shot them mid-flight or mid-hop, small boys pilfered eggs. It was the first time August thought of earning money, of returning to his mother with coins in his palm. Climbing to the high black nests was the least of his concerns—he had a native understanding of trees, being all twigs himself. He knew the parent birds would dive-bomb, so he wore his forest-green cap with the visor angled down over his eyes.

Black-winged bodies exploded from the tree the moment he hauled himself up off the ground. As he gained branch after branch, the crows folded themselves and fell at him, cursing. Reaching for the final bough, he felt a flight feather brush his cheek, a curl of claws at the nape of his neck.

There were three eggs, olive-green with chocolatey spots, huddled together in the dark bundle of sticks. The grown-ups screeched as August ran a finger over the closest shell, finding it silky and warm to the touch.

"It's all right," he told the crows, then repeated to the eggs, "It's all right."

His pockets empty, he backed his way down to the ground.

"Witchery witchery witchery," the yellowthroat sang as it flitted up out of the brush.

August knelt motionless nearby, the lucky green cap twisted sideways on his head. He was making up his mind to shuffle forward for a better look when the thicket rustled again. The cowbird landed hard on a switch that over-arched the yellowthroat's nest. It stole a look both ways, opened its wings like a cape, and dropped. A smudge of brownish grey, it all but disappeared among the woven weed stalks, grass and hair. August leaned closer. The cow-bird was crouching, bobbing every so slightly over the yellowthroat's four dark eggs.

"Glug," it said, "glug glug," and it nailed him with a glassy stare. A moment more and it lifted like dust on an updraft, picked a course through the branches and was gone.

August gasped. The cowbird's abandoned egg was pale, speckled a dozen shades of brown. He couldn't see how it would pass for a second, let alone survive long enough to hatch.

SURSUM CORDA
(lift up your hearts)

August tells himself it's Thomas Rose's recent conversion that's prompted him to place the newlywed couple first on his list of parish rounds, and to some extent this is true.

Something in the butcher's dull gaze puts him in mind of a renegade ram, one that joins the flock solely to mate, then follows its horns away.

At least he needn't worry about the soul of the young wife. He learned a little about Mathilda at the reception, though no one seemed to know her well. She was raised by the Grey Nuns at St. Joseph's until her aunt finally managed to track her down. You can tell, too—she has something of a novitiate's way about her. So different from her aunt. Such grace, such natural piety. August lengthens his stride, his mind's eye lingering on her bowed before him, the crown of her luminous head.

Rose's Fine Meats is closed for the evening, but August knocks on the glass door all the same, unaware of the kitchen entrance round back.

"Over here." The butcher's great block of a head appears from a doorway further down, beyond the storefront, in what appears to be a garage. "Father Day." His broad face moves slowly into a smile. "I'm a little tied up here, but you're welcome." He disappears, leaving the door swinging open.

August pokes his head in just as the butcher tears loose the offal from a hoisted beast, letting it roll forward to land with a slap in a white enamel tub. Thomas looks up from the mess with a grin. "I'd shake hands with you, Father, but—" As if in mock surrender, he holds up his bloodied palms.

August's head swims. His eyes fix on the butcher's rubber boots, two black tree trunks grown up from a bright red field.

"Mucky business, eh?" says Thomas.

The carcass swings gently, hung from its hind legs, sawn and spread open wide. August nods speechlessly.

"To tell you the truth, Father, I love the butchering, but the slaughtering I could do without. I reckon the Indians knew what they were about with those buffalo jumps. No fuss, no muss, and nothing but meat for a mile."

"The Gadarene swine," August murmurs.

"How's that, Father?" The butcher bends again to his task.

"I see your knowledge of the Gospel could use some work." August clears his throat, adopting a biblical tone. "The miracle of the Gadarene swine. Our Lord and Saviour cast the demons from two men who were possessed, sending them into a nearby herd of swine." His eyes glaze over with glory. "The swine ran mad. They thundered off a cliff into the sea."

"Into the sea?"

"That's right, Thomas."

The butcher shakes his head. "Terrible waste of pork."

August's expression sours.

"And another thing, Father, why a whole herd of pigs for only two men? Why not two pigs, an eye for an eye?"

August collects himself. "I suppose that would have something to do with the vast spiritual difference between we who are made in His image and the common beasts of the field."

Thomas lays his knife on a nearby table and turns, proffering an enormous heart. "Are you telling me that couldn't hold a man's demons?"

August takes a stumbling step back. It's vascular and crude, an oversized portion of meat. He presses a hand to his chest. Somehow he's always imagined his own as an alpine pool, crystalline, rocky and cold.

The butcher lowers the heart into a basin of clean water, massaging it, giving it a good rinse. "Hey, looks like we're in the same business, eh, Father?" He laughs. "Washing out hearts."

"I hardly think so," August says weakly, then thinks viciously, *philistine*, the word soothing him, lending him strength. He draws himself up. "I'll be off now."

"Okay, Father." Thomas pats the rump of his kill. "Mathilda'll be sorry she missed your visit."

August flinches ever so slightly at the mention of her name.

"Unless you've already seen her," Thomas adds.

"No. Why would you—why do you say that?"

"Just seems she's down at the church more often than not." The butcher's smile betrays a hint of chagrin. "Makes sense, I guess, her having lived half her life at the rectory. Keeps going back like a bear to its hole."

"Very colourfully put. I shouldn't like to think you regretted your wife's devotion to God and His Church, Thomas. Nor to her aging aunt, for that matter."

"Oh—no. No, Father, I didn't mean—"

August turns his back. "I trust I'll see you on Sunday, Thomas." He closes the door firmly and righteously on his way out.

HIS NAME

Father Day, Mathilda mouths, wide awake beside her husband's snoring form. She's spoken it only once during the course of the day, and once doesn't seem nearly enough.

"Excuse me, Father Day." She said it softly, poking her head in through his office door. "My aunt says to tell you your lunch is getting cold."

23

"Yes, yes, all right."

She lingered for several seconds, but he refused to look up from his desk.

"Father Day." She whispers it aloud now, but it's his Christian name she really craves, the one his mother must've uttered when she first held him in her arms. Mathilda holds her breath, resisting for as long as humanly possible before giving in.

"*August.*" It slips out as she's forced to exhale. A ripe-eared field unfolds in her chest. The butcher saws on at her side.

IN PRINCIPIO ERAT VERBUM
(in the beginning was the word)

With the housekeeper finally quiet above him in her room, August ceases pacing and spreads out his arms. His bedroom is too big. Seminary life has shaped him for narrow sleep—seven years in a room three paces by five—not to mention his bedroom at home, hardly more than a closet, with its rattling window and paper-thin walls.

He reaches distractedly for his bible. Perhaps *Proverbia.* Crossing to the window, he thumbs to a random verse.

Numquid potest homo abscondere ignem in sino suo, Ut vestimenta illius non ardeant? Can a man hide fire in his bosom, and his garments not burn?

He lets the book fall shut, trapping his thin finger in place. The crown of her head. Her creamy lace veil and, beneath it, the part in her auburn hair. It seemed so innocent somehow, that milk-white line of scalp.

He cracks the Old Testament again, skips back to a previous passage, his finger skimming for instruction, the comfort of a judicial tone.

Sit vena tua benedicta— Let thy vein be blessed, and rejoice with the wife of thy youth: Let her be thy dearest hind, and most agreeable fawn: let her breasts inebriate thee at all times—

He sits down hard on his over-plump bed, feeling it swell up to smother his thighs. A shadow rises up at the back of his mind. *Fine words from Solomon*, it asserts darkly. *Three hundred concubines and twice as many wives.*

3

GLORIFICAMUS TE

(we glorify thee)

T he first Saturday, the penitents come out in droves, confession spanning the long afternoon, the lineup snaking slowly through the box. August is snug in his shadowy half—nodding, murmuring, raising his bony hand. So far, so good. Already he's plotting a map of the parish, charting weak spots and fortresses, soul by sinning soul.

Between two voices he presses his eye to the slit in the confessional door. The nave is a mosaic of light. At least a dozen are still waiting, not counting the lone woman seated in a pew, a triangle of head scarf bent in prayer. August squints hard. Is it—?

As if in answer, Mathilda shifts in her seat, drops gracefully down to the kneeler and, in a brief, fluid gesture, holds her rosary up to the light. The palest of pale blue glass. Like beads of water suspended from her hand.

"Bless me Father for I have sinned—" A boy's small voice comes filtering through the screen. "Father? Are you there?"

After the boy, a series of nameless transgressors. August has trouble following their breathy admissions, finds himself counting, *six down, six to go.* Finally, glimpsed again through his peephole, Mathilda rises.

The moment she draws the confessional door shut, he finds himself swamped by a familiar smell. It's not her meadowy wedding scent. Today she exudes dark spices and silvery herbs, rubbed together with plenty of fat.

"Bless me Father," she begins, "for I have sinned."

He mumbles the blessing in response, his hand floating up to sign her with the Cross. *Sausages.* The butcher must have made a fresh batch. She could be wearing a garland of them, so undeniably strong is the smell.

They were August's boyhood specialty, served up by themselves on those nights when his mother was too worn out to cook. He'd push a chair up to the stove and stand on the seat, pricking and turning them, feeling them spit back at him from the heavy black pan.

"Since my last confession, which was four weeks ago, before Father Rock—well, anyway, since that time, I accuse myself of these sins . . ." She trails off.

At seminary, sausages were the rarest of treats. Short, wrinkled fingers, they were a poor substitute for the fat, farm-style links of home. Even so, they inspired such a fierce desire that August thought it best to give them up. He became known for stoically rolling his portion to the rim of his plate. His fellow seminarians waited for this signal, surrounding him like young warriors, brandishing their shiny forks.

"I told a lie, Father," Mathilda says finally.

"A lie?"

She couldn't have chosen a more disarming scent. August would bottle it if he could, anoint himself daily, lift his scented inner wrists to his nose.

"To my husband."

"Oh." The sound thickens in his throat.

"I had to," she blurts. "I didn't want him to—I couldn't bear—on our wedding night—I just had to lie."

"I see." Two tiny words are the most he can choke out. His inner picture of her alters dramatically, the butcher's dark handprints lifting from her flesh, leaving it suddenly, startlingly pristine. The thrill is undeniable. It winds, bone after thorny bone, up his spine.

"Is it a sin, Father?" she asks softly. "I mean, I know about the lying, but the other—"

"Well, no, not exactly." He swallows, gets hold of himself and tries again. "But you understand that marriage is a sacrament—that the *act* of marriage is, well, sacred." The words ring hollowly in his head, bounce around his sinuses, the hidden flaps and recesses of his throat.

"But it's not a *sin*?"

Eagerness in her tone. He feels panicked, a small clawed thing surrounded by fire. "Cast your mind back to the ceremony," he says quickly, "to the words of Saint Paul. 'Just as the Church is subject to Christ, so also let wives be subject in all things to their husbands.'"

"Yes, Father," she presses, "but what about all the women who *wouldn't*, who died because they wouldn't? Didn't God make them saints?"

"Those women were different. They weren't married, for one."

"What about the Virgin Mary? She was married to Joseph, and God loved her best of all."

"I—" He falters. *Virgin.* No longer blue and serene, the word mutated into something forbidden the moment she gave it voice.

"I feel," she whispers, "like I mustn't. Not with him. I feel like it's *wrong*."

He should contradict her, he knows, build a tower of Scripture, ring it round with holy tradition and invite her inside—but he doesn't. *Virgin*, is all he can think. Virgin.

"Three Hail Marys," he croaks, forgetting she has yet to say the act of contrition.

"Is that all?"

"That's all." He retreats into the absolution, lowering himself into the Latin as into a dark and familiar pool. "Go in peace," he concludes, returning reluctantly to his mother tongue.

When she stands, the creases of her dress fall open to release a fresh waft of pepper and sage. His glands respond, producing two thin streams to well up shamefully beneath his tongue.

PORK: POPULAR RETAIL CUTS

Thomas wakes with a diagram in his mind—parts provided, some assembly required. Mathilda's slender back is turned, swathed in a thick white nightgown. She was at church for most of the afternoon, unresponsive at the dinner table, asleep before he could switch off the light. He traces her shape with his eyes, feeling himself twitch and begin to stiffen beneath the sheet. Surely her time will be finished soon.

Ashamed, he turns his eyes to the ceiling, forcing his thoughts back to where they began. The hog in the locker should be plenty chilled. There's church in the morning, so he can't do it then. Besides, why wait when the picture's so vivid in him now?

He steals down to the shop. The locker's a great relief. He stays inside long enough to cool his blood, then shoulders the carcass, lifting the gambrel stick free of its hooks.

It's not long before he breaks a fresh sweat, sawing and trimming, inspiration driving him hard. He'll mar the meat in places, but it can't be helped—now he's started, there's no going back. He carves his components, then carries them to the refrigerated front case for display. It takes some rearranging—he has to remove two of the barred shelves to make room.

He moves quickly, ever conscious of the leaking cold. Down on his knees, cheek pressed flat to the glass, he mounts cut on cut, shoving skewers to hold them in place. Rectangles of jowl pile up to make the bench. The sawed-off hind shanks form a base, tapering down into the two back legs. Fix the trotters for front legs, then lay out the long keyboard of the loin, a cross-section of spine branching down into dark and light ribs. Build up the body behind, rolled picnic stacked on rolled Boston butt. Spareribs stand up for an open soundboard, and before them a white sheet of wax paper, folded into a book of notes.

Thomas slides the door closed and skirts the counter for a look. He glows in the case's green light and in the spread of his own beatific smile. "Imagine, ladies," he murmurs, "the dance of tiny hammers on strings."

BENEDICTA TU IN MULIERIBUS
(blessed art thou among women)

The turnout for August's first Mass is impressive, though he has yet to discern the weekly communicants from those come to gawk at the new priest. The front pews are stacked with small-town gentry—women with shiny pink lips and tightly laced children, soft men with rigid backs. The altar boys have most certainly been culled from their ranks, one fat and sly, the other nervous, unusually small. The scene might have been grafted entire from August's hometown, only in Fairview he wouldn't be standing before the altar. He'd be sitting alone like always, down the end of the very last pew.

He spots the housekeeper five rows back. She's served him every meal he's eaten for nearly a week, but somehow her name never comes to mind. Only "the housekeeper." He can feel her narrowed eyes on him. Earlier, when he entered on the heels of the fat boy, he was certain her face twisted in what could only be called disgust.

Beside her, Thomas Rose is wedged into the pew as though penned. And beside him, Mathilda—so still in contrast to her husband and aunt, so fine, as though she were formed of a different element, something exceedingly rare.

August turns back to the altar, bending to read the Epistle, the gradual, the tract. "*Munda cor meum,*" he solemnly intones, "*ac labia mea—*" In preparation for the reading of the Gospel he begs God to cleanse his heart, to purify his lips as He once did those of Isaiah, sending an angel to scorch the prophet's lips with a lump of burning coal. It's one of August's favourite parts—the muscular descent, the fiery mass in that immortal hand. He opens his mind to the vision, his lips parting, inviting the brand of God.

It doesn't come. In its place, a memory—part pressure, part temperature, part taste. His mother's kiss. Full on his small mouth, welcome yet overwhelming, often a little too open, too moist. He would've been seven or so when he began to suspect it wasn't right, but as always he chose not to speak. Instead he reasoned with himself. It wasn't Aggie's fault. Her lips came in contact with so many mouths, they were bound to get a little confused.

HIS VOICE

His Latin is their little secret, spoken huskily, for her ears alone. When he switches to English, it's almost more than Mathilda can stand—his parables take flight, sending her to the vault and back, grasping after light and air. It all culminates in Communion, his fine fingers laying the host on the tip of her tongue.

"*Corpus Domini nostri Jesu Christi custodiat animam tuam in vitam aeternam.*" He whispers it like a promise, but the lineup shuffles forward, urging Mathilda on. She mutters an amen, then trails after her husband's broad back, the bread of heaven melting to the roof of her mouth.

On the way out, Thomas pumps Father Day's hand as though he were trying to draw water up a well. "Fine sermon, Father," he says heartily, then links arms with Mathilda and draws her away.

At the foot of the stone steps he tilts his head to chuckle in her ear. "Couldn't follow a word of it. Even the

English. The parts I could hear didn't make a damn bit of sense."

Mathilda's mouth falls open.

"Not a patch on Father Rock." Vera stalks past them, her face livid, as though she's in pain. "Mumbles like a schoolboy. No fire in him. Not an ounce of steel."

"Hmm." Thomas nods.

Mathilda bites her tongue. Literally. Traps it writhing between her teeth.

THE HULL OF A SEED

Late on the Sabbath morning, Castor sags down at the base of a black spruce, fitting its skinny trunk to the hollow of his spine. His head lolls to one side. His ass is wet. He balances a half-dead soldier in his crotch.

He's got no say over the visions, never has had. His eye leaves when it pleases, taking his outlook wherever it will. He tried to explain it to Renny once, back before the kid went soft for a rope of golden hair.

"The eye won't set down just anywhere. There's gotta be a good host, see, something with a shine to it, bit of a curve to give back the light. A bottle cap, maybe."

His little brother just sat there with his mouth open. He knew how to listen back then.

"Sure, it happens when I'm drinkin'," Castor went on, "but that ain't sayin' much."

Renny nodded.

"Seems like maybe the liquor sets me off. The look of it, I mean, not how much I get down my throat." He paused.

"Partway down a bottle, if the eye's goin', that's when it'll go. I never been set off by an empty. There's gotta be something left."

Who knows if the boy understood. No way to ask him now.

"It's a cruel wrll," Castor mutters to himself. "Cruer woll, cluel wrol, cruld roe. Hee hee." He composes himself drunkenly, parting his lips in earnest to try again. Only something distracts him—whiskey lapping in the bottle, his own stupid mug in its side.

His eye comes loose, shoots out over trees and blooming weeds, slips down through a crack in the foundation of St. Mary's church. It finds a home in the husk of a flaxseed, one of not many left in the cache.

Close by, in a nest of fine, dry grass, a mother deer mouse hunkers over ten wriggling pups. The cache has sustained her through winter—nearly a gallon of seeds dutifully stashed—and now the season of food has returned. If she doesn't get eaten, she'll eat hearty for months. Wildflowers and spiders—if she's lucky, a salamander or two.

For now, she's laid low with milk, surrounded by nuzzling pups. *Ten of them.* Seven would do better, grow up stronger, have more of a fighting chance. The mother too would grow strong, produce more milk, if she took three of them for meat. She touches her quivering nose to the smallest one, sniffs closely and opens her jaws.

4

VEAL CALVES: STUNNING

The calf isn't the fattest, being the offspring of Sally Gray's one and only sack-of-bones milk cow. It's lame, too, well and truly hobbled by a gash in its right hind leg. There'll be waste, all right. Who knows, the whole thing might end up in the grinder, sell the best of it in patties, the rest in the next batch of mixed sausage.

Thomas paid premium for the calf. Walked around it nodding, saying, "That's a fine animal, Mrs. Gray. I'd be happy to take her off your hands." What else could he do? A young war widow, struggling to hold on to the farm. She had eyes like a spaniel's. Besides, he was doing fine for himself. Better than fine. He could afford it.

Calf stunning takes a light touch. Thomas lifts the hammer, then pauses, his free hand reaching out of its own accord to caress the beast's forehead, the spot where the hair curls softly like that of a small child.

A memory wakens in his fingers. He was all of thirteen, with a full pen of veal calves to drop. Having laid down his sledge, he stood rubbing the first calf's brow, whispering to it, falling headlong down the wells of its eyes. Thomas Senior approached soundlessly. His fingers closed like a handcuff around Thomas's stroking wrist. "This is the killing floor, boy." He squeezed so hard Thomas could feel the blood slow in his veins. "Not the goddamn petting zoo." The calf bawled, and all around them men looked up from their work, grinning. Thomas Senior shoved his son aside, hoisted the hammer and felled the calf. The men gave a guttural cheer. He'd hit it hard enough to kill a heifer. Hard enough even to down a steer.

Thomas continues stroking until the calf closes its eyes. Then swings tenderly, the blow landing precisely where his fingers have been.

VISIBILIUM OMNIUM ET INVISIBILIUM
(all things visible and invisible)

The butcher's propped open his door. August drops his eyes to the ground, but not before catching a glimpse of Thomas Rose's powerful back, his sweat-stained under-shirt a pale continent beside the brown-and-pink mass of a partly skinned calf.

August walks softly, passes unseen. There's a warm evening wind. He kicks up a cloud of reddish dust with each stride, the colour enveloping him, casting his thoughts back to the animal's dangling hide. What good is a skin when it can be split down the middle like that and peeled away? The thought halts him in his tracks. There was a Pope—John XIV, he's almost certain. They flayed him for his faith, his power too, no doubt. Dragged him skinless through the cheering crowds.

From the hollow doorway of Mercy Hardware a figure

emerges, lurching jaggedly across the walk. "Ee-evening, Father!" Its breath is an overproof blast, one eye closed up in a puffy blue pocket, the cheek beneath it raw, as though grated on an unforgiving road.

"Good evening," August answers twice, as no sound makes it out on the first try.

"Cast'er widely," it tells him, thrusting a filthy hand from its sleeve. The thick skin split at the peak of each knuckle, puckered in a row of ancient mouths. August chokes in the hand's swampy smell, lifts his own but finds he can't extend it, instead blesses the creature quickly with the sign.

"Oh yeah," it says, grinning, "right," then wiggles a scabby finger around its head and chest, the effect more a crazy spiral than anything resembling a Cross.

"Excuse me," August whispers with what little breath he has left, turning on his heel and walking stiffly away. It calls after him, an animal sound he can't make out, but he keeps his eyes fixed firmly on the end of the road. The Church of St. Mary Immaculate. Its many-petalled eye.

The housekeeper slaps dinner down in front of him, a white plate bulging with brownish lumps.

"Miss Nickels," he says, careful to keep his tone offhand.

"Yes." She hovers beside him, a little behind even, like a sentry. No matter, he'd just as soon not look at her face.

"I saw a man today."

"Is that so?"

Sarcasm, plain and simple. Still, he wants to know, almost needs to. "A particular man," he continues, "poor, perhaps fifty years old. Inebriated."

She doesn't answer right off. Lets him hang. "Squat fellow?" she says finally. "Built like a forty-gallon drum?"

"Yes."

"Castor Wylie."

Cast'er widely. It was a name the man offered, not nonsense after all. "Is he Catholic?" August asks, feeling the housekeeper move away from him, drawn back to the kitchen, her dishes in the sink.

She snorts. "I shouldn't think so."

"Oh?"

"Wylie's a Scotch name," she calls over her shoulder, twisting the water on hard. "His brother married United."

"His brother?"

She doesn't hear. "In any case, Castor Wylie's not likely to set foot in any church I know."

"No?" August turns in his chair.

"Heathen as they come. Built himself a hovel out in the bog, all made out of bottles."

"Out of what?"

"Lives out there like a savage." She clanks a pot lid hard. "Calls himself *the Seer*, whatever that's supposed to mean."

SUSCIPE, SANCTA TRINITAS,
HANC OBLATIONEM
(*receive, o holy trinity, this sacrifice*)

Eight was too old for stuffed animals, August knew, especially if you were a boy. Still, they were all he had, so he set them on the table in a row—two moth-eaten bears, one toffee-coloured, one black, and a sad-eyed, blotchy dog.

38

Left alone in the house, he could think of nothing but the previous Sunday's Mass. Father Felix had worn violet for Lent, his vestments a shade lighter but just as shiny as Aggie's favourite robe. He had read from Galatians, "'Cast out the slave-girl and her son, for the son of the slave-girl shall not be heir with the son of the free woman.'" August felt the thoughts of the gathered faithful turn toward him. A few bold ones even turned their heads. Glancing up from the enormous lectionary, the old priest met August's panicked gaze. He met and held it kindly with his own.

When she wasn't wearing it, Aggie's robe hung from a tarnished hook on the inside of her closet door. August only meant to check the colour, to see if it was as close as he thought, but the robe felt so mysterious to the touch, slithery and strangely cool. He got gooseflesh slipping it on.

Aggie always kept something to drink in the house, but it would be whiskey or beer, not wine. The closest thing August could find was strong tea gone cold in the pot. He poured it out into Aggie's best cup—bone china with a little cottage painted on the side—then nibbled the corners off four saltines and arranged them on the matching saucer.

He did his best with what little he knew. He began by running his fingers under the tap and flicking water at his flock. Next he genuflected, signed himself with the Cross and began mumbling, now and then bending to touch his lips to the tabletop, or opening and raising his arms. He held a saltine up to the light and said an Our Father before swallowing it, elevated the cup twice to be safe before sipping the bitter tea. Finally, he fed the animals, or pretended to, palming the crackers and slipping them surreptitiously into his mouth.

He had to rush to get everything cleared away before Aggie returned with her shopping basket full.

"What's this?" She laughed at him. "It's a little big on you, don't you think?"

Mortified, he cast his eyes down. The robe sagged from his thin shoulders in puckers and bags, entirely obscuring his form.

BEEF: REMOVING THE TONGUE AND BRAINS

Thomas turns the steer's head face down, runs his blade along the inside of the jaw, loosens the tongue's tip and severs the thick cords at its base. Then takes up the cleaver. A single sharp blow and the tongue comes free from the bone, dragging its fat behind. He drops it into a basin of water and for a moment it seems to swim, a scarlet fish dyeing its surroundings to match.

He got plenty of tongue as a boy. For the family of a slaughterhouse owner—albeit the smallest, most poorly run slaughterhouse on the yards—the Roses ate few prime cuts. Thomas Senior brought home discarded odds and ends, countless buckets of blood, meat too bruised to pass off on the buyers, often a knobby length of tongue. It was the only meat that made Thomas uneasy. He'd seen too many of them working hard in the mouths of terrified cows. His mother watched him choke it down, saying nothing until one of her husband's nights away.

Nights away. The old man crashing in at the crack of dawn, stinking of rye and days-old panties, ground-out butts and dirty hair. Thomas always blessed her in his head—whichever poor, pissed-up girl had taken the bastard on, she'd given his mother a break.

It was on one of those nights that Sarah Rose decided to show her son a little trick. She laid the tongue her husband had left them in a bowl, pressed a small plate down on top of it, weighted it with a fat onion and let it stand.

Thomas retrieves the dripping tongue and scrapes it from tip to base. He can almost see his mother's face before him, the secret little smile she flashed when she lifted that plate. The tongue had reinvented itself—it mimicked perfectly the curve of the bowl. She upended the red dome into a boiling pot, lifted it out pink, carved it at the table like a roast.

"Clever, hmm?" she said softly. "Now you eat up."

And Thomas did, savouring the tongue, really tasting it for the first time, rich and potent against his own.

He comes back to himself, his knife stilled, the steer's tongue lying limp in his hands. He hangs it over the basin by its tip and reaches absently for the saw. His hands know what to do. Open the skull. Lift out the hidden brain.

OREMUS
(let us pray)

It's only his second Sunday and already the crowd has thinned. From the foot of the altar August looks askance at his flock, every member lifting a hand to mirror his, as though he were manipulating them with dozens of tiny wires.

"*In nomine Patris—*" he begins. From among a sea of gestures Mathilda's hand breaches, the lace at her wrist like a ring of foam.

"—*et Filii*—"

It dives to her breastbone.

"—*et Spiritus Sancti*—"

Swims shoulder to shoulder.

"—*Amen.*"

For several long, fidgety seconds he forgets what comes next. The altar boy stares up at him anxiously, but somehow there's room for only a single line in his head. Not even a line so much as a scrap, something left behind by high school English, the play he hated most for the crawling desperation it made him feel.

Juliet leans her cheek on her palm.

Lovesick in the bushes below, Romeo groans, *O that I were a glove upon that hand.*

5

BY-PRODUCTS: BLACK PUDDING

Thomas kneads vigorously, the mixture sticky in his mighty hands. He's read of a dozen variations but makes only one—his mother's and her mother's before. Nothing fancy, she taught him, hog's blood and suet, oatmeal and onion, plenty of pepper and salt. He sells out fast every time. The Scots get a whiff of them on the boil and start circling the shop like dogs.

He fills the stuffer, forces the spout full and slips a length of hog casing over its snout. Turning the crank, he holds the casing in place, supporting the first two inches to be sure of a solid pack. The stuffing sinks down in the hopper, transformed into dark, drooping coils. Thomas flares his nostrils to the familiar—onion pungency, pepper, the comforting goodness of grain. Mere undercurrents in a river of blood.

Maybe that's it. Maybe that's why, after three weeks of marriage, Mathilda still curls away from him in bed, still rises so early and slips away. There's no getting rid of it, Thomas knows, it lingers no matter how you scrub. Not a bad smell exactly, just—powerful. Come to think of it, she does avoid the shop. She's never even set foot in the killing room. He lets out a sigh of relief, embracing the fresh excuse. It's the blood.

It's surrounded him ever since he can remember— puddling darkly, spraying bright up the walls. He'll have to explain it to her. *It's life.* You only have to stick a hog to understand, see how it shoots forth, how it ebbs suddenly as the heart surges its last. Lay your hand to the animal's side and you can feel it leave. Any butcher worth his salt knows you'll never manage a fast chill, a clean cut, without first ensuring a good bleed. Get the life out quick. Whatever's left is yours.

HIS PREDECESSOR

Vera takes to lying in. She leaves Father Day's breakfast to Mathilda, even misses Mass, not showing her face until every last communicant has gone. Even then she moves laboriously, as though each swipe of her cloth causes a rending of something inside. Mathilda follows her, wiping up streaks of polish, erasing smudges from brilliant panels of glass.

It's Father Rock, Mathilda tells herself, believing the grief will pass. After all, it's only been a month and a half since the funeral, precious little time to the woman who fed him thrice daily, sat by the fire and listened to his sermons take shape draft by draft, sometimes even took a pull off his sweet-smelling pipe. Then there was the bickering— never vicious, just a biweekly sparring match to keep them in shape. Maybe one of Father Rock's dogs chewed a curtain hem or stole a chop from the stove. Vera'd get up on her high horse about it, and Father Rock would poke at her until she fell off. They were like an old married couple, really. Mathilda might've been an extra finger on an otherwise perfectly balanced pair of hands.

It was nothing she wasn't used to. At St. Joseph's, the Superior and her attendant sisters were drowning in children. In what had originally been an orphanage solely for boys, girls were still greatly outnumbered, and were appreciated most when neither seen nor heard. The underpaid help were even less attentive—the doorman, the shoemaker, the gardener—all far too busy or too bitter to notice a skinny, silent girl. Which left the chaplain and visiting archbishop, men whose longed-for gazes touched down rarely and were gone.

Vera's come to a standstill beside the altar, leaning on her mop as though on a cane. "Aunt?" Mathilda says gently.

Vera clutches her belly.

"Aunt, are you all right?"

She expects the little woman's head to snap round. *Of course I am*, she'll say, or *What are you gawping at?* or even *Don't I deserve a moment's rest?* Mathilda expects anything but what she gets—her aunt's face swivelling slowly, pale as a votive candle in its tunnel of glass.

"No." Vera grimaces. "No, girl, I'm not."

"Fetch Thomas," Vera says, once Mathilda's helped her back to the rectory, up the long, thin flights to her bed.

"Shall I fix you a bicarb?" Mathilda asks, tucking the blankets down.

"You ought to spend more time with him. Fetch him now. He'll be a comfort to you."

45

"Yes," Mathilda says absently. "I'll go for Doctor Albright."

"Suit yourself." Vera shuts her eyes. "It won't do a stick of good."

Doctor Albright has been practising too long to pull his punches. "It's too far along," he says firmly. "There's nothing for it but to start her on morphine for the pain."

"We understand," says Thomas. "Thank you, Doctor."

His arm is a burden across Mathilda's shoulders. She fears it will buckle her knees.

PANEM CAELESTEM
(bread of heaven)

There was something obscene about a feast. Every autumn, the Fairview Catholic Ladies' Committee put on a fowl supper in the basement of St. Paul's. There was always plenty of everything good—wild sage dressing, candied sweet potato, noodle ring. August overheard all about it at school. He probably could've attended. His presence would've been tolerated, just.

"Did you ever go to the fowl supper?" he asked Aggie the year he turned ten. "You know, when you were—younger?"

Her face went dead a moment, then pulled itself into a smile. "Never mind." She messed a fragrant hand in his hair. "I'll make us a fowl supper all our own."

And so she did. The chicken was so big its breast touched the top of their little oven, so the skin there turned shiny and black. Aggie made his favourites—fresh buttermilk rolls

46

and corn on the cob—and the only green vegetables were cut up small and savoury, mixed with butter and breadcrumbs, and stuffed into the bird's behind. August ate enough for two men—the one who'd left them and the one he would someday become. He was full to bursting long before dessert, but Aggie's pie spilled sliced apples and raisins from its lattice top, and her face looked desperately on. He managed two fat wedges smothered in fluffed cream. Undid his top button and shovelled it in.

It all came up in a hot rush out back of the shed. He went down on his knees while Aggie washed up the dishes inside, barked like a dog until there was nothing but a froth of bile.

Not long after the fowl supper August began showing up early to Mass. Week after week he huddled at the back of St. Paul's, watching the altar boy prepare from afar. He began to anticipate every step, the exact moment of genuflection, the precise order in which the candles came to life. It wasn't fair. The altar boy was one of the schoolyard's cruellest tormentors. He already had his father's double chin—one of many dark profiles August had come to know.

When the warning bell tolled, Father Felix followed the cruel boy into the chancel.

"*Introibo ad altare Dei,*" said the priest, and August mouthed along to the acolyte's reply. He knew well enough what the dead words meant. *To God who gives joy to my youth.*

He went early to confession as well, preferring to avoid the craning looks of those who stood before him in line.

"It's not me, Father," he whispered hoarsely, having finally worked up the nerve. "It's my mother."

Father Felix exhaled audibly.

"Father, I'm worried for her soul."

"My son," the old priest replied, "you cannot confess another's sins." He hesitated. "Perhaps you could offer up a prayer to the Holy Virgin."

"Yes." And August resolved instantly to do so. From now on, his candy money would buy candles in his mother's name, no matter how badly he craved something sweet. Still, if a sin went on unrepented, unconfessed—

"You're a good boy, August," Father Felix said. "A good Catholic. You'd make a fine altar boy—"

August's heart leapt.

"—but we both know the kind of uproar that would cause."

"Oh. Yes, Father."

"I want you to know something, August. As far as I'm concerned—as far as God is concerned—any time you need someone to talk to, even if you just need somewhere to feel safe, you are always welcome in the house of the Lord."

"Okay," August whispered, unable to trust his voice.

"Do you know who Saint Felix was, my son?"

"No, Father."

"Patron saint of those falsely accused."

"Oh."

"I want you to listen to me now," Father Felix said gravely. "While your mother is indeed living in a state of sin—" He paused. "—she is nonetheless a good woman. Can you understand that?"

"But, Father, she doesn't even go to church."

"She used to. I baptized her in this church."

"But—"

"August, your mother has her reasons for staying home while you're attending Mass. The truth is, if she ever tried to set foot in this church, her fellow Christians would drive her out." Again the priest's long, weary sigh. "Do you understand?"

"I—think so."

"Good. Now, have you anything to confess?"

The next morning at the Communion rail, Father Felix looked him dead in the eye. The host fell thickly on August's tongue, and he could swear the old priest muttered the *Corpus Christi* twice. He knew it was breaking the rules, but he held his tongue down low on the way back to his seat and, once there, lifted his hand to cover a false cough. The top wafer was slightly soggy but still in one piece. He held it tightly the whole way home.

He made Aggie close her eyes and hold out her hand. "Father Felix sent it." He placed the damp host on her palm. "For you."

Her eyes opened wide and welled up shiny. Right there in the kitchen she went down on her knees. August watched his mother cross herself slowly and lift the Eucharist to her mouth. Watched her tongue come out to meet it like a cat's.

HIS BODY

Mathilda avoids Thomas gracefully, each day a series of evasions, variations on the central gesture of turning her

49

back in their bed. His breakfast lies alone on the table, a pan lid keeping it warm. She's reaching for the back door when he appears.

"Off again?" He looms in the kitchen doorway, forcing a smile. "I thought they were getting a new housekeeper."

"They are." She fiddles with the knob. "Soon."

"When?"

"Thomas—"

"No." He draws himself up. "No, Mathilda, it won't do. Tend to your aunt by all means, but there's no reason for you to be doing her job. You've got to let all that go."

"All that? You mean my faith?"

"You know that's not what I mean. I mean—giving your life to the Church. So there's nothing left."

"For you, you mean."

"Well, yes." He reddens. "Is that a sin, for a man to want to see his wife more than five minutes a day?"

She doesn't answer.

"I asked you a question, Mathilda."

"It's polishing day," she says quietly.

"What?"

"It's Wednesday, polishing day. I have a lot to do—"

"Damn the polishing!" Thomas bellows, Mathilda staring at him as though two black horns were sprouting from his brow.

"Thomas!" Crossing herself swiftly, she yanks open the door. "Cleaning St. Mary's is a sacred duty. The Church is the *Body of Christ*."

His jaw works on its hinges. She leaps over the threshold before he can summon a reply.

6

ADORAMUS TE

(we adore thee)

Tucked up tight against his massive desk, August shuffles his notes for the week's sermon, reordering them yet again. His mind has been truant all afternoon. The moment he sets it to work, it slips back to the rectory, where a muted drama unfolds.

The housekeeper's taken to her bed, the cancer so far advanced even the doctor was shocked—how had she been up and about at all, let alone still attending to her duties? August could have told him. With help, of course, the help of a loving and devoted niece.

Now Mathilda works alone. Each morning, August awakens to the sound of her arriving early to make him breakfast. Standing at the bathroom sink, he draws the razor slowly down his cheeks, listening to the pipes moan as she fills the kettle for tea. He dawdles while dressing, emerging from his bedroom only after she's mounted the stairs to relieve the night nurse and see to her aunt.

She's up and down those stairs all day. He's caught glimpses of her through the parlour's glass door, bearing watered milk or a wash basin, clean syringes or weak beef tea. All that, and she somehow manages the rectory chores before noon, prepares a hot lunch, then crosses to the church with her cleaning box in hand. Day after day, August finds his meals steaming in the empty dining room, as though they've been laid out for him by some otherworldly force.

Of course, she can't stay on long-term. Married or not, she's too young and—well, people would talk. As soon as her aunt passes, he'll have to arrange for someone new. He should do it now, really—she's running herself ragged—but the idea pains him. No, he decides, better to wait awhile. It might seem as though he's rushing the housekeeper along.

He walks a hand across the green desk blotter, halting at its cushioned edge. Mathilda's been here recently, last evening perhaps, while he was out on his rounds. The desktop gives off an underwater gleam, papers layered and frilled, the paperweight an enormous black pearl. He shakes his head hard, grabs a random sheet from the pile, grips it in both hands and stares. His leggy scrawl swims. Hopeless. He needs a walk, that's all. A little air.

He catches sight of her on his way out. She's standing close by the altar, so close she could lean her hip lightly against it. Her hands move over the monstrance, the left cradling, the right rubbing vigorously to bring out a shine.

The first time Father Felix showed him the monstrance at St. Paul's, August heard *monstrous*, and so it seemed to a little boy—the spindly leg of its stand, its spiky head, the pale, translucent pupil of its eye. He learned the proper term soon enough, but it wasn't until seminary, bent over the fat OED, that he discovered the diverse etymologies of the words. *Monstrous* from the Latin *monstrum*, meaning "portent." Monstrance from *monstrare*, "to show." Still, the two remained twinned in his mind, and he found he could never quite strain all the horror from his awe. It didn't help to find out that, while it now exposed only the host, the monstrance had its origins in those reliquary cylinders that displayed the bodies of martyrs—either whole or in gruesome parts.

Mathilda draws close to the lunula and breathes on the glass, following with a flick of her cloth. August bristles. Surely such intimacy is improper—a mother licking her thumb to rub dirt from a growing boy's face. He should say something. He will. Only now, she's no longer cleaning. She's just standing there, gazing ardently at the body of the Lord.

HIS GIFT

Vera reaches out from beneath the covers and grabs Mathilda's hand. "Lord," she croaks, "you're an oven. How can you be so warm, girl? I'm frozen through."

It's high eighties in the shade. Mathilda's been rubbing ice along her wrists.

"Hah." Vera laughs weakly. "I guess you've still got blood in your veins." Her face contracts with a spike of pain. "Ahnnn," she moans, but when Mathilda reaches for the needle, Vera stops her hand. "No," she says, "not yet."

"All right." Mathilda sits back helplessly. After a moment she begins stroking the pale crustacean that was lately her aunt's right hand. In a single bedridden week Vera's seen more than a decade's decline.

"Fourteen," Vera says wonderingly.

"What's that, Aunt?"

"I was fourteen when I took over St. Mary's. The year Mother finally took to her bed with what they used to call nerves. My father was long gone by then. Yours too—he didn't wait for eighteen before shaking the dust of this town from his shoes."

Mathilda's stroking hand stops short.

"Easy now," says Vera. "It's not him I'm getting at with all this. Not my own father, either. They were useless, the pair of them." She sniffs. "On her better days Mother used to tell me how they were both away on the traplines up north, how they'd be back with a couple of fine fur coats for us any day. Poor fool." Vera's mouth softens. "Father Rock came on the year after I took over. From the moment he clapped eyes on me, he took me for his pet. That was something, too, not that he was a hard man, but to most he was never what you'd call warm."

"You don't say," Mathilda mumbles, but Vera takes no notice.

"'Brilliant,' he used to say, when he saw the glow I got on those candlesticks. 'Like the gold along the roads of heaven, Veronica.'" She pauses, her eyes shining. "You remember that, Mathilda? How he called me Veronica sometimes?"

"Yes, Aunt." Mathilda remembers all right. She tried out the pet name herself once, only to be told sharply never to utter it again. It was strictly between the two of them, like a hundred other things.

Vera smiles secretively. "'I'd better watch out, Veronica,' he used to say. 'Our Heavenly Father may just scoop you up to keep house for Him.'" The pain comes again, and this

54

time Vera's face caves in on itself. "Oh," she gasps, "I loved him! Even then I was sick with love!"

Mathilda gapes. Her aunt gestures wildly to the bedside table, the inadequate remedies there.

Vera sleeps a little after the needle, wakes with a wildness in her eye. "We never touched, you know, not that way." She shakes her head fiercely. "Not once."

"Of course not," says Mathilda.

"Not that I didn't think about it." Vera giggles suddenly, a schoolgirl sound, strange in her ruined mouth. "I did, you know. You won't believe it if I tell you."

"Yes, I will."

"It was a dream I had." Vera would blush if she had the blood for it. As it is, her face smoothes out, momentarily transformed to marble, a carving of someone very young. "It was kissing, that's all—him kissing me, and me parting my lips and kissing back."

Mathilda shifts on her chair.

"I dreamt it nearly every night," Vera goes on. "After a while it got so I was dreaming it in the daylight too, you know, playing it out in my head."

Mathilda nods.

"I was in the confessional one day, the penitent's side, polishing up the leather. Maybe it was the smell of Father Rock in there, I don't know, but the dream came on terribly strong. I kept pushing it away, rubbing it into the kneeler, the seat, but nothing would make it go. I switched cloths and started wiping the screen, and that's when I got the idea."

"The idea?"

55

"More like a voice, really, speaking to me."

"A voice? You mean—?"

"Who, *Him*? I doubt it. It didn't seem like one of His." Vera grins darkly. "But I did what it said. I took out the screen."

"You what?"

"You heard me. I pried out the moulding, and then I could see the screws. I had a butter knife for scraping grease from tight places, so I used that. It took a while, but I got every last one of them out."

"But," Mathilda stammers, "but it's there. You put it back."

Vera holds up a finger. "It *looks* like I put it back. The moulding comes free with a fingernail. The screen's held in with two screws, not even twisted all the way."

"But why?"

"Why?" Vera shrugs. "So I could take it out whenever I wanted." She turns her face to the window's sharp light. "So I could sit in there and look through the frame. And imagine his lips coming through."

Mathilda's heart throws itself about in her chest. "Did he ever—" she asks. "I mean, I know he was a priest, but didn't you ever wonder if he felt the same?"

"Wonder? I know he did." Vera's shrunken hand fights its way under the quilt, fumbles with the sheet and emerges with the smallest of books. It's no larger than a matchbox, well thumbed, bound in leather that used to be red. Though untitled, the front cover bears a golden design— the busts of a doe and buck, simplified and stylized, gracefully entwined.

"My twenty-first birthday." She hands Mathilda the

56

tiny book. "He made me a cake, believe it or not, fresh strawberries and cream. We ate the whole thing, too, just the two of us. Mother kept her bed."

"And he gave you this?" Mathilda measures it against her pinkie. "For a present?"

"He left it in the pocket of my apron."

"You're sure it was him?"

"Look inside."

On the fly-leaf Mathilda finds two cramped handwritten words. *For Veronica.* She strokes the first yellowed page, not daring to open it further.

"It's from the Bible," Vera says. Mathilda moves to hand it back, but her aunt's fingers spring up like a wall. "You read it," she cries. "Read it and tell me he didn't feel the same!"

While Vera dozes fitfully, Mathilda fondles the little book. She averts her face before finally opening it, as though something might leap at her from the page. And leap it does, the moment she takes courage and turns her eyes to the diminutive text.

I sleep, but my heart waketh: it is the voice of my beloved that knocketh, saying, Open to me, my sister, my love, my dove, my undefiled—

Mathilda gasps, her eyes skipping down.

My beloved put in his hand by the hole of the door—

She flicks to a previous page.

My beloved is like a roe or a young hart: behold, he standeth behind our wall, he looketh forth at the windows, shewing himself through the lattice.

"Awooooo—" Vera wails like a ghost in her sleep.

57

Mathilda claps the little book shut and shoves it frantically down the front of her dress.

SED TANTUM DIC VERBO
(say but the word)

Away down the inching Communion queue, August catches glimpse after shifting glimpse of the flowery hilltop that is Mathilda's Sunday hat. Unlike most, it's actually pretty—tiny violets between dark cloth leaves. She moves closer. Nectar and velvety petals. He can smell them now, artificial though they are.

Defrocked. The word rises unbidden, unaccompanied by the dreadful image it normally evokes—a great dark bird with its magnificent wings cut away. Suddenly a frock is something whispery in the fingers, perhaps that pale blue one she often wears.

Her husband steps up to the rail, extending a disturbingly wide tongue. He takes the host the way a child takes a cookie—grinning stupidly and munching it down—then draws aside like a thick curtain to reveal his young wife.

Not the blue after all, but a green one he's never seen. Before he can stop them, August's eyes peel the dress away, fabric dropping in loose coils to reveal delicate, almost edible flesh.

Can he have fallen so far in a single month?

He blinks hard, but naked Mathilda remains, eyes downcast, lips parting to receive the host. Naked, that is, but for one small thing. It's barely a hat at all, really, it's so unobtrusive, as though the violets are part of her, having pushed their way up through her scalp.

Next in line, a bent old man clears his throat, its phlegmy rattle yanking August back. The dress returns in an instant, curling darkly to hide her glorious form. August's hand convulses, hoists a wafer and places it on her waiting tongue.

MEAT FOR HEALTH

She won't touch her meat. She'll cook it dutifully, but for a week now Mathilda's eaten around whatever Thomas provides, lamb chops or roast chicken, tender little veal rosettes. He's not blind. She's never had a big appetite, but at least she used to try—pick at her spare ribs and push them around on the plate.

It eats at him. Every untouched cut.

"Mathilda," he says one evening as she lifts a forkful of peas to her mouth, "you're not eating."

Her mouth full, she chews and swallows before answering. "Yes, I am."

"You know what I mean. You're not eating your meat."

She lays down her fork. "I can't stand it," she says quietly. "I can't."

"What do you mean, you can't stand it?" He tries to laugh, ignoring the rushing sensation in his neck. "A butcher's wife who can't stand meat?"

She looks up at him, the longest, straightest look she's given him yet. "Is that what bothers you?"

"What?" he splutters. "No, I'm—I'm only thinking of your health."

"I feel fine."

"Well, you won't for long."

She lowers her gaze. "Is that a threat?"

"What?! What the—no! I just—I meant your health will suffer. You'll get sick, is what I meant, if you keep this up." He shakes his head. "Jesus."

"Please don't."

"Don't what?"

"Take the Lord's name in vain."

"Sorry." He saws a chunk off his T-bone. "Mathilda, honey, I just want you to be healthy, you know, strong. For your own good." He takes a deep breath. "Maybe for a baby one day soon."

She shoots her chair back from the table. "I don't feel well."

"Honey, what is it?" He reaches for her hand, his touch making her flare.

"It's this meat," she says hotly. "Mounds and mounds of it. It's disgusting. It's making me sick!"

His fingers draw back as though burnt.

"Doesn't it bother you?" she demands. "Cutting up all those animals, hacking them up into bits?!"

"Mathilda," he says, keeping a choke hold on his tone, "human beings eat meat. It's God's will."

She blanches, her face contorting like that of an outraged child. "Since when?" she shouts, bursting into tears. "How do you know? Who says?!"

"The Bible."

She stares at him. "What?"

"Whose offering did God honour?" he asks quietly, glaring at his steak, gripping the rim of his plate.

"He—"

"Abel's. Abel's offering, not Cain's. God wanted meat, Mathilda, not rabbit food. Abel gave Him lamb."

"What would you know about it?" she mumbles. "You're *Presbyterian*."

Thomas explodes. "You think Catholics are the only—?!" he yells. "Dammit, we read the Bible! Not to mention all the crap I had to learn for the privilege of marrying you! *Corpus Christi*—isn't that what they're serving down there? The poor bastard's body and blood?!"

Mathilda leaps to her feet and hammers up the stairs, slamming the bathroom door behind her.

"Mathilda!" Thomas howls, his voice breaking over her name. He's gone too far. Lost hold of the reins, felt the old man grab them and gallop away.

ET NE NOS INDUCAS IN TENTATIONEM
(and lead us not into temptation)

Surely, to be tempted is no sin. August stares sleeplessly into the convergence of beams above his bed. Even the saints were tempted, he reasons, even Christ Himself. His hand fumbles at the scrolled base of the bedside lamp, twisting the little serrated knob to spread a circle of light over his shoulders and head. Better.

Beside the lamp, a precarious tower of books, the top volume winking glossy black letters from its yellow spine. *Confessions*. There—Saint Augustine was tempted. More than tempted. He succumbed, lost the path and found it again, then had the tremendous courage to record his travails. August reaches out greedily, sitting up a little, shoving a pillow in at the small of his back before cracking the book.

My soul being sickly and full of sores, it miserably cast itself forth, desiring to be scraped by the touch of objects of sense.

August nods eagerly. That's what it is, a sickness.

Don't scratch. Aggie bending to lift him from the slippery baking-soda bath, pulling white cotton socks over his small hands. *They'll get infected if you do.* He faced himself in her long mirror, three years old, a scrawny, pot-bellied child, enough like a plucked chicken without the pox.

He skips ahead.

I defiled the spring of friendship with the filth of concupiscence—

His eyes cloud over with chagrin. It's true, he thinks savagely. A fine young woman confides in her priest, and he rewards her with sinful thoughts and a lustful gaze. Well, no more, he resolves with a sudden righteous surge, no more. Encouraged, he flips forward.

His concubine gone, the saint laments, *my heart which clave unto her was torn and wounded and bleeding.*

Duo in carne una. A red ribbon of Genesis crosses the backs of August's eyes. *Wherefore a man shall leave his father and mother, and shall cleave to his wife: and they shall be two in one flesh.*

One flesh? Then how a sickness? Vaguely upset, he finds himself jumping again to a fresh page.

The eyes love fair and varied forms—

He jumps again.

For pleasure seeketh objects beautiful, melodious, fragrant, savoury, soft.

"Fragrant," he says aloud. "Savoury." His mouth dries out. Suddenly desperate, he rifles madly through the book, as though searching for some memento left pressed between pages—a dark violet, a brittle, hand-shaped leaf. The word *Thou* catches his eye. He thrusts his face close to the type.

Thou flashedst, shonest and scatteredst my blindness. Thou breathedst odours and I drew in breath and pant for Thee.

Words inscribed hastily, no doubt, an outpouring of the saint's sensual regard for his God. August should be transported, should feel himself brimming over with the wine of devotional love. He realizes this, even as he feels keenly the lack.

HIS COUNTENANCE

Locked in the bathroom, Mathilda reads feverishly long after Thomas has given in to a heavy, disenchanted sleep.

"'His eyes,'" she murmurs, "'are as the eyes of doves by the rivers of waters, washed with milk, and fitly set.'" She looks heavenward. *His eyes.* For a moment they float above her, ringed like targets, the colour of rainy slate.

She turns hastily to what is fast becoming her favourite line. "'I am my beloved's,'" she whispers, "'and my beloved is mine: he feedeth among the lilies.'" She can see him— not all of him, just his naked shoulders and face—crouched in a fiery meadow, the red goblet of a wood lily at his lips.

63

The image is terrible, wonderful. It spurs her on to more mysterious parts, the passages that move her in a manner she can't begin to understand.

"'His countenance is as Lebanon, excellent as the cedars.'"

Pages later she stumbles on another, deep and inviting as a country well. "'The mandrakes give a smell—'" She pauses. *Mandrakes.* Are they animals or plants? Their smell skunky or sweet, fetid or delicate or divine? In the end it doesn't matter. The word itself thrills her to the marrow of her bones.

7

HOC EST ENIM CORPUS MEUM
(for this is my body)

After his run-in with Saint Augustine, August grows mistrustful of the mind's twilight, as rife with questionable stirrings as its mirror in the natural world. He confines his bedtime reading to the one book that still seems fitting after prayer.

Quam speciosi pedes, the Blessed Apostle Paul writes in his letter to the Romans. *How beautiful are the feet of them that preach the gospel of peace—*

August looks up from the page. The feet? Without thinking, he yanks at the cotton blanket, bunching it up to uncover his own. Toes the length of a child's fingers, nails shiny, cut a little too close. He points his feet toward the door, then flexes them back, marvelling at their quiet strength. So many twigs and pebbles of bone. Down the end of the bed, his overlooked extremities seem suddenly miraculous. He sweeps them like windshield wipers, delighted by their synchronous grace.

He lifts an eyelid to dancing sheers and a thundering, greenish sky. The air is terribly close. He's on his belly, right arm skewed beneath him, his bottom rib damming its blood. The hand's asleep, nestled dead against the mass of his groin. It could be the hand of another, for all the sensation it affords.

He presses dreamily against it, contracts his pelvis and presses again, feeling himself grow hard. A third tentative thrust and the hand stirs, shocking him awake all the way. It's like walking in on somebody, catching them red-handed—only the hand in question is a sickly shade of blue.

August rolls off the slab of his arm, feels life return torturously in a stream of needles and pins. The hand arches its back. He grabs it, braiding the fingers with those of its more sensible twin. *"Pater noster, qui es in caelis—"* he mutters fiercely, burying himself in prayer.

BY-PRODUCTS: HEADCHEESE

The hog's thick snout and drooping ears are tough, so Thomas boils them with the dewclaws and toes, letting them soften a bit before adding the rest of the head, the heart and tongue, the loose, leftover skin tied up in a cheesecloth sack. When everything's tender, he picks the hot meat from the bones and chops the larger chunks down to size.

On the second boil he gives some thought to casing. He's cleaned the hog's paunch for a bag, but by the looks of things he'll have a fair portion left over. Not enough to bother making links, though. He may as well pour it out in a pan.

The thought pricks out a memory from his mind—seventh grade, the last year the old man tolerated him wasting his strong arms in school. They were doing art.

66

Greasing their faces with petroleum jelly, sticking straws up their noses, tilting back for the papier mâché. Some of the kids didn't like waiting for the moulds to dry. One under-sized girl lost it, tore the whole mess from her face and ran bawling down the hall. Not Thomas. The mould felt cozy. He was sorry when it came time to lift it off.

Pouring in the plaster, he felt an indescribable excite-ment, an all-over electrical itch, as though he'd never looked into a mirror and was about to confront himself for the very first time. The results were less than thrilling. When the mask came free, it was altogether too smooth, a pale whitish grey. It was the largest in the class, true, but otherwise just as unremarkable as the rest. He accidentally knocked it to the floor, where it cracked across the eyelids and lips. The mould was better anyhow. It held a more accurate impression of him in its hollow bowl.

It was one of the few items he brought with him to Mercy, along with a yellowed photograph of his mother, his butchering book, a change of shorts and money in a brown paper sack. He keeps it in the top dresser drawer, right out in the open. He'd gladly tell Mathilda all about it, but she just folds his boxers and stacks them away beside the face of his youth, never once thinking to ask.

Thomas legs it up the stairs, and in moments he's back with the mould in hand. He wipes the concave features with a bleached cloth, then lards up his fingers and begins rubbing fat into their cavities and cracks. For the moment he forgets all about the paunch. The mixture's perfect—soft but not sloppy, the gelatin spread evenly throughout. He ladles the headcheese into the mould, then carries it to the back cooler with care.

Two hours later, the mask springs out lively, florid and expressive on its plate. Thomas displays it on the top shelf with sprigs of parsley cresting back from its brow.

Mrs. Carstairs is the first of many admirers. "Oh, Mr. *Rose.*" She presses her fat fingertips to her mouth. "It's you, isn't it? It's *you.*"

"I'd've been about twelve," he tells her with a wink. "You can see for yourself the ravages of time."

HIS SMELL

Mathilda has waited patiently at the end of the line. Stepping into the stifling box, she lowers herself to the kneeler amid the countless odours of those who came before. She draws close to the screen, catching a whiff of male pungency from the other side.

"Bless me Father for I have sinned—" She hesitates, hearing him shift in his cassock at the sound of her lowered voice. "It's been a month since my last confession, and since that time I've had—impure thoughts." She plays with the hem of her dress. "And not just once, either."

He takes too long to answer. Far too long. Sounds strangled when he finally speaks. "Yes, my child. And have you—"

"I can't help it!" she cries. "It's the Bible!"

"The—Bible?"

The matchbox rattles in her hand. She fishes out a red-headed stick and strikes it, illuminating the tiny book in her palm. She's kept the page with a thin ribbon, something fairly safe to start with. Deepening her voice for the part of the groom, she begins. "'Behold, thou art fair, my love; behold, thou art fair; thou hast doves' eyes within thy locks—'"

The match dies against her fingernail, releasing a smoky, disquieting smell. Taking his silence as a kind of assent, she lights a second. "'Thy lips are like a thread of scarlet,'" she reads softly. And more softly still, "'Thy two breasts are like two young roes that are twins—'" The match curls up black and she shakes it out. She can hear him breathing now. "You see, Father?" she says. "I can't help it."

Still nothing but the hammering at her temples, the drag of his laboured breath. She's reaching for another match when he forces a loud cough.

"Ten Hail Marys," he wheezes.

"But, Father—"

His thin door opens and falls shut. Footsteps—measured, almost mechanical—carry him away.

ET VERBUM CARO FACTUM EST
(and the word was made flesh)

August was taught the *Canticum Canticorum* as metaphor—Christ the groom, his spouse the One True Church.

Tossing in his sheets, he suspects it may in fact be what it seems—*The Song of Songs*, a fragrant comb of words steeped in the honey of sex. When sleep finally comes, he dreams of Mathilda's mouth opening beyond the screen.

Dentes tui sicut greges tonsarum— Thy teeth are like a flock of sheep that are even shorn—

69

Of all the lines that might, it is this one that surfaces, her lips parting to utter it, both eye teeth revealed. Gleaming fangs turned fleecy and soft, they leap out, lead the others ewe upon lamb. The whole flock passes magically through the mesh, engulfing him in a woolly white stream.

He wakes with damp pyjamas, the hand a sticky phantom lying spent beside his deflating sex.

The male seed is the medium for original sin. So Saint Thomas Aquinas taught, and though many dissented, August was never so sure. Thus was the Redeemer born of a woman undefiled, delivered guiltless, completely untouched by the stain.

August holds his palm to the moon's weak light, staring at it as a murderer would, his colourless emission as damning as any blood. In his guilty, sleep-addled state, it seems his hand is thinning out, becoming translucent, a bony lampshade lending warmth to the lunar chill.

Corrosive. The semen is eating his flesh.

He throws the covers aside and leaps to his feet, the offending member thrust out before him, its clumsy brother fumbling at the knob of the door. Three leaping strides and he's in the bathroom, wrenching wildly at the grey-trunked faucet marked *H*. The tap belches and spits, then blasts a brownish stream. His good hand becomes a vise, closing to hold the other down while the temperature rises through pleasure to blistering pain. The hand turns a dangerous shade. Still he holds it under, defying all instinct, burning himself good and clean.

Halfway across the crowberry patch, Castor freezes, listening hard. After a moment it comes again—an unmistakable bumbling, a feathery-legged shuffle in the scrub. He grins. There isn't a rock or a good-sized stick within reach, so he pulls the mickey from his belt and smacks it against his palm.

"Fool hen," he calls softly. "Foo-oool hen."

True to its name, the fool hen pokes its head out from behind a nearby spruce, flashing the red eye patch of a male.

"Hey, buddy," Castor croons, "it's only me." He advances slowly, gripping the bottle around its neck. "You trust ol' Castor, huh?" The bird blinks at him. "Maybe that ain't such a good idea." Two feet from it now, he halts. "Sorry, buddy." The bottle comes cracking down. Castor remains bowed over the fallen bird, staring deep into his mickey, unable to move.

His eye settles in the arc of a morphine vial. St. Mary's housekeeper sits propped up in bed, worrying something shiny in her hands. At first Castor thinks *rosary*, but as the necklace slips her grasp, he catches sight of a fine gold chain, then a hinged heart the colour of a new penny. She opens her mouth in what must be a cry of frustration, snatching it back up from the quilt.

He knows the locket well. His eye landed there once, saw naked poplars through the rectory's kitchen window, watched the housekeeper's raw hands plunge into the steaming dishpan, the niece's pale arm reach in close for a teacup to dry.

The housekeeper's lips move in a muttered curse or prayer. The little heart's a tadpole in her fingers, a determined, slithery force. Finally, she gives up on her hands and wedges it like a nut between her teeth. It surprises her, springing open in two shallow halves. Only one side holds a picture, too small for Castor's eye to make out. She gazes at it for a moment, then begins picking at its edge with her nail.

In an instant he's back in the bog. The fool hen lies senseless at his feet, its black breast turned to the sky.

HIS SUFFERING

"Take them." Vera shoves the only jewellery she owns into Mathilda's hands. "Take them now." Her eyes narrow. "That way I know for certain they'll go to you."

Both chains are simple, plated gold. The locket is red gold, smooth and strangely plain. It pales beside the crucifix, white gold and fully two inches long, the hanging Christ so finely wrought Mathilda can make out the stringy muscles of His thighs, the heart-rending hole in His side. She lowers the Cross onto its back in her palm, the way the soldiers must've lowered it after He died. Stroking Him tenderly with the tip of her finger, she looks up to find Vera's eyes have glazed over with the drug.

Mathilda unclasps the thin chain at her neck and lays her confirmation crucifix aside. Vera's is so much more solid—somehow deeply adult. She tucks it inside her dress, feels its cool back meet her skin.

72

It swoops forward as she bends over the little book. *A bundle of myrrh is my well-beloved unto me.* She smiles crookedly. *He shall lie all night betwixt my breasts.*

AGNUS DEI

(lamb of god)

Her eyes are mirrored signals flashing code from the pews. Try as he might to look elsewhere, August meets them upon entering, and again after the Gloria's adoring refrain.

"Dominus vobiscum," he says throatily, extending his arms, believing he can distinguish her clear, steady voice from amid the congregation's reply. He flings his gaze wildly over the flock, and still it returns to her, her moon-shaped face serene, a fit setting for the unearthly reflections of her eyes.

Later, during the minor elevation, he is again distracted, this time by the smarting of his burnt palm against the chalice's curvaceous stem. Impatient with himself, he calls up images of the Saviour's spilled blood—the stitchwork forehead, the hammered holes, the wound in His naked side. It works, if only for a moment. Behind him, Mathilda's impassioned recitation of the Our Father rises head and shoulders above the rest. He takes a breath and soldiers on, praying earnestly for protection.

His long fingers snap the host in two, place a half on the paten and crumble a corner off its twin to dissolve in the wine—as the faithful are absorbed into the Church, he was taught, as they doff their individual skins, becoming one in the bloodstream of Christ.

"Agnus Dei—" He solemnly addresses the Lamb, begging for mercy, begging for peace. After the prayers before Holy Communion, he inclines toward the altar and strikes his breast, wincing. *"Domine, non sum dignus—"* He repeats the profession of humility three times, thinking miserably, I'm not worthy, it's true.

Since his first Communion, August has savoured the host, looking forward eagerly to ingesting the corporeal fact of the Lord. The doctrine of transubstantiation posed no problem, no mystery even—he could taste Christ's presence in that fine wafer, his palate discerning the very purest of flesh.

Now, nearly weightless, the Blessed Sacrament falls like an imaginary blow on the budding surface of his tongue. *Insubstantial.* No ripeness, no resilience, no reward. He clasps his hands carefully, but instead of praying, he wills his throat to close, his saliva to run dry. It's no use. Despite all his best efforts, the host melts and slips softly away.

Shaken, he mumbles insensibly, uncovers the chalice and sweeps the powdery crumbs from the paten into the sacred cup. His hand stings terribly. He drinks shallowly from the Precious Blood, raising the spotless cloth to wipe any trace of his lips from the rim.

At long last he removes the ciborium from the tabernacle and lifts its arched lid, exposing the hosts for the Communion of the faithful. The moment of veneration is fleeting. *Ciborium*, he thinks, from the Greek for "the seed cup of a flower." Reaching inside, his scalded fingers begin to throb.

8

PRAECINGE ME, DOMINE
(gird me, o lord)

Rat Creek ran deep the year August turned thirteen, rising up in its gully to form more of a river than Fairview had ever known. Just where the muddy turn of it came snaking into town, the water pooled to meet a flat outcropping of rock. Normally good for nothing, the rock made a natural pier, a black magnet for teenage boys.

August could hear them from where he sat sinking into the old horsehair loveseat his mother had finally relinquished to the porch. Their sound splashed up out of the coulee and washed toward him across the side field—the laughter boyish, cresting at times into a squeal or an abandoned yelp, then shifting to something deeper, a bellowed threat, the tried-on shout of a man. August listened to them day after day, poring over the latest book he'd borrowed from the church office, all the time telling himself he couldn't possibly care less.

Then one day—a day so hot he felt the bare soles of his feet would ignite—he stood and pivoted toward their swimming sound. He knew what awaited him. As far back as he could remember, he'd been resolving to give up trying to fit in.

There were six of them, all around August's age. He watched them from behind the old willow that had its roots spread out crazily down the bank. They were jumping in one after the other—cannonballs, scissor-legs, awkward, splashy dives—disappearing and bobbing back, stroking hard for the outcropping and hauling themselves out, as though there were no pleasure to be had in the water, but only in breaking its surface, in feeling it rush up around you and swallow your yelling head. From where August was standing, they made a circle of sorts, their brown bodies rotating in a wheel.

Until one of them chanced to look up.

"Hey!" The boy's fat finger rose to inform. "It's him. It's that son of a *bitch*."

Burnt necks swivelled.

"What'cha doin' out, sonny?" said another. "Your mama got a *gentleman caller*?"

Yes, thought August, your father. Didn't speak it, though, kept his tongue. He'd learned long ago there was no right answer, just as he'd learned they couldn't chase him if he could force himself never to run, or that it was no fun for them to beat on something that wouldn't fight back and wouldn't even cry.

Now it was almost always just words, and even those lacked their former force. As little boys they had understood how wrong, how downright evil it was for a woman—no matter how lovely, and even then they knew she was—for a woman with no husband to receive *paying* gentlemen in her home. Now those same boys could feel manhood beginning to colour their blood, and the change made them not so sure. Some of the wilder ones made it their business to pass close by Aggie's place on their way fishing. Some even stole into her backyard to slide silk stockings from the line—stockings they would press to their faces, even to their bare bellies, once they were safe in their beds.

Still, the *son* of a woman like that—

They left off jumping into the creek. When the last boy hauled himself out dripping, they spread out in a line, hardening their bodies to make certain August understood.

They were like one of those cut-out garlands, six little figures in a row. August looked down through the spaces between their legs and saw the water, six muddy triangles of cool. Maybe, he thought slowly, if I walk upstream a ways, I'll chance upon a better place.

He turned to go, but instead of the wide field his eyes met three big, bare chests—more brown, rippling triangles, only these were turned tip-down. Two of the men had soiled undershirts hanging like tails from the hips of their pants, but the middle one had his tied in a headdress, Lawrence of Arabia–style. Their hands and heavy workboots were black with grease. Railway men. August stole a look at their hard faces, figuring the middle one had been to see Aggie for sure.

"Ain't you goin' in, boy?" Arabia's hand came down on August's thin shoulder, black hair steaming from the pit of his arm.

"I—I—" August stammered.

"C'mon." The hand spun him lightly, and then August was slipping down the bank with Arabia right behind him, to where the other two were already stripping to their shorts. Arabia reached up to tighten the shirt's knot, then unbuckled his belt, motioning for August to do the same. Together they stepped out of their pants, and then the four of them tossed their clothing onto the bushes and walked out onto the coveted face of the rock. The boys broke and parted like a gate. Arabia's two buddies strode through like it was their birthright and jumped in tandem, throwing up a watery wall. But Arabia was different. He took his time, nodded hello to both sides, then pressed the palms of his hands together and followed his fingertips through the air, parting the surface with his nails and sliding into the creek like a knife through chocolate cream.

The boys began to smile now, relaxing their formation, a few of them whistling approval through their teeth. August held back. Arabia was underwater, nowhere to be seen. The two buddies were already climbing out, one with the look of twisted cable, the other hard in his own way, more like the rock they stood on, substantial and smooth. The boys elbowed each other to let them pass. Finally, a white cloth sphere surfaced on the far side of the creek, more than a little way down.

"Hey, boy," Arabia called out, and it was perfectly clear which boy he meant. "Ain't you comin' in?"

So August did. Took the rock at a run and launched himself flailing into the creek. It took him in whole. With a sucking, silty rush it drew him down until his feet met snaky weeds, then pushed him gently back up to the air. Back on the rock, the others were following Arabia's two buddies like ducklings, trying their best to stand out from the brood.

August stayed in, partly because Arabia did too—each of them a little apart, submerging to pull through the water, surfacing to let the water pull at them—but mostly for the feel. Smooth enough on the face of things, the creek was strangely alive below. It touched him all over—his chest and legs, his hands and throat, even the patch of new down at the small of his back. He turned that patch to the mild current, felt the shorts flatten to his behind while they billowed out bag-like in front. The water reached up through the leg holes, stroking him *there*.

Suddenly Arabia was hauling himself out, the other two shaking water from their hair. August struck for the rock— he wasn't waiting to find himself unwelcome once they'd gone. Back on dry land, his body lost its fluid grace, returning to the unwieldy collection of bones he'd come to know—with one small but immeasurable difference. The same boy who had pointed before now pointed again, though this time he aimed lower, as though his finger's trajectory was meant to pierce August through the belly rather than the eye. They stared—the boys, then the men— every one of them bent his gaze to the swelling in August's shorts. His hands came together to shield it. He looked up to meet grin after wicked grin.

"What're you starin' at?" Arabia reached up to untie the undershirt, uncovering a mass of coal-black, curling hair. The armpit hair that matched it bled out over his chest before narrowing to divide his belly with a line. "Never had a hard-on, I guess." He wrung out the water. "Must be babies still."

August watched the pointing hand fall, then the turned-up corners of all those grinning lips. Arabia pulled the damp undershirt on, drawing it slowly over his shoulders and down his front. "That means you're a man, is all," he told August, and the other two nodded and smiled. Then, like a team of workhorses, they turned as one body and started away up the bank.

August struggled into his pants. Around him the boys were getting fidgety, the railway men above them now, nearly cresting the bank. *A man.* He knew better than any of them what that meant.

There were those who preferred the back door. August watched them out his narrow bedroom window, so many shadow puppets against the shed—the postmaster's jabbing chin, the blacksmith's nose, a certain town councillor's jowls. Then there were those he didn't have to spy on, the ones who came brazenly up the front steps, who knew to wait if Aggie's tasselled shade was down, and often did so on the porch, helping themselves to beers from the cooler. Sometimes, during the harvest, there'd be two or three of them waiting their turn. Men with no wives, or wives in other provinces, or wives who wouldn't dare open their mouths to complain.

August didn't stay with the boys, and he didn't follow the railway men either. Instead, he scrambled up the far side of the old willow and started running, following the creek's cutting shape away from town.

He kept on long after the stitch took hold in his side. When he finally reached the bluff, he dropped to his knees in the poison ivy patch and, like a dog in any carcass it finds, began to roll. Saint Benedict threw himself into the nettle bed to fend off the demon lust—August knew this for a fact, one of many he'd swallowed whole from the pages of Father Felix's books. But even there, down on his belly among the venomous leaves, he could feel himself growing hard. There was nothing to do but stand. And once standing, to run.

Back at the house, Aggie was lying down in the parlour with a cigarette between her lips and a pink washcloth draped damply over her eyes. August ignored her, stalking through to the kitchen, where he dragged the carving knife from its shallow drawer.

"August," his mother called out, "be a love and stick the kettle on."

He didn't answer, didn't comply. Instead, he laid the blade flat against the fly of his pants and, with a slow chopping motion, slid it down.

"August?" Aggie called.

He could feel the leafy poison in his blood, the itch spreading out to open him in a patchwork rash.

"Honey? Are you all right?"

The knife clattered to the floor. Aggie pulled off the washcloth in time to catch the back of him, his angry hand slamming the door.

He was winded, his legs jelly, by the time he reached St. Paul's. "I—have to—huh, huh—confess," he wailed like a stuck bagpipe, his mouth inches from Father Felix's face. Then he sprinted for the stuffy box.

It was some time before the two came to understand one another, Father Felix questioning softly, August weeping wretchedly, scratching like a primate between replies.

"My son," the old priest said finally, "this is no great sin. Becoming—excited is, well, inevitable. It's what you do with that feeling that matters."

"It is?"

"It is."

"But, Father, don't you ever feel like you'd be better off—you know—without it?"

"Without it, my son? You mean desire?"

The word flared hotly in August's ears. "No," he muttered urgently, "I mean *it*."

Father Felix drew back from the lattice. "August, you haven't been thinking of—?"

August didn't answer.

"Now, August," Father Felix began severely, "you remember the words of Saint Paul in his first letter to the Corinthians, 'But now God hath set the members every one of them in the body as it hath pleased him.'"

"But—"

"He also wrote, 'And such as we think to be the less honourable members of the body, about those we put more abundant honour; and those that are our *uncomely parts*, have more abundant comeliness.'"

August sniffled. "But he didn't mean the *body*, did he, Father? He meant the Church."

"Well, yes," Father Felix admitted. "The Church is a body with Christ at its head. But you mustn't forget, August, Christ was also a man. He had all the—parts you and I do. He too was created in the image of God."

"Yes," August assented miserably. "But didn't Christ—"

Father Felix waited a moment before asking, "Didn't Christ what?"

"Didn't he say, '—and there are eunuchs who have made themselves eunuchs for the kingdom of heaven'?"

The priest shook his head hard in the gloom. "Eunuchs in the figurative sense only. He meant celibates, my boy, priests."

"Oh."

"Listen to me." Father Felix sat forward again. "He meant spiritual eunuchs, August. Real eunuchs aren't even allowed to become priests in God's Church."

"They aren't?"

"No, they aren't. It's like free will. How can God be sure you want Him if you haven't any other choice?"

Choice. August felt himself nodding, calm coming over him like a spell.

"Do you see, my boy?" Father Felix said anxiously.

"Yes, Father." The reply was honest, absolute. "I do."

9

HIS HEART

On her hands and knees behind the altar, Mathilda reaches around the thick base of the crucifix, her cloth returning full of dust.

One of the worst places, that. Vera took her on a tour of St. Mary's dirt traps not long after Mathilda first arrived. Taught her how dust was just a soft word for filth, how it was everywhere, riding invisible currents, eddying, bedding down thickly in its favourite haunts.

Mathilda wipes until the cloth comes back spotless. Satisfied, she drops it into her cleaning box, feeling absently down the front of her dress. The crucifix hangs loose, but the locket's smooth back adheres to her sweat-dampened chest. She frees it and, on a whim, unclasps the chain. It would be normal to open it—press the tiny button that holds the two half-hearts closed—but Mathilda already knows it's empty. Maybe Aunt Vera kept Father Rock's tiny portrait in there, took it out to have with her when she dies. That thought is sad enough, but anything's better than imagining the locket forever void.

Mathilda has only two photographs of her own. The first was a parting gift from the Grey Nuns, a fuzzy group shot that shows them assembled at the leafy border of the orphanage grounds. Each mouth is grim, each forehead marked with the black fold of bonnet that mimics a widow's peak. Layered, immovable, the women who reared her resemble nothing so much as mountains, a range of them seen from the plain.

The second is a good deal clearer, a dual portrait taken in a cluttered Winnipeg studio shortly before Vera bustled Mathilda onto the train to take her, as she so blithely put it, home. Mathilda's nine-year-old face is a blank, round from bone structure alone, not a morsel of flesh to spare. Her bobbed hair has been carefully, almost painfully combed, her dark dress ironed so it shines. She stands with a thin hand clutching the arm of an enormous wingback chair. Strangely, it is the chair that most draws the eye, so oversized and ornate as to make Mathilda's grave little aunt seem an exhibit of sorts, something one might come upon in the musty bowels of a museum.

On rare occasions Mathilda removes these two photographs from her top dresser drawer and lays them out side by side. Before and after. A precise document of the break at the midpoint of her short history, the halfway mark in her life so far. To the left of these two she places the picture she doesn't have, the one she so definitely refused.

It was her first morning in the rectory, the first morning she'd ever awoken in a room of her own. Dawn was breaking, and already she was scrubbed and dressed, seated at the kitchen table in a cloud of porridgy steam.

"Here." Vera thrust the sepia square at her with a jabbing motion. "It's the only one I've got. You might as well have it."

Mathilda didn't reach for the photograph as her manners prompted her to. Instead, she folded her hands carefully in her lap and allowed herself a lingering, fretful glance.

The boy looked to be about twelve. Hands thrust deep into the pants pockets of a wool suit, hair rearing up out of the shape it had been licked down to, he eyed the hooded camera with scorn.

"It's your father, girl." Vera waved the photograph so the boy vacillated before Mathilda's eyes.

"Yes." Mathilda looked down into her bowl.

"You don't want it?" her aunt said sharply.

Mathilda twisted her hands. "No," she said. "No, thank you."

Coming back to herself, Mathilda shifts on her knees, suddenly aware of the floor's unyielding nature against her bones. She's about to rise when something dark catches at the top of her eye. Not five feet up the back of the huge wooden Cross there's a small pit. It's no deeper than a fingertip, which is more than deep enough to provide a hiding place for grime. It's filthy. How is it possible she never noticed it before?

She wraps her finger in the cloth and pokes it into the pit, twisting as though she's cleaning an ear. It comes out black on the first few passes, then brownish and finally clean. Mathilda sits back against her heels, spotting the necklace on the floor at her knees. In her ardour, she's allowed it to drop. The chain lies separate, having snaked free of the locket's loop during the fall.

She plucks up the small, coppery heart. Without a thought in her head she runs a hand up the Cross's back until her middle finger dips down into the pit. As though cast to order, the locket fits snugly into place.

Thomas slaps a forequarter of beef on the cutting block, outside up. It's twelve ribs long, the thirteenth left behind in the hindquarter, like the one Adam gave up so God could build him an Eve. Thomas fingers the edge where it should be. Imagine constructing a human body around nothing but a single rib. *A woman's body.* Just think of it— they were buck-naked, the two of them, and without an ounce of shame. In the two months since he married her, Thomas has only ever seen Mathilda fully dressed, or draped in that white nightgown of hers, the one that brushes the floor when she walks.

Of course, the no-shame arrangement only lasted until that business with the snake and the tree. He never liked that part. From the first time his mother read him the story, he thought God had gone too far, making them self-conscious like that, the fig leaves and all, making them hide. Having seen so many animals without their skins, Thomas knows damn well what naked means. Beauty. Muscle and bone. The secrets of Creation laid bare.

The door jingles behind him, making him jump. He turns to find Pauline Trask in a too-tight dress, splotchy white flowers on a background of navy blue.

"Mr. Rose." She drags her pointy heels across his floor.

"Mrs. Trask," he replies, and then, without thinking, "You're looking well."

"Well?" She gives her handbag a little swing. "I'm many things, Mr. Rose, but *well* isn't one of them."

"Oh?" He flushes, wiping his hands on a cloth.

She drops her eyes and smiles, a crooked canine slipping

out from between her lips. Her fingertip traces along his counter, as though she's drawing in spilled salt. "Is that chicken nice and fresh?"

"Very nice." His eyes skip to her flowery front and away. "Came in this morning."

"I'll take two good legs. Oh no, what am I saying, Albert won't be back until tomorrow night. Better just give me one." She looks up. "Go ahead and leave the thigh on—no point watching my figure when he's never around to notice."

"Oh, now." Bending to slide open the display-case door, Thomas feels his trousers bind painfully at the crotch. He selects the best piece. "How's that one look?"

"Gorgeous."

He's keenly aware of her gaze, feels it prickling on his shoulder as he tears off a sail of brown paper, on his forearms as he wraps up the leg.

"How much will that be?" she asks, unclasping her purse.

"On the house." He hears himself say it, a silent panic thrilling in his chest.

"Why, Mr. Rose." She plucks the little parcel from his hand. "How can I ever repay you?"

He should make a joke of it, he knows, say something—anything—to ground the charge that crackles between them. Instead, he watches her turn and scrape slowly across the tiles. Even grins when she flashes him a wave from the door.

Mathilda presents her aunt with a spoonful of applesauce, but Vera turns her face away. "Tried to take him," she says bitterly.

"Come on now, one mouthful."

"Take him away."

"Who?"

"*Who?*" Vera comes close to shouting. "*Him.* Father Rock."

"Oh." Mathilda gives up for the moment, setting the jar and spoon aside.

"Those McGintys wanted to take him away."

"Only to the funeral parlour, Aunt."

"Beauty parlour, more like. Did they think I'd let them do him up like some kind of doll? Lipstick on a man like him?"

"Don't excite yourself."

"Not on your life." Vera's eyes glitter. "There were those that were against it, I know, but there wasn't anybody going to lay that man out but me."

"Hush. You did a fine job, too. He looked fine."

"First time I ever saw a man without his clothes."

"Without his clothes?"

"I had to wash him, didn't I? Get him into his vestments. Got to look your best when you meet your Maker, Mathilda. Smell your best, too."

"Yes," Mathilda stammers, "of course."

"He had to be dead, my one and only naked man." Vera smiles ruefully. "Those dogs of his were good as gold. I was going to put them out while I did it, but they all just lay down around the bed with their chins on their paws. Just about the only time I'd seen them all quiet."

Of course she let the dogs stay. Mathilda indulges in a moment's resentment, recalling how she tried to help that day, how Vera snatched the basin from her hands and slammed the bedroom door in her face. She feels a wave of grief. Not simple mourning—more the acute misery an overlooked child experiences at the mention of the favourite's name. Father Rock's dogs. A chaotic mass about his legs, the old ones dying in their baskets, now and then a new puppy for the pack. He was always touching them, sweeping his broad hand down a rippling back or resting it on a panting head.

"No better way to know something than to clean it." Vera digs under her pillow and produces a square of pale blue flannelette. "This is the cloth I washed him with. I made sure to wipe his face last."

VENI, SANCTIFICATOR
(come, o sanctifier)

"Miss Nickels?" August raps lightly on the housekeeper's bedroom door. "It's Father Day." He hesitates when she doesn't answer, then opens it a crack. "Miss Nickels?"

Her mouth gapes like a cave. He fears she may be dead, then spots the flick of a pulse in her stringy neck. "Miss Nickels," he whispers, "I've come to administer the Holy Sacrament." The room smells of breath and urine, of flowers gone rank in the vase. He breathes a sigh of relief when she doesn't stir, draws back and silently closes the door.

It's hot at the top of the rectory stairs, more of a landing than a hall, with a single small window and three dark, glossy doors. The one to the bathroom hangs ajar, leaking antiseptic scent. The third—the one that faces the housekeeper's—is closed. August stands perfectly still, listening for movement in the house below. Nothing. He fits his palm to the glass doorknob, closes his eyes and twists.

The room that was Mathilda's is even more cramped than her aunt's. August sets his Communion case down on the child-sized desk and steps to the window, looking down on St. Mary's northern wall. The Stations of the Cross progress two per painted window—*Jesus Falls the First Time* sharing a frame with *Jesus Meets His Mother*, *Jesus Falls a Second Time* alongside *Jesus Speaks to the Women*, *Jesus Falls a Third Time* paired with *Jesus is Stripped of His Garments*.

Beside him, the ceiling slopes claustrophobically to a skinny bed. Its bedclothes are gone, no doubt washed and folded away. The grey-striped mattress is perhaps two inches thick. Dead centre, three stripes wide, there lies the ghost of a bloody stain.

HIS BREATH

Mathilda's face is flushed, her hand dancing fitfully where the white nightgown gathers in folds at her lap. *Awake, O north wind; and come, thou south—* She halts. It's a hot night, but the bathtub's fat lip is cool through the cotton at the backs of her thighs. She can hear Thomas snoring, loud enough to carry through two doors and the stretch of darkened hall between.

"'Blow upon my garden,'" she reads aloud, "'that the spices thereof may flow out.'" The hand has a will of its own. It works steadily, drawing up the nightgown like a blind, tucking it aside. "'Let my beloved come into his garden—'" She inhales sharply. The book drops. Lands splayed open wide on the tiles.

"Bless me Father for I have sinned. It's been four weeks since my last confession."

"Yes, my child?" His voice is strangely removed, as though he's piping it in from elsewhere.

"And since that time it's gone beyond thought."

"Yes?"

"I touched myself," Mathilda says quickly, "*there*."

Again the shifting cassock, the sound a priest makes when he squirms. "And was there—volition, my child?"

"No. Well, yes. It was my hand. My hand was—doing it before I knew what was happening."

He clears his throat abruptly. "I see. Yes." He hesitates, begins again. "You know that Christian marriage is the embodiment of Christ's espousal to His Church—"

"Yes, Father, but—"

"—and that the act of marriage was created by God for the sole purpose of procreation, and is permitted only within the sanctity of the marriage bond—" His voice wavers.

"I know, Father."

"Good."

"It's just—I was lonely. In that way."

Amid the silence, the sound of him swallowing hard. "You're a married woman," he offers weakly.

92

Her voice comes back plaintive as a child's. "I was lonely."

He responds the only way he can. "Do you repent of your sin and promise faithfully never to sin again?"

From there they slip into the ritual dance—contrition, penance, absolution, position, advance, retreat. This time it's Mathilda's turn to bolt.

Once outside, she steadies herself against the heavy church doors. She'd been feeling all right—contrite even—until he spoke that word. *Sin.* It was the way his tone softened around it. The way his authority bowed.

It's business as usual the following week—August laying the host on Mathilda's tongue, Mathilda laying his meals on the table. For the most part she keeps out of his way, absenting herself when he ministers to her aunt, giving him few chances to avert his eyes. Once, backing down the stairs with the bucket and mop, she's certain she hears his long step halting, arrested for a moment in the hallway below. And once, she makes so bold as to straighten the parlour with him in it.

"You don't mind, do you, Father? I won't take long."

He nods tersely and returns to the book in his hand. She moves about, smoothing doilies, plumping cushions, aligning books. Father Rock's grim-faced portrait has gone askew. She grabs the gilt frame in both hands and guides it back.

"How is your aunt today, Mrs. Rose?"

His voice is a cool breeze at her back. She turns.

"She's—weak, Father."

He looks past her. "She must draw strength from the Lord," he says after a moment, bending again to the written word.

Come Saturday, Mathilda takes her place quietly at the end of the confessional line. No one bats an eye—it seems fitting she should go last, being a servant in the house of the Lord. Once inside, she draws her dress up to meet the padded leather bare-kneed. This time she makes no pretence of confession. She doesn't ask for his blessing, merely draws the book from her brassiere, drags a match along the striking strip and reads.

"'Thy lips, O my spouse, drop as the honeycomb: honey and milk are under thy tongue; and the smell of thy garments is like the smell of Lebanon.'" There again, *Lebanon*. Mathilda pictures dark-skinned bodies wrapped loosely in sheets, the sheen of sweat, unknown spices piled high in coloured bowls.

She licks her fingers to pinch out the match. He sighs. Relief? No, regret, she's sure of it. She strikes again. "'How beautiful are thy feet with shoes, O prince's daughter!'" She pauses, thinking she may have heard the softest of groans. "'The joints of thy thighs are like jewels,'" she rushes on, "'the work of the hands of a cunning workman—'" The flame eats a hole in her finger pad and she cries out, dropping it to smother in the folds of her dress.

"Are you all right?" His voice is urgent. "Are you hurt?"

She pulls the seared finger from her mouth and presses it to the screen. His lips touch down like lightning, swelling through to kiss it better in tiny bulging squares. Then he's gone. She can hear him running, his black oxfords clattering like hooves.

10

JUDICA ME, DEUS
(judge me, o god)

ugust was fifteen the summer Aggie believed she'd finally found their ticket out. Ernie Payne was seventy if he was a day, once something big in the next town over, now rattling around his fancy house like the last biscuit in the tin—wife buried, kids flown off, foundation beginning to give way. Ignoring his night blindness, he'd driven the long road to Aggie's on a tip and presented her with the remnants of his desire. Half a dozen such trips and he'd been moved to declare his love— an old man's love, passionate and possessive as a child's.

Aggie could scarcely believe her luck. "I hardly have to do a thing," she told August, laughing.

Ernie took them away to a fellow Elk's cottage on the lake. They played family—Ernie the mildly cracked patriarch, Aggie his keeper, August the hollow-eyed teen. Aggie wore new cotton dresses sprinkled with flowery prints, shopped for groceries in the nearby town, prepared whatever sweet or greasy concoction Ernie craved. She kept the cottage neat as a pin, herself too, as though all those years she'd gone around with her dark hair coming loose, she'd been dying to wear it smoothed and fine. Of course,

95

underneath all that tidiness lay Ernie's needs. August got to know the look in the old man's watery eye, went out wandering before he was told.

Brushing through a lakeside clearing one heated afternoon, he found himself surrounded by large, thin-winged flies. They cleared the way as he passed, lifting in shimmering waves, then sifting down to rest again among the nodding grass. They were legion. He found them clinging to bushes and trees, silvering a broken fence, a pile of discarded tires. Up close he discovered their loveliness, so many slender abdomens arched like lyres. Each one emitted the faintest all-over pulse, a minute, insistent surge, which, viewed en masse, set the whole field swimming like a sea.

At the Treat Shack, August accepted his heaping cone, laid Ernie's shiny coins on the counter and, quite against character, heard himself ask, "What are they?"

There could be no doubt to which *they* he referred. The flies were so thick on the sky-blue clapboard, the treat lady had to thrust her fat hand out through a little door in the screen, scoop up the money and yank it back.

"Fish flies," she answered, pulling a sick face. "I guess you're not from around here."

"They're beautiful," he murmured, to himself as much as her.

She snorted. "Not for long."

There were more than enough rooms in the cottage for August to have one of his own, but he chose to remove himself, bedding down in the musty canvas tent he'd set up at the foot of the sloping yard. The fish flies covered it now. No longer a pasty yellow, his little home winked like mica in the gathering night. He left the door flaps rolled up so he could watch them on the screen, and beyond, the undulating body of the lake. He dreamt of wings, thousands of them, a soft translucence caressing him head to toe. Woke sweating, bewildered, his boxer shorts plastered to his thighs.

The tent was besieged. He didn't dare step out for fear they would swarm him, so he let the shorts grow gluey against him, buried them shamefully early the next morning among the sand willows that sprouted from the beach.

The fish flies didn't drink blood or suck sap or gnaw great, gaping holes in the trees. There wasn't time. They were born, they mated, they died. Before long the ground was black with them. Aggie swept dark piles off the porch, thick bands marked the tide line, the lake grew a bobbing, blemished skin. They rotted like anything else. For a week August walked in misery, inhaling their carrion stink.

When Ernie fell down dead of a stroke while shaving, it came as no great surprise.

HIS TRADITION

Mathilda saws three thin slices from the loaf and butters them with care. Dipping the ladle into the soup pot, she fishes for the prettiest chopped vegetables, the heartiest chunks of beef. After arranging the bread in a fan shape around the bowl, she carries Father Day's lunch to the dining-room table, where she's already laid a perfect place. She smiles at the sound of the front door. In the two months since she took over Vera's duties, he's never once been late for a meal.

She retreats to the kitchen, one ear cocked to the scrape

of his chair. Leaning into the stove, she pours a dipperful
of soup through the strainer, collecting the amber broth
in a cup. On her way up the stairs she pictures him eating—
dunking the bread so it softens, closing his lips on the
spoon.

"There you are." Vera struggles to raise herself up on
the pillow. "Come here."

Mathilda balances her tray on one hand, drawing the
door closed behind her. "Don't try and talk, Aunt," she
says gently. "You need your strength."

"What for? To die?"

"Hush."

"I won't hush, I'll have plenty of quiet soon enough."
She hooks a finger into the pocket of Mathilda's apron. "I
made myself an old maid for him, is that what you think?"

"No. No, Aunt."

"Well, it wasn't like that. He was God's territory, all
right, but I set up house in a little corner of him all the
same. Like a squatter," she says giddily, then sinks back
into her pillow, spent.

A squatter? Mathilda pictures her aunt sitting neatly,
almost daintily, in her chair before the fire, Father Rock
pacing close with a fistful of pages, pausing now and then
to mumble a line aloud, or to shove a scribbled passage
between Vera's gaze and the lacework in her lap. If Vera was
a squatter, what did that make Mathilda—kneeling at the edge
of the rug with the dogs splayed out between her and the
hearth, or bent over her schoolbooks at the kitchen table, or
staring holes in the blue rose wallpaper of her tiny room?

"I knew it was in there." Vera's voice makes her jump.
"I've been having the pains for more than a year."

Mathilda sets down the tray. "You knew?" She feels for the chair back and sits down hard.

Vera nods. "At first I thought it was my sin. You know, loving him—impurely for all those years. Who knows, maybe it is."

"No!" The protest leaps from Mathilda's mouth, startling them both. "I mean, you're not—you're a good woman."

"Maybe." Vera smiles thinly. "Anyway, whatever I thought, I fought it. Gritted my teeth when it flared up and forgot it the moment it settled down." She pauses, her voice hollow when she speaks again. "I gave in to it when he died."

"What do you mean?"

"Just what I said, I gave in. More than that, I egged it on. When the pain came, I opened the gates and let it run. I'd lie in bed at night stroking where I thought the tumour might be." She lifts her eyes to meet Mathilda's horrified gaze. "It's true. I talked to it, still do. *Grow.*" She pats her distended belly. "Come on, you little bastard, grow."

ET A TE NUMQUAM SEPARARI PERMITTAS
(and never suffer me to be separated from thee)

Morphine's softened the housekeeper—she looks up without a trace of hostility as August utters the entrance blessing and steps awkwardly into her room. Mathilda turns on her chair, watching him steadily in the vanity mirror.

"Leave us alone now," the housekeeper says mildly.

"Yes, Aunt." Mathilda rises, passing close by August on her way out the door.

"That's not necessary," he blurts. "I mean, family are welcome."

But the housekeeper waves her chicken-foot hand. "Go on."

Repeated visits haven't steeled him to the smell. The sound of the door closing fills him with an acute and irrational dread, as though he's just been sealed into a crypt. After a moment's ignoble hesitation, he pushes the feeling aside and takes a lunging step toward the bed. He hurriedly arranges the Blessed Sacrament and the oil of extreme unction on the night table, then mumbles his way around the little room, shaking droplets of holy water on the sick woman's belongings while avoiding her gaze.

Though her face remains placid throughout the following series of prayers, he can't help but feel she's waiting him out, uttering her responses by rote. Sure enough, her head bobs eagerly when he pauses after the last amen. She looks up at him through glittery eyes and rushes headlong into the sacrament of penance.

"Bless me Father for I have sinned." She hesitates, and August bows his head politely. "It's been—well, decades since my last real confession—"

He looks up sharply in time to catch the tail end of a twitchy little smile.

"—and since that time I accuse myself of these sins." She takes a long, sucking breath. "I loved," she says finally, "and I didn't do a thing about it."

August nods, dumbfounded. "Continue, my child."

"That's it."

"That's it?"

"Yes. Only—" Her breath quickens. "Only there's something I wanted to ask you, Father."

"Yes?"

"After we die—in heaven, I mean—are we the same?"

"The same?" He gathers his wits. "Well, death is the beginning of our true life, a life infinitely richer than that which we know on this earth." He shoots a glance at her expectant face. "In heaven," he continues, "God shows Himself clearly to those who are blessed—"

"Yes, yes," she interrupts, suddenly fretful, "but what about *us*? Are we changed? Will we know each other? Will we know our—loved ones when we meet?"

"Oh. Well—"

"The thing is, Father, we never kissed." She kneads a loose fistful of flannel sheet. "Do you think maybe, in heaven, I could kiss him?"

"Kiss him?" August draws back. "I shouldn't think so," he stammers. "Love is—*different* in heaven."

"Different?"

"More spiritual, selfless. You won't have the same—desires."

"I won't want to kiss him?" she asks, her voice forlorn.

"Well, yes," August replies feebly. "I mean, no, you won't."

The housekeeper closes her eyes. "No," she says quietly. "That can't be right."

II

MEAT FOR VITALITY

Thomas takes to watching his wife leave. He feigns sleep when she rises, listens to her move about the kitchen beneath him, then hurries to the window in time to watch her emerge from the back door. She walks slowly down the lane, her gait languorous, a maddening lilt and sway. *Waltzing Mathilda*, one of the packers at the slaughterhouse used to sing. Thomas's eyes follow her fine heels like dogs.

It's not normal. She's his wife, dammit, and every night she turns rubbery and cold, like a white length of tripe in their bed.

Take her. The thought speaks aloud. *It's your right.*

Suddenly he feels warm, a little feverish. Then clammy. He steps back shakily from the pane.

If only she'd eat a little meat. Flesh feeds flesh, fires up the blood, gives the body its mortal heat. Just think of those Eskimos—nothing but seal and whale and bear, and look at them, the buggers live in snow houses, they're little furnaces, every one.

He'll have to work on it, keep at her—nothing forceful, just a gentle, relentless push. After all, it's nearly three months now, and he's had nothing but a dry kiss on the cheek.

Three months makes an anniversary of sorts, their first quarter-year. He could make dinner, insist on doing everything himself—close the shop early, lay out candles and wine. He flushes warmly at the thought of serving her. She's relaxed, maybe even a little tipsy. *You're spoiling me*, she purrs, smiling like a huntress and digging in.

He'll make something really special, impossible to resist. Crown roast. Lamb? No, even better—veal. He grins wildly. He'll make a real show of it. Pile up the potatoes and call her his queen.

THE WHORL OF A SPHERE

Castor's vision of the housekeeper's niece is fleeting, his eye resting only briefly in a green-swirl aggie lost in the grass. It's night, and she's down on her knees in the lane behind her husband's shop, arranging sticks and dried leaves in a little pyre. She sets a match to it, making herself lovely in its sudden licking glow. Castor's pulse quickens at the light on her throat. He feels a terrible urge to gather her red hair in his hands and preserve it from the threat of the flame.

He returns unwillingly to his body, sprawled in its arm-chair beside a badly smoking lamp. It's eerie, the way his eye so often seeks a fire. As though it too remembers, and is determined he should never forget.

The Roseville house was an old clapboard tower half a mile outside town, far from his daddy's white family on the hill. John Wylie had lost both legs from the knees down out East on the ships before coming home to Manitoba to marry the girl he'd always loved. The fact that Mary Lariviere was the finest looking woman in Roseville did nothing to change the purity of her blood. *Squawfucker*. Some said it to Wylie's face, others behind his back out of respect to his stumps.

The bedrooms in that old house were on the second floor, Wylie having insisted that was where bedrooms belonged. As soon as he was big enough, Castor helped his mother carry her crippled husband up the narrow stairs.

Castor was fifteen the night it happened, old enough to have hauled Wylie up to bed on his own. The engine was what woke him. By the time he'd shaken the sleep from his head and stumbled to the open window, three men were dragging a large wooden box from the bed of a truck. They hunkered down around it and there came a flickering, as though all three were lighting cigarettes at once. As Castor turned to go wake his parents, a terrible squealing arose from below. He spun back to the casement, saw the men stagger backwards as the crate burst open in flames.

Fire shot in all directions, running crazy zigzags through the grass. At first Castor thought they were gas trails, but then one of the burning strips leapt into the air, showing itself to be alive. Several of the flaming creatures—*weasels?*—tore into the dead lilacs that were crumpled like newspaper around the house. Castor's feet took root. He covered his eyes. Heard drunken laughter and spinning tires, the growl of the truck's escape.

The door flew open behind him. His mother was wearing one of Wylie's undershirts and nothing else. Already Castor could see smoke curling up behind her, hear a devouring rush from below.

"Jump!" she yelled. "Jump for the tree!" And she disappeared into the thickening smoke. He stood motionless, whimpering. She was back in a heartbeat, the baby in her arms. "Jump, Castor!" She rushed at him.

"But what about—"

"Jump!" she screamed. "NOW!"

He scrambled up onto the sill, felt her palm at the small of his back, and sprang. The elm was like a giant leaf pile laced with sticks. It cut and battered him as it broke his fall.

"Castor!" His mother stood above him at the window, backlit by the terrible blaze. Her face was savage. She held the baby out like a gift, and Castor struggled to his feet, extending his bloodied arms. He braced himself. And then she did it—shut her eyes and let her month-old baby fall.

He took the shock of it into his body, staggering forward on impact, twisting violently to put himself between little Renny and the ground. He hit hard, his head bouncing so the world around him wavered and went dark.

When he came to, Renny was squalling on his chest amid a shower of sparks. Behind them, the house let out a deafening roar. Stunned as he was, Castor knew what he had to do. Keep hold of his baby brother, get up on his feet, and run.

HIS MOUTH

Mathilda's inky eyes have sunk deep into her skull in search of sleep. She's been up all night, trying everything she could think of to rid herself of the little red book. After endless aborted attempts at ripping it page from page, she stole out to drown it in the back ditch. Unable to bring herself to submerge it, she built a small fire and let the book dangle, crying out at the last second and snatching it back.

It nestles in its customary corner of her bosom now, as once again she brings up the rear of the confession line. She shuffles forward like a sleepwalker, sinking heavily to the kneeler when it's finally her turn. Bowing her head, she remains silent for as long as it takes the last few penitents to leave, then unearths the book, rattles her matchbox like a fetish and begins slowly to read.

"'Who is she that looketh forth as the morning, fair as the moon, clear as the sun—'" She pauses for as long as the flame will allow. "'—and terrible as an army with banners?'"

She moves quickly in the sudden gloom. Pries out the moulding, finds the two screw heads with her fingers and twists. Vera had it right—in moments the screws bounce off the kneeler and roll away. Mathilda lifts out the screen. She can just make him out, drawn back in terror to the corner of his box. Her fingers move methodically, slipping buttons from holes, reaching back to release hooks from their eyes. She scratches a match to life and gives him a good long look. When the light dies, she lifts her bare breast and holds it to the open frame. At first nothing but the faintest of scrambling sounds. Then his mouth. It fumbles for a moment, discovers her budding nipple, and latches on.

CUTS FOR SPECIAL OCCASIONS

It never occurs to Thomas, not once, not even a knock on the back door of his brain. The thin-lipped, high-stepping priest? A stick man. An old man really, too intent, too particular for his years. Thomas feels sorry for him—another faggot rolled up in the cloth.

No, if anything it's the Church. Moderation is best in all things, and in religion most of all. It gives him the willies, truth be told, all that smoke and mirrors, and the poor sap rambling on in some old girl's nightie. The building, too. Those gory windows, the way it hulks over its dead end, looking down on all the sinners of the town.

St. Mary *Immaculate*. Mathilda turned woman there, with nobody to guide her but a spinster aunt. Before that a gaggle of nuns. Thomas shakes his head. No wonder she doesn't know what she's about.

He has the table laid out fine—a snowy cloth, the good dishes, even a fistful of flowers from the back lane. The wine is icy. He's read how you can get away with white when it's veal—not that either of them would know the difference. Still, he'd flinched at the thought of serving red.

She's late getting home. "How dirty can the place get?" he mutters, then turns to the oven to fret over his master-piece. It's looking a little dry. He lowers the dial to *warm* and turns again to the window, debating whether he should baste it again.

She's coming. Even dragging her heels in the dust, Mathilda manages a slim-hipped sway. Thomas runs to the stove, transfers serving dishes to the table, lifts the drip-ping crown roast onto its white and waiting plate. Her hard shoes on the back stairs. His heart pounds. He sits. Then stands. She walks in to find him somewhere in between.

"Mathilda." It's all he can think of to say.

"Hello, Thomas." Her eyes widen as they move over the table. "What—?"

"Three months," he blurts. "It's our anniversary, a quarter of a year."

"Oh." She stares at the gleaming wineglasses, the fat bottle, then fixes on the meaty crown, its blunt-boned petals splayed. "I—" She blanches suddenly, alarmingly, as though someone's pulled the plug on her blood. "I don't feel well, Thomas. I think I need to lie down."

He should say something, he knows, offer to help as she teeters up the stairs, ask if she needs anything, perhaps an Aspirin or a cup of tea. But he can't. He sits down heavily in his chair. Hears the bedsprings moan and fall quiet, a smothering quiet, so it's all he can do to draw a breath.

His hands reach out for the roast. Slowly, ceremoniously, they lift it high and bestow it sizzling upon his head. Hot grease trickles down his temples. He stands carefully and takes a few mincing steps, like a charm school student balancing a stack of books. A few more steps make a circle, and from there he progresses to a series of figure eights. Dignity, he tells himself. It's tricky, all right, but he never once reaches up to hold it on.

PONE, DOMINE, CUSTODIAM ORI MEO
(set a watch, o lord, before my mouth)

On his knees in the cramped office, August weeps uncontrollably, begging forgiveness before an oily depiction of the Sermon on the Mount. When he finally manages to lift his gaze, it fixes not on the Saviour, but on the light that surrounds Him, yolky gold bleeding off into white.

Halo?

No, that's just the head. There's a term for it, August knows, this glow a sacred body gives off. He distracts himself with the search, moves his mouth to try and shape it, follows its trail through the shadows of his brain. In the end he has to give up. For the life of him, he simply cannot come up with the word.

12

ALTERNATIVES TO BEEF

That goddamn Church.

Thomas stands in the road out front of his shop, staring down to where St. Mary's squats. The nurse must have relieved Mathilda by now. She's probably stayed on to scrub the church floor, when every other man's wife is at home tucking his children into their beds. By God, the wind lifted her skirt the other day and gave him his first real look at her knees. They were knobby and red. That place is taking her finest years.

All down Train Street the boulevard elms are beginning to turn. Thomas walks heavily back to the shop, locking the door behind him. He's not quite done for the day. Five minutes before closing, an old man he'd never laid eyes on came in dragging a grizzled billy goat on a rope. They were rank with urine, the two of them. Thomas was about to gently usher them both out when he noticed the old fellow was shaking. Tremors ran down his arms, his head wobbled, his jaw worked sideways like a cow's. The moment he freed a gnarled hand from the animal's leash, it led his arm in a grotesque involuntary arc.

Then there was the animal. It was black and white, not mottled but half-and-half, hind and fore, as though its maker had taken a snowy goat by the heels and dipped it headlong into a vat of ink.

"Ever seen one like it?" said its keeper, his rebel hand waving.

"Well, no," Thomas answered, "can't say that I have."

"Welsh black-neck," the old man said smugly. "You won't find another in these parts."

"Is that a fact?" Thomas breathed awkwardly through his mouth in their pissy cloud.

"It is." The old man cleared his throat. "You can see for yourself the bugger's had it."

It was true. The old billy was a sight, a swollen bag on four rickety, threadbare legs. Mucus gathered in the corners of its eyes and in the black crevices of its nose. Its hooves were so badly overgrown they curled up like a sultan's slippers.

"Yes sir," Thomas agreed loudly. "I'd say so."

"He's for the dogs," the old man yelped. "Terriers, see, Scotties. I breed them."

"Yes," Thomas said patiently. "I see."

"I'd butcher him myself, but with these hands—" His head shook with added violence. "—I'd probably slit my own throat."

"Never mind that now," said Thomas. "I'd be happy—"

"Good." The old man thrust out the leash, a yellow zigzag in his hand. He had tears in his eyes. Or maybe they were just watery. It was impossible to tell.

Now, as Thomas wraps the sinewy, foul-smelling meat in brown paper, the goat's head gazes up at him from its basin on the floor. He can feel its stare, the same bug-under-glass tingle he gets from the crucifix at Mathilda's church. Do they have to show Him like that, so waxy, just the way He would be after losing so much blood? Maybe she's cleaning it right now—his young wife lovingly swabbing those big white feet. The thought makes his right eye flicker, the cheek beneath it twitch and dance.

He can't stand it. He has to do something, anything, to win her back. A miracle, that's what he needs. He remembers something Mathilda told him once, back when he was learning catechism and he let her go on about the one holy Catholic and apostolic Church just to hear the sound of her voice. Miracles. In some countries—hot countries, where people more naturally acted things out—Catholics bought little body parts made of silver or tin and affixed them to Crosses or to the church steps as a way to beg miracles from God. Heal my lame foot, Lord. Heal my heart.

He nudges the basin with his boot. The goat looks so sad, a faithful companion cast aside. Of course he couldn't nail it to the Cross, or even leave it on the church steps—only a madman would do such a thing. Still, there is that hedge. Surely, beside the steps is close enough.

HIS HEAD

In the confines of the sacristy, Mathilda bends to her basket, slides her hands under a freshly ironed surplice and raises it to its rightful shelf. Her chest muscles follow those in her arms, lifting her delicate breasts.

She's left the door open behind her. He makes a small sound drawing it closed, but she knows better than to look around. The lone window drops a rectangle of crepuscular light. She lets him watch her in it, bending again to the basket at her feet.

It's no surprise when his hands land on her hips, or when one of them lifts the hem of her dress while the other wrestles her panties down. He's gulping—she can hear him—gulping air like a child who's been sobbing too long to stop. He lifts his own hem then, fumbles to free himself, pushes at her, finds his way in. She bites her lip so it bleeds when he tears her, but it's worth it, so worth it to have him inside. Moments later he cries out like a puppy and falls listless against the curve of her back. She cradles his head between her shoulder blades, as though balancing a heavy stone.

He backs away from her the moment he pulls out, and she turns to find him smoothing his cassock with shaking hands. He won't look at her. Instead, his eyes find the basket, his vestments freshly bleached and pressed.

Then, as though the floorboards are pivoting beneath him, he turns.

"August—" she pleads.

"Father Day," he says strangely, his hand on the door.

ITE, MISSA EST
(go, you are dismissed)

August bolts himself into the office with trembling hands, whirls, and flattens his back to the door. His eyes dart about the room. He'd never budge the prie-dieu, or the walnut cabinet for that matter, weighted down with so many leathery books. The desk must weigh a ton, but the chair—it's a heavy oak throne, the maroon seat rubbed shiny, still moulded to Father Rock's behind. August lunges for it, grabs its thick arms, drags it groaning from behind the desk. Then freezes. He's caught sight of himself in the cabinet's cut glass door, the hysterical mask of his face.

He sits down hard in the chair. Stares empty-headed, then comes back to himself with a start and sits forward, straining his ears. Nothing. She's not coming after him. Even if she were, would she really try to break down the door? He lets out a single sharp bark of laughter, then curls down to hide his face in his lap.

How, in God's name? *How?*

He hadn't expected to see her there. He was just passing, head bent to the breviary, and there she was, a fine painting framed by the door. There was no face to contend with, only hips, a lifting hem, a revelation of hidden lace. The light went out in his head. His eyes were two tunnels to the shape that was her, the threshold and perhaps half a dozen steps the only obstacles to be overcome.

Overcome. Yes. As though his body were a fleshy vehicle, something utterly alien at the wheel.

Like sleepwalking.

What are they called, those female demons who come to men in their sleep? *Succubi.* That's right, from the Latin, "to lie beneath." August looks up. Nods gravely, beginning to understand.

HIS DUTY

Mathilda moves about the rectory kitchen in a daze, her hands preparing the only thing Vera can still stomach, a watery cup of tea. She'll carry it up now, see if her aunt needs a shot, sit by the bed until the night nurse arrives.

At first she was sure he would follow her, confess his wretched love and take her in his arms, this time face to face. But perhaps it's better this way. Too much at once and he might panic, sicken even, like a man gorging himself after a prolonged fast.

She mounts the stairs slowly, feeling her thighs brush one another lightly with every step.

"Aunt?" she calls softly into the little room. A cone of yellow lamplight hovers beside the bed. Vera's sleeping face is turned away, her grey hair loose on the pillow like a girl's. Mathilda pads toward her, sits the cup down to steam silently beneath the lamp's fringed shade.

There's something about Vera's hand—the way it lies palm up on the quilt, slightly cupped, as though offering something unseen. Mathilda skirts the bed swiftly to stand trembling on the other side.

The nurse takes care of everything. She draws the sheet up over Vera's face, telephones Thomas and Doctor Albright, looks high and low for Father Day. Mathilda lets Thomas lead her back to their flat over the shop, lets him tuck her into bed, turns her dry eyes to the wall when he offers a hot cup of tea.

LAVABO INTER INNOCENTES MANUS MEAS
(i will wash my hands in innocency)

The office darkens around August and still he grips the chair's arms, his fingers curling possessively, like a king's. At some point he hears the heavy groan of the front doors.

A woman's voice—not *hers*, but familiar—calls out for him in the nave. Footsteps in the hall and again, "Father Day?" followed by a bout of knocking on the office door. He lets go of the chair and covers his ears, holds the pose long after the knocking stops.

In the end it's neither duty nor despair but discomfort that forces him to stand. His bladder full to bursting, he shuffles to the priest's WC. It's been too warm for trousers. Slowly, painstakingly, he draws up the cassock, revealing black ribbed socks and boxy knees, two bloodless, ramrod legs. One hand holds the heavy cloth bunched at his waist while the other hooks a hesitant thumb over the waistband of his shorts.

Faced with handling himself, he's filled with a sudden, nameless dread. Or not so nameless. It's not the idea of finding it changed—somehow marked, larger perhaps, or darker—but the idea of *not* finding it, of finding it gone. Having wished it, almost willed it more than once, he prays fervently that it not be so.

It's late, very late, when August finally unlocks the office door. Mathilda's left the vestibule light on to illumine the rose window from within. The nave is gloomy and surprisingly cool, as though subterranean, untouched and untroubled by the heat of day. There's even a draft. August can feel it on his bare throat, the backs of his hands, rising up under the cassock's black bell. The centre aisle gapes, forcing him to move stealthily along the wall.

The font burbles in its alcove, a dove-grey basin, water spilling from a pair of cupped and proffered hands. August bends slowly from the waist. The hands are masterfully rendered. So loving, so infinitely strong. He's close enough to discover veins in the marble, fine wrinkles where the flesh might crease.

"Help me," he whispers, lowering his face like a drinking beast. The hands are cold—shockingly so—adamantine, almost cruel. He snorts water up his nose and chokes.

HIS RETREAT

Early the next morning Mathilda calls out to wake Thomas as usual, slamming the back door on his reply.

Not a soul along Train Street. Not a sound in the rectory. She pauses for a moment at the foot of the stairs, looking up. Vera's bed will be empty now, her body removed in the dead of night, the McGinty brothers having slid it quietly into their shiny hearse. No point going up. She continues through to the kitchen, rolling up her sleeves as she walks.

Her heart leaps shamelessly at the sight of an envelope propped against the kettle. The seal's licked shut, so she tears it, unfolding the white sheet to reveal a block of his cryptic hand.

Mrs. Rose,

I am informed that The Church of St. Mary Immaculate in the Parish of Mercy is to employ a new housekeeper, effective today. She is the widow Stitchen, formerly of a small prairie parish to the west of town. As I have elected to pick her up myself, I will have no need of a morning meal. If convenient to you, I will be available to discuss the details of your aunt's funeral tomorrow.

The Diocese is most grateful for your service during your aunt's illness and passing. You will, of course, be duly compensated.

   With deepest sympathy and the blessing of Christ our Lord,
      Father Day

Mathilda drops the nameless envelope in the garbage. She removes Aunt Vera's sharpest paring knife from the drawer, lays the note on the cutting board and begins slicing it into narrow strips. One after another she lifts the paper ribbons to her mouth. Her eyes vacant, she stares dead ahead, shifts on her feet and chews.

13

PER IPSUM, ET CUM IPSO, ET IN IPSO

(through him, and with him, and in him)

T wo hours before Vera Nickels's funeral is due to begin, August still can't decide on what to say. He hunches over a blank sheet, his long fingers choking the pen. He never liked the woman. There was something in her gaze that went clean through his skin and poked about, as though she were charting his innards, every darkness he harboured, memory and deed.

Still, there's no denying she had a fierce devotion to the Church. He nods sharply and scrawls the word *fierce*.

What else? She looked after him for a time, grudgingly but well. Looked after Father Rock too, don't forget, not to mention Mathilda. *Mathilda*. He hasn't laid eyes on her since—since before he left her the note. Her ox of a husband took care of the funeral arrangements, saying softly, "The wife's beside herself, I'm afraid. Thought it best to let her rest." August kept the desk between them, and by the end his hands had stopped shaking. There was nothing in Thomas Rose's rather humbled demeanour to suggest he knew. *Best to let her rest*. But surely she'll be at the funeral, pale and delicate in black, gazing up at him from the mourning pew.

He catches himself. The point is, the housekeeper took excellent care of her niece. By all accounts she went to a great deal of trouble to locate her older brother's abandoned girl. August scribbles *abandoned* alongside *fierce*.

He's distracted by a sound, something brushing through the fine-boned saplings outside. It would be only normal to look out, but the office window is set too high, designed to afford illumination only and not access to the countless diversions of the world.

Again the brushing. It's almost human, only gentler, more at home among the trees. He pushes back quietly from the page. Steps first onto the chair's creaking seat, then up onto the flat face of the desk. From its edge he can see perfectly—the long window divided in three, its middle pane centred on a white-tailed buck. He holds his breath. The animal is unspeakably handsome, its hide both glistening and dull, as though it were cut from still-wet clay.

It lowers its velvety antlers to a sapling poplar's greenish bark, begins rubbing in short, nodding strokes. The thin tree trembles, shedding a yellow cascade. Tine by tine the fine brown velvet wears away, hanging crimson about the buck's ears. Skinning itself, thinks August, a chill skipping along his spine.

The tree bark darkens. The buck's true antlers emerge.

HIS MARK

Mathilda sends Thomas to the funeral without her and burrows down sick in their bed. She's not faking, either.

Every peal of St. Mary's bell lodges like a hatchet in her skull, her gut churns bilious and sour.

She tells herself it's the sin that's making her ill—so much easier than facing his rejection, the death of their newborn love. She can't even confess to make it better. *Bless me Father, for I had knowledge of you in the sacristy.* She squeezes her eyes shut. If only she could go to another church, one where the priest could still speak to her in the anonymous voice of God.

She could invent a friend in a nearby town, or perhaps even a reunion at the orphanage. The mere thought of travel is enough to exhaust her. In any case, to confess would be to wipe her soul clean, and isn't the stain of him better than nothing?

EMITTE LUCEM TUAM
(send forth your light)

The summer of August's seventeenth year, the sky opened to hammer down hailstones the size of eggs. Broken-necked chickens went down scratching in their yards. All around Fairview, cattle bled from their backs, their skulls—one lost a big brown eye. Dogs and horses ran mad while the crops lay down and died.

August was caught out in it, wandering the fields. The hail tore his clothes, cut his scalp, then the backs of his hands when he laced them together to form a helmet of flesh and bone. He did the only thing he could—bent his body at the waist, threw his long legs out in front of him and ran. More than once he went down in a heap on the ruined wheat, unable to keep his balance among the icy stones. When he reached the road, he found them bouncing, flying back up at him from the ground. He pounded on with his mouth clamped hard.

In town, every windshield had caved. The streets were deserted, not a sound but the thunder of hopping hail. Hands still glued to his head, August passed doorway after doorway—Thompson's Fine Furnishings, the Ideal Café, the Sons of England Lodge—skidding onward to St. Paul's.

The hailstones were like giant marbles on the church steps—he had to go down on all fours to make it up. Shuffling forward on his knees, he reached out for the door. His bleeding fingers on its handle worked like throwing a switch. Just as suddenly as it had begun, the hail came shattering to a stop.

Silence. He hauled himself up slowly, turned and saw the pavement strewn with glassy, steaming stones. Faces came out of doorways, then feet, stepping gingerly, as though testing the solidity of the ground. August lifted his eyes. The sky was torn clean, almost blinding.

Father Felix was nowhere to be found. The church was deserted, yet August assumed his customary place, sliding quietly into the last pew. After feeling himself all over to tally up cuts and pulpy spots that would bruise, he eased down to the kneeler and began muttering whatever came to mind. An Our Father followed by a few Hail Marys. Several Glory Be's. He even got partway through the Litany of the Most Precious Blood but couldn't remember what came after "Blood of Christ, shed profusely in the Scourging." Having run out of words, he reluctantly opened his eyes.

The light amazed him—shafts of it mid-air, pools on the floorboards or trapped among the pews, great unnamed shapes shimmering on the walls. Crimson lapped over cobalt, gold over living green. He knelt long enough to witness its movement, a glacial benediction blessing every surface it stained.

The window above his right shoulder depicted the feeding of the five thousand. He craned his aching neck and saw the scene for what it was—the crowd so many hungry shards, the shoreline broken, even Christ Himself a collage. Strips of lead held the elements in place, but it was the mounting, the holding up that allowed meaning to shine through.

Aggie was curled face-in on the parlour sofa when he got home.

"Where have you been?" Her voice came weakly through the cushions.

"Out."

She rolled over. Her eyes were swollen, the greasy black pencil melted halfway down her cheeks. "August!" She scrambled to her feet. "Who did this? Who?!"

"What?" Then he realized what he must look like—black hair matted with blood, shirt ripped, skinny arms mottled pink and blue. "Nobody," he assured her, "I got caught out in it."

"What?" Her hands on his face like a blind woman's.

"The hail. I got caught in the hail."

She felt down over his sharp shoulders and squeezed his arms.

"Ow!"

She let her hands drop, stepped back and burst into tears.

"Hey," he said, bewildered, "it's okay. I'm okay."

"N-no." She backed up to the sofa and lowered herself slowly, wincing when her bottom touched down. She cried hard then, shoulders jumping, face in her hands.

August had seen that wince before. She had trouble walking after some of them, let alone sitting down. "Did something—happen?" he asked. "Did somebody—"

"Get me Our Lady." She pointed toward the high corner shelf, then sat up a little straighter and started wiping at her eyes. August obeyed. The foot-high porcelain madonna was heavy. He needed both hands to lift Her down.

"Give Her here." Aggie's face was a streaky mask now. She looked up at him through the eyeholes, one hand grasping the Virgin firmly about the waist while the other felt up under the ceramic blue folds of Her robe. The stopper came out with a kissing sound. Then money, a rush of coins carrying bills with them, all colours, each folded in a tidy square. Aggie caught and pooled it in the lap of her dress. "I've been saving," she said quietly.

August stared. It couldn't have been easy. They'd been through the same lean years everybody else had—Aggie accepting a sack of cabbage at times, or a couple of fresh-killed chickens—back when the whole top layer of the prairie seemed to be blowing off, the two of them sweeping and sweeping, stripping the beds daily to shake out the filth.

She laid the hollow statue on the glittering pile, reached up and took hold of her son by his wrists. "This is for you," she said, "so you can get out."

He hadn't known until that moment.

"Mother—" He knelt down to tell her, knowing it would be the happiest day of her life. "Mother," he said again, "I've been called."

LIBERA NOS A MALO
(deliver us from evil)

August finds it by smell. Having unlocked St. Mary's great front doors from the inside, he pushes them out into the morning. A foul sweetness hits him full in the face. Something dead in the bushes. He knows the odour well, having grown up where the land and all its creatures met the fringe of a prairie town.

He shakes his head. There should be someone to look after such things, a proper caretaker, not some once-a-week gardener to run the lawn down to scrub and hack mercilessly at the gnarled old grape. Certainly the priest has enough to concern himself with. Still, there's no getting past it—the reek of death is no fit aroma for the stairway to the house of the Lord. He pinches his nose and descends.

Three steps into the caraganas he parts a bushy clump and draws back. It's formless under a faceted blanket of flies—formless, that is, but for the points of two chipped and yellowed horns. Disgust bottoming into horror, he tears a leafy switch and swats at it, seed pods rattling a fine black rain. The flies lift in a greasy cloud. Skinned of its hide, the goat's head is somehow both more and less human. The eyes are wide open, one staring whole, the other pecked to a jelly. Both are raw about the rims, as though irritated by a flood of tears. Something's eaten a half-moon from the upper lip, exposing the stumps of an animal sneer. It's the last thing August sees before the flies regroup in a darkly jewelled mass.

Around him the bush grows murky, confused. August sits down hard, raking his fingers through feathery leaves on the way. Only one man in town would have a goat's head lying about—certainly only one who could skin it with such skill. *He knows.*

In seminary they studied the faithful of the world. To his amazement August learned of practising Catholics who, though they venerated the Holy Virgin and Her Son, went about their lives in the Old Testament way. These were the kind of men who left the heads of livestock to say they had called. August hammers at his forehead with the heel of his hand. *Keep thee far from the man that hath power to kill.*

The butcher knows, all right. What other possible explanation?

One. A thought like a voice. *One other explanation, far worse. One other with an affinity for goats.*

Dread bubbles up from the soil around him. August sniffs his sleeve, his fingers, finds the head's stench clinging to him like smoke. With no thought for who might see him, he scrambles to his feet and explodes from the bush, taking the church steps like a man possessed.

THE HAPPY COUPLE

Castor's tried several vantage points over the years, but the alder thicket is the best by far. It'll stay dense enough to hide him until at least mid-October, and it's on a little rise, so he can see all three outbuildings, a couple of boxcars and a good portion of the platform.

He's been waiting for over an hour. He doesn't need much, just a glimpse, enough to assure him his little brother's alive and well. He wouldn't be fool enough to approach Renny. Not after what happened two years ago, the last time they came face to face.

The new station was only half built then, a timber framework open to the stars. Castor prowled around its periphery until he found what he'd come for—sacks of lime, cement and sand, piled like pillows on the ground. They turned out to be heavier than he'd bargained for, but the moment he spotted the wheelbarrow, it was problem solved—he could manage three of them now, even make it back for a second run.

He was bent over a sack of sand, grunting like a boar, when a pair of coverall legs appeared. Holding his hands out in surrender, he straightened. There wasn't much light, but he would have known that silhouette anywhere. "Ren!" He let out a sigh. "You scared the pants offa me."

"Shhh!" Renny crouched down, pulling Castor after him. "You been drinking?"

"Just maintenance."

"Christ, Castor, what're you doing here?"

"What's it look like?" Castor grinned, but Renny wasn't laughing. "I need a proper house, Ren, the shack's fallin' to shit."

Renny turned his face away. After a moment he stood and hoisted a sack of cement onto the barrow. Then another. Then turned on his heel and ran.

Castor takes hold of the nearest alder's trunk and closes his eyes. He opens them just as Renny steps out from the station's side door, lifting his hand in a wave. Castor turns his head in time to see his brother's wife swing a silver lunch pail in reply. Elsa's hands are purple up past the wrist. She must still be working at the jam factory, bringing Renny his lunch on her break.

It's strange she hasn't quit that place and had a kiddie by now. It made sense while Renny was overseas fighting, but the war's been over for three years. Maybe she *can't* have them. Castor flashes on the time his eye landed in their bathroom faucet. Elsa hunched over on the toilet, bawling. Down around her ankles, the crumpled panties fair ruined with blood.

Renny jumps down eagerly from the platform and meets up with her at the first switch. He ignores the lunch pail and takes hold of her hand, drawing close to whisper in her ear. She gives him a glare, but not a real one, because a second later she whispers something back. His face splits wide open in a grin, and he turns and pulls her after him, like a boy leading his mother to a bullfrog in the grass. When they come alongside an open boxcar, he lets go of her hand a moment, just long enough to vault himself up on deck. He reaches down to haul her up after him, the two of them disappearing behind the heavy sliding door.

Eight years. Renny was gone for half that time, but all the same, it's been eight years since the two of them tied the knot, and they're still carrying on like newlyweds. Castor feels a two-pronged pang. He was jealous at the wedding too, sick with it. It didn't help matters that Renny had chosen one of the linemen to stand up with him. *Best man.* Castor was well oiled before he even set out for the church. Once there, he lurched down the aisle, opening his jacket to show the guests his bottle, explaining just exactly how the visions came on. Renny and the lineman took hold of him by the arms and half-carried him to the empty back pew.

Elsa gave him a poison glare upon entering, then shone smiles left and right all the way up the aisle. The second she and Renny were done signing the register, she came for Castor like a broody goose. "If you care about your brother—" she said to him through her teeth.

"Well, sure I care—"

"Shut up and listen. If you really care about his happiness, if you want him to be able to hold his head up in this town, you'll walk out of here and never come back."

"Aw, now—"

"The town drunk," she hissed. "The village idiot." He lowered his eyes, and that was when she came in for the kill. "Look, it's Uncle Castor," she sang in a little-girl voice. *"Run!"*

Suddenly Castor doesn't feel much like sticking around to watch Renny and Elsa emerge. Besides, it's high time he got his hands around a bottle. He can feel the ghost of a tremor coming on.

14

SICUT IN CAELO, ET IN TERRA
(on earth as it is in heaven)

August stood awestruck before St. Peter's Catholic Seminary, flanked by the two suitcases that were all he'd brought with him from home. It was the largest building he'd ever had cause to enter. Its landscaped grounds swept gracefully down to the Thames—only the Canadian cousin, but to August it was the finest river in the world.

"Entering seminary is a life and death decision." So began the Rector's speech of welcome. "*Life* because you are choosing to give your life to the Church and to Christ our Lord." He paused dramatically. "*Death* because you will pass a sentence of death on the life that came before."

August smiled. He'd taken the bus to the London depot and a taxi from there, but that wasn't how the escape played itself out in his mind. He could picture himself standing in the street out front of his mother's house. He'd been waiting so long he could scarcely believe it when the time finally came. The bird was the colour of smoke, the size of a winged horse. It circled before landing, blocking then revealing the sun. August didn't question, he simply threw a long leg over its back, dug his fingers into its silky ruff and held on. The dove lifted him away just as Fairview began to sink, collapsing in on itself like a dying star.

He tuned back in for the speech's denouement.

"—from the Latin, *seminarium*," the Rector said gravely, "meaning 'seed plot', the ground where one plants, say, a crop of corn." Here the Rector removed his thick glasses with tremendous delicacy, as though he were revealing an occult truth by exposing his squinty eyes. "As in any cornfield," he continued, "there are those who grow sweet and healthy in their husks, safe in their silk, golden in the sight of God." He smiled thinly. "And there are those the crow picks clean."

SLAUGHTERING HOGS: STICKING

The hog's a giant. It took just about everything Thomas had to scald it, dragging it up and down in the steaming vat, first by its hind legs, then by a massive hook through its lower jaw. It was a hairy bugger, and scurfy too. He was at it forever with the bell scrapers, and still the beast had to be scrubbed and singed all over twice before the final shave.

Its jowlless head sits on a plate now, the tongue and eyes carved out, along with the waxy core of its enormous ears. Thomas has already opened the carcass to find little blood trapped in the chest—the sign of a professional kill.

Most slaughterhouses stuck their hogs hanging after yanking them off their feet with a length of chain, but Thomas Senior was from the country—he'd grown up sticking hogs on their backs, so on their backs was the way it was done.

For months after Thomas botched his first sticking, the old man checked up on him when he was killing hogs. Even when everything looked perfect, Thomas Senior would squat down and stick his fingers in the wound, exploring the shape of it, feeling for the cut-macaroni ends of arteries and veins, counting how many Thomas had got. When he was satisfied, he stood and walked off without a word. When he wasn't, he stuck his own knife in, then Thomas's fingers, to show him how it ought to feel.

Thomas cuts down between the hams and splits the aitchbone with a saw. Then loosens the penis and lets it hang, to be pulled out later with the guts.

He'd always dreamt of escaping, but it wasn't until his mother passed on that the dream began to walk with him through his waking days. He was twenty-seven when Sarah Rose died. It was merciful—a blood clot breaking loose somewhere and shunting steadily toward her brain. The morning was peaceful, his father not yet returned from the night before. Thomas was hunkered over the paper to the soft scrape of her whisking eggs behind. She didn't make a sound—at least not with her mouth, just her small body crumpling, the same thud as a two-month calf. It was all over before he could pick her up, not so much as a twitch or a moan.

The day after the funeral he was boning beef. "No sense mooning," Thomas Senior had grunted at the graveside. "You and me back to the grind bright and early." And so they were, Thomas donning his mother's apron to cook the old man his breakfast, a panful of hissing bacon and the last of her home-baked bread.

When the others knocked off for the day, Thomas stuck around, the narrow blade frantic in his hand. The old man looked in, said, "Lock up, willya," and was gone.

The moment he heard the door slam, Thomas reached in under his rubber apron for the newspaper he'd smuggled in, stuffed down his shirt front, bleeding ink over his belly and chest. He spread it on a dry corner of the table and began piling up bones, folding up three sheets per parcel, setting the grey lumps aside.

Thomas was a whiz with the boning knife—he controlled it like a claw—but today he'd been sloppy, left so much meat on the bones that he'd felt the others exchanging looks. Let them. Not one of them had a feeling bone in his body, except maybe MacLeod, and he'd been out on the killing floor dropping steers. Thomas had never told MacLeod about feeding the dogs, but he had a feeling the quiet half-breed would understand.

The others hated the stockyard pack. Some of them even laid out rat-poisoned livers and hung around to watch the skinny mongrels wolf them down. At least once a week he rolled bundle after bundle down the dark side alley, watching the toothy shadows tear into each one, so grateful they swallowed the bloodied newspaper too. Many had died from eating what they were given, but that did nothing to cut the hunger of those that were left.

He was folding up the final sheet when a black box ad caught his eye. *Butcher shop for sale. Fully equipped. Sole butcher to town. Apply Town Hall, Mercy, Manitoba.* His heart kicked hard. He traced the ad with his knife tip and lifted it from the page, folded it up small and drove it deep into the front pocket of his pants.

He could hear the dogs scrapping outside. Gathering up the bone parcels in his arms, he hurried to the back door, a crazy grin splitting his face. "I'm coming," he called out, laughing. "Daddy's coming."

Thomas felt like a country bumpkin on the streetcar. He'd lived in St. Boniface all his life but had only crossed the river to downtown Winnipeg a handful of times, and those with his mother, to the looming Hudson's Bay and back. He asked the driver to let him off close to the library, an institution he knew nothing about, save the words an elementary school teacher had planted in his brain. *A library is a kind of heaven. You can learn anything you want there for free.*

He wandered the stacks, trailing his hand down spine after spine. Famous painters, tuberculosis, birds of Canada, the Baptist Church. His head swam. Half an hour before closing he did the unthinkable—approached the aged librarian at her desk.

She nodded wordlessly, swivelled in her chair and yanked out a long, skinny drawer. Her knobby fingers flew through the cards, alighted, pulled up three and scratched particulars on a small green pad.

Thomas panicked. "I can't," he stammered. "I don't know—"

She sighed and nodded again, then leapt up like a woman half her age and led him at a run through the shelves. One of the books was perfect—small enough to smuggle home, with detailed blueprints for retail cuts, both fancy and run-of-the-mill. Thomas burned the midnight oil for a week, slipping the book under his mattress and catching an hour's sleep before rising to work. He carried the dotted diagrams in his mind, laid them out over carcasses to better understand. The old man caught him idle, intent on a quarter of beef, and cuffed him upside the head.

A month had passed since Thomas spotted the ad. He'd located Mercy on a map, counted and recounted what money he'd managed to save. It was a surprising amount, really, given his piddly pay. And then there was his mother's rainy-day fund, one of the many secrets they'd shared, a flat English toffee tin flaked pink and gold, kept under the nest of her prize layer in the ramshackle coop.

He couldn't bear to write and see if the butcher shop had already sold. The way he looked at it, that shop was his only hope.

Rose's Slaughterhouse bred two kinds of men—dead-eyed shufflers and nutcases, the kind who lopped off fingers in their brutal haste. Thomas Senior liked to keep a good mix. The shufflers showed up on time, while the snaky ones kept up the pace. Thomas could feel both types inside him, loitering like bums, waiting for his will to break. So far, though, he was still an exception. Him and MacLeod, the smooth-skinned Metis from The Pas—the only one Thomas talked to, even though it was rare to get an answer back. MacLeod was unmatched as a cutter. Carcasses divided themselves eagerly for him, like loose women removing their clothes.

It was just the two of them at the greasy lunch table, the others hooting and hollering outside. Thomas Senior had two fat male rats in a cage, and was taking bets on which would claw the other down. No longer able to keep it to himself, Thomas fished in his breast pocket for the ad. MacLeod gave it a good long look, like he was trying to figure how much it was worth. "You got money?" he said finally.

"Some. Enough, I guess. Maybe."

MacLeod sipped his strong, foul-smelling Thermos tea. "So go."

"Yeah," Thomas sighed, tucking the square of newsprint away. "He'd skin me."

MacLeod nodded. "Do a piss-poor job of it, too."

Thomas laughed. It was true, the old man never could get a clean cut—raggedy hides and splintered bone were a sure sign of his work. Every beast he handled gave meat that was fear-toughened and bruised.

MacLeod's metal cup struck the table. "Tonight," he said firmly.

"Tonight?"

"You go out in the shipment tonight."

It was a truckload of pork sides headed for Ontario. Thomas could bail out partway to the provincial border and find his way somehow from there. *Find his way somehow.* It was an exhilarating phrase.

It was crazy, he knew, but it just might work. Also, MacLeod reminded him, it was free, and he'd need every cent he had when he got there. Besides, Thomas was no artist, but even he could see a kind of beautiful symmetry to the plan.

They picked a crate with a good-sized knothole for air. MacLeod piled the pork sides in around him, then nodded and nailed the top down without a word.

Thomas figured the truck's speed at about forty-five and counted off miles with a box of matches and a pocket watch.

He made his break when the driver pulled in for coffee and pie. MacLeod had used finishing nails—a couple of cramped kicks and the lid gave way. Thomas pushed aside three fatty slabs and sat up like a vampire, banging his head on the metal roof.

Jesus. He broke a clammy sweat. What if they'd stacked him at the bottom of the pile?

Shoving the meat aside, he climbed out awkwardly, lit a match to get his bearings, then hammered the lid back on loosely with his fist. He kept his eyes closed to clamber backwards down the stack, preferring his own dark to that of the rig. The door opened mercifully from the inside. He hoisted it up just high enough to roll out onto the gravel lot.

Road signs told him east from west, one promising not far to the turnoff he needed. It didn't take long to leave the truck-stop lights behind. It was still spring, still cold. Every now and then there came the howl of an engine, headlights tearing a white strip through the night. Thomas stopped to catch his breath. The earth was spinning. He could feel it— the planet and him on it—spinning through space.

HIS LOVE

It takes three full weeks of sick mornings for Mathilda to stop kidding herself. The truth hits as she's scrambling eggs for Thomas's breakfast, gagging in their putrid steam.

Later that same day she catches a glimpse of Father Day through the shop window, scurrying past on the far side of the street. Her stomach kicks at the sight of him. She excuses herself from the chicken livers she's weighing and runs upstairs. After splashing frantically at the sink, she looks up to meet herself, wild-eyed and dripping, in the mirror. He's thinner, no doubt about it, rings of blue misery beneath his eyes. It could be as simple as guilt. Or maybe, just maybe, it's love.

Come Saturday, she reclaims her position at the tail of the line. There's a faint tarnish on the brass handle of the confessional door, a tarnish that wouldn't have been there in Aunt Vera's time, or during her own brief reign. She kneels down, feeling instinctively for the frame. The moulding won't come free. Beneath it, she imagines not two screws but eight, every one of them tightened down. She skips the preliminaries.

"Father—"

"*Bless me* Father," he replies stiffly.

"I'm pregnant." It's the first time she's said it aloud. "Did you hear me? I said I'm—"

"I heard you."

"Well?"

"Well—" He pauses for what seems like forever. "There's certainly no sin in that."

"*What?*"

"'Your wife shall be as a fruitful vine on the sides of your house,'" he quotes distantly, "'your children as olive plants round about your table.' Psalm one hundred and twenty-seven. Perhaps you recall it from the marriage ceremony."

"But—" Mathilda stammers, "but you know I've never been with him."

"So you say."

She's struck dumb.

"Is there anything you wish to confess?" he asks coolly.

Her eyes fill instantly with tears. "Go to hell," she whispers.

"What's that, my child?"

"That's right." She presses her mouth to the lattice. *"Your child."*

"Back already?" Thomas is closing up shop when Mathilda returns.

She sets about helping without a word, pulling down the four wide blinds. He's scrubbing the block when she rounds the counter and lays her cheek to his back. He freezes. Stands stock-still as she nudges him from behind—first her chin, then her small breasts, then her hips. She feels a tremor run through him, feels it double in strength when she presses her pelvis into his tree-trunk thigh.

"Now," she tells him, and he turns slowly, one hand on the counter, steadying himself like a boxer at the ropes. She rubs her entire length down his, feeling him harden under his blood-spattered coat. He groans and stoops forward, lifting her as though she weighed no more than a spring lamb. "Now," she says again as he pounds up the stairs, *"now."*

He can't help but be a little brutal—a big man who's been saving it far too long—but Mathilda wants it that way. She keeps her wits about her, remembering to yelp when he enters her, to clutch helplessly at his heaving back. Afterward, he won't let go. He drops off with her locked in his arms, so she lies there breathing shallowly, watching the lengthening shadows climb the walls.

Later, when dark has fallen and Thomas has finally shifted in his sleep, Mathilda manages to wiggle free. She rises and pads down the hall. Crying softly, she rocks herself on the toilet, willing her husband's seed to drain away. It's only the beginning, she knows. Having opened the floodgates, she'll have to let him rage and flow. It hardly matters. There's no reason to keep herself now.

She's brought the faded little book with her. She can barely make out the words for trembling and tears, but she forces herself, whispering them aloud like a curse. "'I opened to my beloved; but my beloved had withdrawn himself, and was gone: my soul failed when he spake: I sought him, but I could not find him; I called him, but he gave me no answer.'"

She spreads her legs and drops the book into the toilet's bowl. Reaches across herself to flush it away.

15

HOSTIAM PURAM
(a pure victim)

M rs. Stitchen is a middling housekeeper, if that. After only a month in her care St. Mary's has taken on a distinct pall. August runs a forefinger along the banister on his way down the rectory stairs, turning the fingerprint up fluffy and grey. Not that he minds a little dirt—he's developing a new fondness for it, in fact. The hank of black hair that once fell to his eyes now sticks to his scalp when he rakes it back. Beneath his cassock he's beginning to exude the undead odour of the pitifully poor.

It's just that soap and water—even cold water—seem suddenly self-indulgent. All that fresh scent and foam, not to mention the dubious action of rubbing one's body with a nubbly cloth. No, nothing wrong with a little dirt. It's the new housekeeper's mothering he can't stand. She knows her place well enough not to badger him directly, but that doesn't prevent her from drawing him a bath each morning, laying out an assortment of candied soaps, inquiring every other day where all his dirty laundry might be. He deflects her insinuations by ignoring them, finding this method singularly effective—except when it comes to the matter of food.

A broad, ample-bosomed woman, Mrs. Stitchen is deeply distressed by August's hollow cheeks.

"You could use a good feed, Father," she announced the moment she first crossed the rectory threshold, as though *Father* were the name of some neglected family pet.

"Thank you," he began icily, "but I'm not—"

"Nonsense," she called over her shoulder, abandoning her cases in the hall and cutting a beeline for the kitchen as though she could smell the way. "Sausages and eggs is what you—" And the rest was mangled amid a clanking of pans.

It took several mornings, but he wore her down to four slices of toast and a pair of hard-boiled eggs. The eggs took some doing.

"Soft-boiled feeds the blood, Father," she insisted repeatedly, then, under her breath, "and if anyone's blood could use it—"

"That is an old wives' tale, Mrs. Stitchen." He paused to let the insult sink in. "In any case, runny yolks sicken me. If you want to put me off eating altogether, you're going about it the ideal way."

The next morning two eggs rolled loose on his plate, the little silver cups nowhere to be seen.

Hard-boiled are easier to hide. He can peel them slowly while she watches, sprinkle each with salt, then set them aside and nibble absently on a corner of toast. When she returns to the kitchen momentarily—and she always does, for there's inevitably a pie in the oven or stock on the boil—he slips one or both of the eggs into the pocket of his robe.

Mrs. Stitchen stared hard at the striped bathrobe the first morning he wore it to the table. "Protects the cassock," he told her wearily.

The toast is tricky. No matter what he says, she butters each slice until it drips. He has to line his pockets with wax paper to keep the grease from bleeding through.

He takes his tea clear. "For the throat," he tells her firmly, morning after morning.

"Then at least a little sugar, Father," she pleads.

"I think not."

It's not that he eats nothing. Every few days he slips and wolfs a chicken leg or a wedge of pie, some animal part of him reaching for it, working his frantic jaws. Still, a chicken leg every few days isn't much. Thin to begin with, August is growing gaunt.

It's nothing so extraordinary. After all, the Church was built on the bones of men and women who cared nothing for their mortal flesh or, more accurately, who knew full well what evils the body harbours, and were more than willing to slip its chains. August will carve it away, every cluster of fat, every muscular string. No meat for a demon to feed on, no blood for the Devil to fire. Cell by cell he'll chisel himself a new body—a saint's body—one with luminous, paper-thin skin and creaking bones.

"*Mea culpa,*" he says softly, slicing the eggs lengthwise before dropping them with a splash into the porcelain bowl. "*Mea culpa—*" He lets the toast float and soften. "*Mea maxima culpa.*" He grips the smooth handle, flushes and grins.

Father Charlebois was famous throughout St. Peter's for his lectures. Legend had it he once delivered a series of talks on Saint Francis barefoot, a length of rope cinching his tattered robe, his voice bird-like in the shadows of his cowl. To teach the meaning of martyrdom he made a trip to the knacker's for the dark, marbled eyes of a horse. "What does it take to follow in the footsteps of Christ?" He walked down the rows with the eyes on a large blue plate. "Sancta Lucia had her eyes plucked out, and still she kept sight of the Lord."

For the very first class of August's first year, Father Charlebois arrived with a white ram in tow, its head bowed under a pair of massive, curling horns. Without a word the little priest drew a long knife from his briefcase and turned to the class. One after another the young men's voices dropped away.

"Who among you shall kill this beast?" he demanded.

Many shifted in their seats, but August remained quiveringly still.

"You realize it was a priest's role to do just that," Father Charlebois went on, "before the Lord God sent His Son, our Saviour, to this earth."

The class relaxed a little, releasing a composite sigh. Only August held tight. He was seated at the back, old habits dying hard, but even so he could smell the animal's greasy coat— feces and grass ground into something nameless, familiar and disturbingly rank. The ram looked up, pinned him with its dumb gaze and released a low, threatening bleat.

Father Charlebois's child-sized hand shaped itself to the ridged spiral of the ram's left horn. "Before the coming of Christ, this was all people understood. The slitting of throats, the charring of carcasses—*this* was how they worshipped, how they atoned, by sending their messages to God on a river of blood, a column of stinking smoke."

Slowly, ceremoniously, he lifted the knife, presenting it as a knight presents his sword. The classroom was utterly silent, thirty seminarians suspended in autumn light.

"Sacrifice." The word rang out. "They understood that much, but what they were unable to grasp was the *kind* of sacrifice God required. The prophets knew, certainly, but who else?" Father Charlebois jabbed his knife heavenward. "That is why God gave us His Son. *His Son.*" He paused. "And Christ? Christ gave us Himself. What more can you give? Not a stand-in, not a scapegoat, but your *self.*" He lunged at them, gesturing from one to the next with his blade. "That is what God requires!"

A collective shudder ran off in waves from the centre aisle.

"Before the coming of Christ, the priest offered the victim to God. But Christ was both priest *and* victim. He didn't perform the sacrifice, he *became* it. The action acted on the actor. Perfect circle, perfect offering, perfect rite!" With that, Father Charlebois laid down the knife. "None among you shall kill this beast, because those days are gone. You're the rams now, boys. That's what we're doing here—get it?"

HOSTIAM IMMACULATAM
(a spotless victim)

August dreams a banquet, soaking his pillow in drool. The table is broad and soft. Dead centre lies something the size of a turkey, crisp and brown, flecked stuffing spilling out from its end. Potatoes burst their skins beside Christmas oranges piled high, two or three of them partially peeled. A jellied salad, jellied ham, custard trifle in a cut glass bowl. All this and more—yet it's the bread he desires, round and simple, its crust inscribed with the slash of a knife.

He takes it in his hands, tears it and, like the egg in an Easter loaf, finds a baby August curled at its heart. His infant self is naked, belly smooth and drum-like, sex a shelled peanut, limbs creased and dimpled at their joints. The little legs stir and, in stirring, grow together as though fused. One limb now, it pales visibly, hangs quivering from the infant's tiny hips. Horrified, August drops the bread, only to have it bounce back at him from the table's quilted expanse. He wakes a split second before the baby-loaf hits him in the face.

The invisible worm—

Again, high school English, the only poetry—excepting Holy Scripture—he's ever known. How is it now? He reaches down into his memory and hauls up the line, squinting hard in what little starlight his window allows. *The invisible worm that flies in the night in the—howling storm—has found out thy—*what? It's no good. The snatch of verse circles and skips back to its beginning, spinning scratchily in his troubled brain.

16

MEAT FOR STRENGTH

Thomas's prayers have been answered. St. Mary's new housekeeper has been into the shop many times now, a stout, talkative woman, fond of a fatty cut. Mathilda says nothing of the change—she's simply home. Ever since her aunt died, she's been a constant labouring presence about the place, sewing new kitchen curtains, hanging wallpaper in the flat, sticking her head deep into the oven and scrubbing long after any grease can be seen. She's even taken to standing beside Thomas behind the shop counter, weighing while he wraps, accepting money while he trims to order with a smile. In his bliss Thomas fails to notice how reserved his regular customers have become.

She gives herself to him whenever he asks now, but never like the first time, when she came to him in the shop. She probably frightened herself. Truth is, she frightened him a little too, her passion was that fierce.

He's wrapping two nice pork chops for Elsa Wylie when Mathilda falls. It's just as though somebody's shot her, the way her body lifts up a little before collapsing in a heap. Blood on her blue dress. Thomas crouches over her, helpless. Elsa, normally strong-minded to a fault, drops her shopping basket and begins to cry. Old Mrs. Kimball steps out from behind her. A nurse in the Great War, she rounds the counter and takes command.

"She'll keep it for now," Doctor Albright stage-whispers, drawing the bedroom door closed. Thomas hulks before him, a poor fit for the hallway, shifting like a steer in the chute.

"Keep it?"

"The baby."

"The—?"

"You didn't know? Never mind, young thing like that, no mother to teach her, she probably didn't know herself."

Thomas blinks rapidly.

"She's pretty weak." Doctor Albright squints through his glasses. "Any idea what's sapping her strength?"

"She won't eat right," Thomas mumbles. "I keep telling her."

"What do you mean, *right*?"

"Well, not much."

"Uh-huh. And?"

Thomas's face is a misery. "She won't eat meat."

"No meat?" A smile cuts into the doctor's cheeks, but he arrests it, bends it down into a thoughtful frown. "Well, that won't do. No sir. You'll have to see if you can't tempt her."

Thomas nods. "Yes, Doctor. I'll try."

"Good. Even so, it'll be touch and go. I'm putting her on bed rest for the whole of her term." He lays a hand on Thomas's shoulder. "Between you and me," he says hoarsely, "she could lose the little nipper like that."

FILII EVAE

(children of eve)

When there's any post to speak of, Mrs. Stitchen lays it out on August's desk, centred on the blotter like yet another unwanted meal. Today she's culled a letter and set it aside— a pastel envelope smelling of spicy blooms, addressed in a loose, womanly hand.

August doubts Aggie actually perfumes her letters. It's more likely just the touch of her fingers, the brush of her hair, even the lick of her tongue. It's the scent she's always worn, and like many in her walk of life she's always worn too much. As a small boy August never dreamt his mother's smell came from a bottle. He believed she exuded fragrance just as naturally as the purple bushes that marked the coming of spring in every Fairview yard. Except Aggie exuded year-round. And for some reason she was the only woman in town who left such a heady trail.

Men lifted their noses like dogs when she passed them on the street. Older boys asked confidentially, almost kindly, "What's that perfume your mama wears, August? Sure smells nice." They laughed when he told them shyly he didn't know, but the laughter sprayed like nails, and he realized they meant to hurt him even before one of them hissed, "Wonder what she's coverin' up?" That was when August understood—beneath her sweet, shifting cloud, his beautiful mother stank.

During his seven years at St. Peter's, Aggie wrote faithfully once a month, her letters arriving on or around the full moon. He was lonely enough to answer them promptly, even eagerly, until somewhere deep into the second term, when he found himself summoned to the Rector's office.

"Mr. Day," the Rector began, "it has come to my attention that you have received certain letters. That is to say, letters of a certain kind."

August's heart shrank. Besides Father Felix's two notes on St. Paul's stationery, Aggie's fragrant missives were the only correspondence he'd received. He'd read each one only once. He couldn't risk keeping them for what little guilty comfort they might afford—Aggie was too easy in her language. She mentioned her customers often, sometimes even by name. *You know Tommy Weiss. Well he fell head over boots off the wagon again and whose doorstep do you think he landed on?* August absorbed every word, then burned the evidence—cremation in a pencil tin at the sill of his little window, ashes fluttering up into the dead of night. He'd never considered the possibility of steamed-open seals, his mother's secrets already perused.

As if in answer to his thoughts, the Rector spoke again. "No one has read your mail, my son. You know we employ the honour system here at St. Peter's."

"Oh."

The Rector planted his elbows on the desk and clasped his spotted hands, eyeing August along their knuckled range. "August, is there anything you wish to tell me?"

August sucked his lip miserably. *He that loveth father or mother more than me is not worthy of me.* And yet— *Honour thy father and thy mother.*

"Well?"

August tried to swallow and found his throat blocked by something the size of a fist. "I know she's not perfect, Father," he choked, "but she's my mother. I'm all she has."

"Your mother?"

"What? I mean, pardon me, Father?"

"Your mother sent you those—scented letters?"

"Yes. Why, what—? Oh." August felt himself colour from the collarbones up.

The Rector's hands relaxed and fell apart. His leaden mouth drooped into a smile. "We just assumed—the soft colours, the perfume—"

"I know." August shook his head hard, as though the priest's voice was hurting his ears. "I've told her not to wear so much."

"What's that? Nonsense." The Rector chuckled lightly. "Now that we know it's not a *sweetheart*, what does it matter how your letters smell?"

It matters. It's possible, even probable, that Mrs. Stitchen has jumped to the sweetheart conclusion as well. Why else separate the letter like that? Why single it out?

Rage, sudden as a blood clot, explodes in August's brain. *"The silly bitch,"* he says through his teeth, meaning first the cattle-hipped housekeeper, then Aggie, then all of them—the whole damnable sex. He yanks the bottom desk drawer out and sweeps the flesh-toned envelope into its mouth. Slams it shut with a thunderous clap.

THE GLINT OF A BLADE

After a blur of distance, Castor's eye lodges in the cleaver's gleam. The sheep hangs sightless, suspended by the tendons that worked its back hooves. Already skinned, its hind legs are hopelessly thin—it seems impossible that they and two others could've borne such bloated weight. Its pelt hangs open like a coat, the breast muscles gathered in a stripy pink vest.

The butcher's black apron and boots give off a greasy shine. His right hand balled up into a fist, he divides the animal from its skin with short, gentle jabs, taking care not to tear the membranous fell. He's smiling. Talking to himself—no, singing. Castor has no way of telling which song, but it's something tender by the look in the butcher's eye.

Left hand holding the pelt taut, he works it free of one hindquarter, then the next. Fists down to the shoulders, peels the skin to each foreleg where it's split. Then the neck, knuckle and thumb, teasing until it loosens and gives way. The sides slip off nicely, but the rump takes time. He works his way gradually up to where the pelt clings about the root of the tail. The curved knife sudden in his hand, he carves around the anus, yanks up the bung and ties it off.

Freed from the stumpy tail, the pelt pulls easily from the back, falling loose to the nape, where it hangs like a fleecy cowl about the sheep's head. Nothing left but to sever it from the skull and face. Moments before Castor's eye pulls out, the butcher reaches again for his knife. Still smiling. Still moving his lullaby lips.

17

COGITATIONE, VERBO, ET OPERE
(in thought, word, and deed)

Father Shea specialized in teaching the art of the sermon, stressing the priest as God's instrument, the invention through which He gave His divine music voice. August pictured himself part cello. Imagined the bow dragging mournfully across his hollow chest, pulling out chord after celestial chord.

Shea was an ugly brute—a barnyard face on a body the cassock couldn't hide—but his looks fell away like a costume the moment he parted his thick lips and spoke. He began simply, as a rule. "A parish priest must be a man of faith."

Anticipation rippled down the rows.

"And more. He must also be possessed of an ardent desire to *communicate* that faith."

About there August closed his eyes. It wasn't the words themselves—they were plain enough—it was the way they emerged, each breaking the seal of Father Shea's mouth as though it were the silk of a cocoon.

"To communicate, one must be *in communion*, and to be in communion is to speak out from inside the words." Father Shea paused. "The sense inside the sound, that's what people listen for, that's all they're truly willing to hear. Words are empty vessels without intention, without thought. Bring the thought to the very lips, d'you see, bring it further, fling it out." He made weigh scales of his misshapen hands. "Every noun its measure, every verb its proper pace. Horses are not lemons, d'you see? *Horses.*"

August could hear the source, the very sound *horses* grew out of, the beasts themselves giving rise to their name.

"Hum now," Father Shea directed them suddenly, "all of you, try a few notes." And they did, dissonance rearranging the room.

"Feel that? Now think of your head as a church. Try again." This time he talked over their sound. "Let it echo through the chapels of your sinuses, high up into the vault of your skull. Keep your throat open—it's the aisle, the passion rides up on a breath." He silenced them with a sharp wave. "That's when you're really preaching," he said into the hush. "When you can *feel* the Word resound."

SICUT ERAT IN PRINCIPIO
(as it was in the beginning)

August is kneeling at the prie-dieu in his office, deep in evening prayer, when the buck returns. He halts mid-murmur, cocks an ear to parting bushes, an imagined lifting of hooves. Muffled through stone and glass, there comes a low, insistent baaing. He rises as though bidden, clambers quietly to stand again at the edge of his desk.

It's not alone.

The doe steps prettily. She turns her eyes the buck's way, liquid dark, and again the buck baas, lifts a hoof and sets it down. She leads him into the open, the snowy yard unmarked but for the record of their steps. The buck bends his swollen neck as though bowing to the doe's hind end, his antlers the hands of a man, the shape they assume when forming themselves to a woman's ribs. The doe halts for him. Allows him to draw close, to mount her in a single fluid move.

More than two months have passed, yet for a moment August can feel her, the soft backs of her thighs, the curve of her hips where his fingertips dug in. His position seems suddenly precarious, as though the desk is tilting, threatening to throw him off.

In the between-tree shadows a shifting, a gathering of forms. Lost in the cloud of their own scent, the deer remain intent, unaware. August is no help. Even if he weren't so light-headed, he hasn't the bush sense to know.

A split second before it happens, the buck lifts his head, raising his antler-hands to the sky. They break from the trees—yellow, dappled silver, one liver-coloured with enormous paws. They are dogs and not dogs. Crossbred to be pets, beloved mutts, they're losing fur in clumps now, their origins clearly visible in bared haunch-blades, ribs, fangs.

The buck hasn't time to disengage, the dogs attacking as though he and the doe are one body, a giant, two-headed deer. Less organized than wolves, the pack forms a snarling patchwork, one tearing at the doe's belly, two fastening into haunches, the largest sinking its teeth into the buck's thick neck. August yells pure sound—a warning after the fact—then stands whimpering, his hands clenched and helpless at his sides. The brawling mass traverses his window

155

third by third—the buck goring the yellow dog, tossing it yelping through the air, others leaping back from the doe's slashing hooves.

All at once the knot loosens and lets go. The little black dog, thrown to the poplars, rebounds off a trunk and lies stunned. The mottled grey drags a cracked foreleg. The yellow bitch slinks open-bellied into the bush. Of those left standing, the pale-faced show blood while the dark ones appear innocent and clean. The pack dismantled, these few pace at a safe distance, silently working their jaws.

The deer come apart. Stand quivering, then turn the torn flags of their tails and run. None give chase. The battered dogs dissolve back into the shadows that brought them.

"Dogs," August tells the empty office. "Dogs?" Then it dawns on him. The question surfaces every so often on his parish rounds. *Those mutts ever turn up? Ever see anything of Father Rock's dogs?*

BY-PRODUCTS: MINCEMEAT, CANADIAN STYLE

The buck was brought in field-dressed, heart and lungs left in, chest and belly cavity spread open with sticks. The hunter'd done a messy job at the throat but declared it didn't matter, he wouldn't bother mounting a head that small.

"Fine animal all the same," he went on, patting its torn rump. "Reckon he drained out nice, cut him with the head downhill."

"Yes," Thomas answered tersely. He felt strangely protective of the carcass. "I'd best get on with it," he said, turning his back. "You can come for the meat tomorrow."

Lying on its side now, stripped of hide, head and hooves, the buck is almost womanly—fifteen or so, before life's hardness starts turning them soft. Thomas grows forgetful as he works, continually misplacing his butcher's terms, thinking *deer* instead of *venison*, *breast* for *brisket*, *thigh* for *ham*.

He loves game meat. It has such flavour—too much for some. Colour too. It's the oxygen, of course, more red blood cells in an animal that gets to run. But isn't that just another way of saying freedom? Isn't it the wildness that transforms their very fibres, the fact that they can't be owned?

Thomas lifts the deer's tenderloin from its hiding place along the spine. Such a delicacy. He wraps it with painstaking care.

Even after the hunter's picked up his meat, Thomas can't get the idea of venison out of his mind. His mother made mincemeat with it once and only once, following a recipe she'd clipped from a neighbour's discarded magazine. Thomas Senior had always been a skinflint when it came to home and hearth. When he got wind of what all went into the mixture, he blew his top. *Lemons! Candied citron— just what in the hell is that? Christ, woman, look around you, does this look like the fuckin' Ritz?!*

He was right, too. No matter how Sarah Rose tidied and cleaned, the house was a dump, sprung up like a weed among the stockyards so the stink had them pinned on all sides. Summer days it got so thick even the lifers could smell it. More than smell—at times Thomas felt he could bite off a chunk, chew and swallow it like a mouthful of shit.

But that mincemeat. It might have been the only time the house smelled sweet, the only time he breathed long and deep there on purpose. She made it on a Sunday so Thomas could stay home with her after church and help. He did so gladly, chopping and stirring, not resting until the very last quart was capped.

She surprised him by leaving a cup or so in the bottom of the pot. She cut slices from a dense white loaf and plastered the warm mincemeat thick. The taste matched the smell—surpassed it even. His tongue was transformed, a fat butterfly landing on bloom after bloom.

Thomas begins to plot. They'll have some of the ingredients at Conklin's, and the rest can be ordered in. He slips out of his apron, taking his coat from the hook by the door. On the way out he flips his little clock-faced sign.

He has no trouble getting his hands on the meat—so many of them kill for the sport alone. The last of his special order arrives care of Conklin's delivery boy. The kid leans his bike up against the shop window and enters triumphant as a hero returned, holding up a bag of bright oranges and a flagon of vinegar, tarragon waving like a pondweed inside. Thomas over-tips the boy, then sets about getting the venison on right away. He covers coarse chunks with water, adding a kitchen-string posy of celery, parsley and bay.

When the meat falls away from the bones, everything gets chopped in together—apples, peel off, oranges, peel only, lemons, whole. He doesn't cut corners. The famous candied citron, a whole sack of sugar, top-grade molasses, enough suet to grease up a cow—it all goes into the big black kettle, and before long, magic billows out from beneath the lid. It's heart-rending. Exotic yet familiar, the smell of both home and away.

He stirs the pot six times during the course of an hour, then ladles the steaming contents into sterile glass, finishing each jar off with a little ceremony—two tablespoons of brandy more than good enough to drink. He's screwing the last lid down when he hears Mathilda moving around above him. Her footsteps halt at the top of the stairs.

"Thomas," she calls plaintively, "what's that I smell?"

He'd planned to make tempting little tarts, but Mathilda can't wait that long. She sits up in bed, digging her soup spoon into the still-warm jar. Soon she's shovelling the mincemeat in, dropping glossy blobs on the lace neck of her nightie, sporting a dark circle around her lips. "Oh, Thomas," she moans more than once, the blood flaring in his lap so he has to look away.

The spoon scrapes bottom, and before she can ask, he's bounding down the stairs for a second jar. She's gorging. She could make herself sick, but the thought never occurs to him, and if it did, he wouldn't give a damn. Her hunger thrills him. He perches at the edge of the bed, watching her gobble and wolf, his heart dancing like a drunk in his chest.

Somewhere in the bottom third her pace slackens, the spoon dangling instead of digging between bites. He takes it from her fingers and scoops deep into the jar. Her eyes are glassy. "Open wide," he whispers lovingly, and she does.

18

ET CUM SPIRITU TUO

(and with thy spirit)

As the snowdrifts deepen, August passes through
torpor to a kind of jumpy blur. Finding himself
unable to sleep for more than a few hours a night,
he takes to prowling, his dress woefully inadequate to the
bitter cold. He leaves by the rectory's back door, turning
away from civilization to the scrub and poplar forest west of
town, keeping his bearings by the glint of St. Mary's mod-
est spire.

Early one December morning, after countless half-
circles at the end of his tether, he finds he has finally
walked himself numb. He halts, realizing dully that he
must turn back or freeze. Still, he stays rooted to the spot,
as though waiting for someone—or some *thing*—to arrive.

Exhausted, he draws the lids down over the icy balls of
his eyes. When he lifts them, the gloom is parting, folding open in two enormous muted wings. He hasn't time
to cry out. The owl plunges into the snow barely a yard
from his boots, struggles for a moment and sits up with a
beakful of wriggling fur. Three blinking gulps and the kill
disappears. Wings elongating like shadows, the great bird
lifts soundlessly, swimming up from the forest floor with

measured, sensuous strokes. August strains his eyes, but even staring, he can't pinpoint the moment it vanishes from sight.

He almost turns, almost departs without noticing what's left. The owl's impact cast in the snow—wings splayed out for drag, facial disc feathery about the curve of the beak. The talons go deepest, thrust forward as though lowered from the belly itself. August stoops closer. Even something of the nameless prey. Three round drops, a scarlet ellipsis on the snow.

MEAT FOR APPETITE

Mathilda is his and his alone. For two months now she's kept her bed as ordered, refusing to see anyone, claiming she's too worn out to face a soul. Christmas season or no, Thomas doesn't even think of hiring a nurse. Instead, he takes on afternoon help in the shop.

He's a parlourmaid on the stairs, up and down, the pink flush of service in his cheeks. She's eating like a farmer now, growing thick under the blankets as well as round. She'll tolerate the odd potato or handful of peas, but most of her demands are for meat, four or five meals a day, with sausage rolls or Cornish pasties to hold her between. Thomas buys her a little brass bell and drops everything to answer its call. More than once he leaves a customer hanging—ground round half wrapped, a pile of chops teetering on the stainless scale.

That first Christmas at St. Peter's, August found himself among those chosen to ride out beyond the city limits and gather evergreen boughs. He and a dozen others hunkered down in the truck's bed, their backs vibrating against its slatted sides.

Over the coming years his fellow seminarians would do more than ignore him. They would call him Professor, mimic his hunched walk, knock his books to the floor. One Passiontide they would go so far as to string him up in the gymnasium, weave his arms and legs into the knotted climbing net, and leave him hanging there, head down. For now, they were content to talk around him, laugh across him, shout hymns at the passing moon. Even as August marshalled his spirits and lifted his voice, he remained separate, a sad tenor standing out from the choir.

Ordinary people looked up from the store-lit streets as they passed. Young men in uniform saw *St. Peter's Catholic Seminary* on the truck's door and scowled at them, a cargo of cowards. Young women turned up their faces, discerned handsome from worthless, offered smiles. A few of the seminarians smiled back, one lifting his black-mittened hand in a wave. August cast his eyes down. Won't last the year, he thought, and felt briefly warm inside.

He was close to frozen through by the time the truck turned down a dark side road and shuddered to a stop. They piled out like cattle, stamping their feet, nostrils flaring to the crystalline cold. Each was issued shears, a basket, an electric torch. They waded into the snow-choked ditch on command.

"Not too far," Father Gillis warned. "Fifteen minutes and the horn brings you back."

Most paired off, but August struck out clumsily on his own. It wasn't long before the snow muffled the others' voices, lending them the cadence of children playing far away. Then August was the one and only man, surrounded by the tall, well-meaning bodies of trees. He switched off his torch. The snow gleamed about his boots, about the scabby grey trunks of the pines.

On the fields around Fairview the sky had stretched him, often empty but for the eerie plainsong of a hawk. Here the treetops huddled to form a socket for the moon.

I'm free, he thought suddenly, looking up like a rabbit from its hole.

By second year, August had given up trying to join in during afternoon recreation. Instead, he spent the time bent in study or in prayer. He was in chapel so often he could feel the skin thinning out over his elbows and knees, the scented wood wearing at him, opening invisible holes through which the Holy Spirit might enter, or, better yet, through which his own imprisoned soul might one day flee.

When not praying, he read voraciously—Butler's *Lives of the Saints*, the *Summa Theologiae* of Saint Thomas Aquinas, *The Dialogue* by Saint Catherine of Siena, anything at all by the incomparable Augustine. My namesake, he told himself dreamily, knowing full well it wasn't so.

Aggie had told him often enough the story of his naming,

of his coming into the world. She was out walking by the Olsons' back fallow, up to her waist in a field of their wheat. "I carried you high," she liked to brag. "Still had a better figure than most in this town."

It came on sudden, so sudden she sat down hard, flattening a circle of wheat around her. "Sure I had a little pain before that," she told him, "but I just put it down to gas. That's how come I was out walking, I was trying to work it out." She always laughed before the next part. "Worked it out all right. There was no stopping you once you decided. I barely had time to get my knickers down."

She had to bite through the cord, her teeth the only sharp instrument at hand. There was nothing to wrap him in but the dress on her back, so that was what she used. Night had come down hot and dry by the time she had the strength to walk home, so at least it was dark when she emerged from the tall grass in nothing but wet panties and a bra.

"Anyhow, that's how I named you. Late summer baby born in a field, no better word than August for that. Besides," the story rounded off, "it's kind of like Aggie. Got a bit of yours truly in the sound."

HIS ABSENCE

Mathilda can feel herself expanding by the day. It's more than her condition. At three and a half months the baby's a compact ball, rising modestly while the rest of her spreads out. Thomas is partly to blame. He looks in on her even when she hasn't rung, his face an open rib cage, displaying

164

his ardent heart. "How's my queen?" he asks. "Hungry?" Puffy and immobile, she finds herself powerless to resist.

It's just as well she's been confined to her bed. Never mind the fact that she's already outgrown everything but her nightgown—the truth is she couldn't bear to drag her dead love and its consequence around town.

Yet her own mother must have done just that. She too carried a mistake, the work of that errant boy in the picture, the one with the unruly hair.

Like the rest of her, Mathilda's mind is getting soft. It returns time and again to the dancer, lingering, allowing questions long held at bay. How far along was she when Jimmy Nickels bolted? Three months? Six? Did she curse the life in her belly, or did she perhaps take comfort in it? A little piece of him broken off inside her. A consolation prize.

19

AB OMNI PERTURBATIONE SECURI
(secure from all disturbance)

August loved Latin—such musical precision, a perfect system through which to divide and conquer the world. He thrived within its bounds, just as he thrived within the tolling structure of the seminary day. St. Peter's broke life into pieces and portioned it out. For the first time in his life August began to feel secure.

Until.

Late one night, in the heart of the grand silence, there came a moaning through the wall beside his bed. Someone else might have thought the moaner was ill or in the grips of a nightmare, but August was all too familiar with the sound of sin. He lay frozen in his bed, just as he'd lain frozen the night he heard his mother being killed.

She'd cried out over and over, and the thing that was murdering her must've had more than one head, because it answered in the voice of a bull, then a coyote, then a bear. August heard it leave by the slamming back door, then a hush, and he knew with a childish certainty she was dead. The next morning, Aggie folded down his quilt to find him curled at the foot of his little bed. "Wake up, sleepyhead," she said softly, and he opened his eyes and screamed.

Now, as he buried his head under the pillow, his neighbour moaned louder, as though it were somehow fundamental to his release that he be overheard, that he not arrive at his whimpered climax entirely alone.

August found himself looking out for the young man at morning prayer. Even though they'd slept separated by a wall for three years, August knew him only by sight, never having bothered to remember a name. The neighbour had the look of an invalid about him—watery eyes, fine cheekbones, flaxen hair. The mouth he'd moaned through was pink—it formed itself sweetly, almost girlishly, around the words of supplication and filial love. Watching it move, August felt a sickening response in his groin.

Not long after his arrival at St. Peter's he had chosen the flamboyant Father Charlebois for his spiritual adviser. Their next tête-à-tête wasn't scheduled for two weeks, but August wasn't sure he could wait that long. He requested a special session and spilled his contaminated guts. When he finally grew quiet, Father Charlebois seized hold of his hand, sandwiching it only partially, as his own were so pitiably small.

"My son," he began gravely, "there are times when a Man of God must do battle with the Prince of Darkness." He lowered his voice, as though they might be overheard. "No weapons, you understand. *Hand to hand.*"

August nodded. He knew all about combat—what it meant to be shaken so your tongue slapped in your mouth, kicked blue and breathless, shoved face down in a filthy ditch. *What happened?* Aggie bending over his latest wound, her hair loose, fingers greasy with the flowery salve she was rubbing into his knuckles, his cheek, his knee. The answer always a lie. *I tripped. I fell.*

He'd fought back at first, slight though he was, but it only brought more of them piling on. In the end there seemed to be little use in defending his mother's honour—after all, everything they said or sang about her was true. He realized it lying on his stomach with a larger boy's knee in his back. The ditch water he lay in was hopping with chorus frogs. A blue-spotted salamander stared out at him from a snarl of weeds. Surrender, he thought, play dead. And it worked.

Father Charlebois's eyes were burning. "You never know when he will strike, August. Even after years of faithful service, Satan can come at you like a rabid dog, and when he does, there's nothing to do but beat him back!" He released August from his grip and sat back, his smile almost disgusting in the way it cracked open and spread. "Remember the war in heaven, my son."

August looked up, bewildered. "But Father, those were angels."

The priest's finger shot out like a striking baby snake. "The point is," he shouted happily, "we won!"

CURED MEATS: HAM

With food in her belly and the radiator on high, Mathilda yields easily to the ever-present temptation of sleep. Her eyes flutter open on January then February light, the growing swell of herself beneath the quilt and, very often, Thomas jammed up against the bed on a small wooden chair.

On St. Valentine's Day he sits waiting for her to awaken, a heart-shaped box of chocolates folded to his chest. At length she stirs, peering out at him through her lashes.

"Thomas," she murmurs, as though talking in her sleep.

He takes her hand in his, holding it a little too hard. "Yes, love?"

"Do you know when I first noticed you?"

Her tone is almost tender. He swallows loudly. "No, when?"

"At the Labour Day picnic. You remember, you were stuck behind that table, slicing up ham."

"Sure."

"You were looking at me."

He smiles sheepishly. "I was always looking at you."

"Yes, but this time I noticed. This time I looked back."

"You did?"

"You wouldn't remember. You were distracted by the crow."

"Crow? What crow?" Then it comes to him—the sudden weight of it landing, its claws flexing into the flesh of his scalp. He shudders, recalling how he bellowed and danced, how the bird lifted as suddenly as it had arrived, left him hopping amid a laughing crowd. "You saw that?"

"Yes."

He laughs weakly. "I guess it was the meat. They're carrion birds, after all."

"Maybe, but it didn't seem that way to me." Her voice is barely audible. He has to lean in close to hear the rest. "To me, it seemed like a sign."

"A sign?"

"Like when Our Lady knew to accept Joseph." She closes her eyes. "Only with him I think it was a dove."

"Oh." Thomas chokes on the little sound. His wife's hair glows like dark honey, ranging over the pillow in slow

169

streams. He touches a strand. "I always knew. From that first morning when I walked into town. Fourth Avenue looked empty except for you."

It's hard to read her face. That might be a strange kind of smile.

"Mathilda?" he says softly. "Honey, are you asleep?"

MISERERE MEI
(have pity on me)

August hasn't laid eyes on Mathilda since she told him, yet his image of her continues to evolve. She'd be six months along by now. Just as she no doubt grows large in the curtained bedroom above her husband's shop, so too she expands in his mind.

He reads feverishly by the bedside lamp—*Or know you not, that your members are the temple of the Holy Spirit?*— then drifts off to dream of her lying huge and prone, a jungle-bound shrine, her belly its central dome. She's marked all over with an ancient tongue, dancing characters and runic designs. Snakes coil thickly, looped like vines from the huge-leaved trees. One drops in a bright pattern. Slides a slow, scripted *m* over her stony thighs.

August wakes bathed in sweat, feels the small hot head thrusting up where the pyjamas have twisted painfully about his groin.

"Why, Lord?" he cries, the words taking shape before he can think them down. "A serpent built into me, embedded in my flesh?" He clasps his hands hard to keep them innocent. "It's too much, Lord," he howls softly. "It's cruel."

And if thy right hand scandalize thee, cut it off—

He thrashes his head from side to side. No. We are forged in His image. His to create and His alone to destroy.

For it is expedient for thee that one of thy members should perish—

No. *No.* Father Felix explained all that, remember?

SLAUGHTERING: PRIMARY CONSIDERATIONS

With the April melt, Mathilda grows hungry for news of the outside world. Thomas delivers, bringing stories like bright garnishes on every plate—sometimes gossip from the shop, sometimes an item from the flimsy *Mercy Herald*. By early May he's begun to tell her of himself. First the shadowy closeness of mother and home, then a little of his father, the yawning slaughterhouse, its windows casting slabs of light.

"I fainted, you know," he confesses, "the first time I had to stick a pig."

"You did?" Mathilda opens her heavy-lidded eyes.

"Sure." He grins. "Hit the floor." He leaves out the thrashing he got when he came to, the half-stuck animal shrieking on its side, the old man jamming the heel of the knife back into his shaking hand.

"I fainted once." Her eyes fall closed again. He's used to it now, the serenity of her lidded gaze. "At confirmation, I stood up too fast after taking Communion—at least that's what everybody thought."

He nods sympathetically.

"But that wasn't it."

"It wasn't?"

"I had a vision," she says quietly. "Just for a second, but for that second it was like my whole head flooded with light."

"Boy," says Thomas. "That's something, all right. Was it—I mean, what did you see?"

Her eyes move like fish under their lids. "Christ."

"Oh."

"He was floating above me, you know, on the Cross. His face was far away, kind of blurry, but his feet were right over my head. They were so close I could've reached up and caught hold of the nails."

Thomas searches for something fitting to say, but it's like riffling through the closet of a man half his size.

"I told Father Rock about it after," Mathilda says, opening her eyes.

"You did?"

"I went to see him in his office."

Thomas pictures the towering, snowy-haired priest. Sees him pacing behind that immovable desk, shaking his big head silently, almost threateningly, while Thomas struggled through the lesson of the day. "What did he say?"

"He said I was imagining things." Her mouth trembles ever so slightly. "I told him, no, Father Rock, I saw Him, I swear, but he said if I hadn't imagined it, then I must be telling a lie."

"He never."

She nods. "He did. He said it was wicked of me. He said I was deceitful and vain."

"Vain?"

"To try and make myself the centre of attention. To try and take the attention away from Him—the Saviour, he meant—on such a holy occasion."

"The gall of him," Thomas says angrily. *"The gall."*

She tilts her round face his way. "You believe me, Thomas, don't you?"

There's something new in her tone. Something, if he's not mistaken, very much like need. "Yes, love." He touches her cheek. She doesn't flinch. "Yes," he repeats firmly, "I do."

GRATIA PLENA

(full of grace)

It took a letter from Father Felix to arrange for August's ordination to take place at St. Augustine's in Brandon, rather than at home. The old priest picked Aggie up bright and early on the day, sat in her little kitchen sipping tea while she fussed with her hair, called out to remind her to go easy on the makeup and maybe put on something a little plain. She complied gracefully, emerging in a dark brown dress that clung like melted chocolate to her thighs.

Long past the blush of youth, Aggie still took effortless command of a room. August watched it happen—the turning heads on his fellow deacons, the sliding eyes on more than a few of the priests in attendance, though not, thanks be to God, the archbishop himself. August stared at the ground as he passed, but he could still feel her, a dark softness in the middle pew, strangely mighty, almost frightening in her way.

When it came time to prostrate himself before the archbishop's throne, August did so eagerly. He knew the position well. Back home, he'd lain like that on the rippling grass or, in winter, face down in the snow. Not often.

He kept it for emergencies, nights when the rhythm of Aggie's bedsprings threatened to split his skull, when he couldn't bear to witness yet another heart-rending cry. He'd stumble out into the field that backed onto their house, sometimes in his pyjamas, boots and coat, sometimes just pyjamas and bony bare feet. It didn't matter if he caught his toes in a dog hole or cut his heel on a curl of wire—nothing stopped him until he made it to the heart of that field. Once there, he'd flop down on his belly, spread out like a starfish and grab fistfuls of grass, or powdery, compacting snow.

Prostration was meant to make him feel helpless, he knew, humiliated even, but in truth he found it comforting. So comforting, he nearly forgot he was meant to be listening for the voice of God. *You have not chosen me, but I have chosen you and ordained you.* August strained his inner ears. Nothing. He waited so long, the parish priest cleared his throat, his echo approximating the hoped-for words. August rose to a dizzy sickness, the blood draining to pool warmly in his feet.

The archbishop's hands settled heavily on his head, and he wobbled a little under their weight. Dozens of men had touched him there. Pudgy hands, sticky with sweat. Old, almost fleshless hands. Hard hands, a seemingly endless stream of railway men and farm hire snaking through town. They patted his head as though they were uncles or family friends, pressed pennies into his waiting palm. *Go get a sugar stick now—or a licorice whip, or a chocolate dollar— go on now, make yourself scarce like a good boy.* The man in the striped suit was no different, save for the value of his coins. Two whole quarters—enough for a stack of chocolate bars, or more two-a-penny candy than August could hold. He opted for the latter, turning the front of his shirt up like a pea-picker's apron, loading it with the most sugar his money would buy. He forced it all down, up to his eyes in the reeds beside Rat Creek.

All through his teens August washed his hair each and every day, ignoring Aggie's talk of pneumonia, scrubbing until she swore he'd go bald.

"Tu es sacerdos in aeternum," the archbishop pronounced, and August felt himself sway forward as the pressure of those hands lifted away. It was irreversible, that phrase. *You are forever a priest.* He stepped back to don his chasuble, grinning like a bloody fool.

20

QUARE ME DERELIQUISTI?
(why hast thou forsaken me?)

For months now, August has endured bowel seizures and blackouts, random nosebleeds and aching bones. Hunger and exhaustion are whittling him down to that simplest of instruments, a hollow length of reed. He can feel himself growing holier by the day, and so, it seems, can his flock. They sit forward in their pews now when he speaks, staring as though they can see clean up to heaven through his burning black eyes.

Mathilda's image comes to him less often now—at times bridal, at times heavy with child. Either way, his body is too wasted and wrung out to respond.

In spite of this, he finds he can feel spring in his veins. The mild evenings trouble him, as do the sticky buds, the opening of countless green eyes. Sack of bones that he is, he feels his pulse quicken to the change. Though somewhat less wretched, he finds himself more restless than ever before.

Come nightfall, he prowls an ever-widening loop. He recognizes landmarks now—a jutting stone here, there a tree struck by lightning, one half living, the other mere remains. On the night of June the first, he looks up from his wanderings to find he can no longer make out St.

Mary's spire. Strangely, he feels not panic but an inhuman sense of calm. He presses on. Low scuttlings through the leaf mould underfoot. Now and then something louder—larger—a greater displacement of space. The buck? he thinks hopefully. Then a slinking shadow-thought—the dogs?

"The Lord is my shepherd," he whispers, feeling the truth of it, His holy presence somewhere very close by, leaning heavily on a luminous staff. "Lead me, Lord," he croaks to the trees, then nods and hastens forward, deep into the burgeoning dark.

Singing. Not far, by turns raucous and thickly sweet. He weaves toward it through the brush, recognizing neither words nor tune, but the voice as one he's heard before.

Castor Wylie's built himself a twiggy fire. He's dancing a jig of sorts in the space cleared by a fallen tree, one hand waving aloft while the other grasps a fat, sloshing bottle about its neck. "Father!" Castor bellows mid-leap, even though August feels sure he's stationed himself where he can't possibly be seen. "Hey, Father!"

August peers out cautiously from behind his bushy pine. Castor hops and reels closer, tilts the whiskey to his mouth and does a little caper to swallow it down. "Father Daytime, right?" A yellow stream escapes his lips, winding a course through his patchy, mouse-grey beard. He stops dead. Lets his short arms hang and stares up into the night sky. "Pretty dark for *Daytime*," he says solemnly, then cracks up, snorting, slapping his thigh.

"It's Day," August says weakly.

"Okay." Castor nods, grinning. "Day." He turns and jumps the little campfire, then lowers himself into a teetery crouch, motioning for August to do the same. "C'mon in, Father."

And for some reason August does. He holds his palms out to the fire, his knees going off like gunshots as he squats.

"You'd snap easy," Castor says mildly.

August picks up a forked stick and prods the coals. "You live around here?"

"Too close to town for the likes of me. I got a place out on the bog." He thrusts the whiskey bottle out across the pitiful flames.

August waves it away, but the bottle remains. "No, thank you," he says, and still the whiskey hangs before him. "I don't want any."

He looks past the bottle to find the old drunk's eyes have grown milky skins. Scrambling backwards, he crosses himself frantically, as though beset by a cloud of blackflies. Yet, on second glance, Castor seems peaceful, almost miraculously still. No Christian, to be sure, but perhaps no worse. August suddenly remembers the Shepherd, recalls being led to this place.

His gaze somewhere deep in the glowing liquor, Castor speaks. "There's a woman—"

August stiffens. "No," he answers loudly, "no woman."

"A woman," Castor insists. "Long dark hair."

"I told you, there's no—oh." *Dark hair.* August swallows a sigh. The poor sinner's hallucinating, harmlessly mad. August lowers his head in sympathy, like a neighbour at a wake.

"Nobody'd touch 'er," Castor mumbles. "Not a soul." His cracked mouth hangs open for several moments before adding, "Cut 'er tits off. Both of 'em, clean off."

August looks up as though called. Saint Agatha, Virgin Martyr. Not a hallucination, but a holy vision. *Calls himself the Seer.* August squeezes his eyes shut hard in hopes of seeing her too. "Where is she?" he whispers hoarsely. "Is she here?"

After what feels like forever, Castor's soft answer sounds in his ears. "Far."

"Yes," August mutters, feeling foolish, "of course." Away across the ocean, back through an ocean of time. It was a Roman prefect who wanted her, who cast her into a house of ill repute when she had the temerity to call herself a bride of Christ. *Nobody'd touch 'er.* She emerged from the brothel unmolested, such was her natural dignity and grace. So the prefect had her hung upside down on a pillar. Had her breasts twisted off like pears.

August nods as though bowing, chin to chest. The message is clear—the body tormented, the spirit set blissfully free. He opens his eyes to find Castor toppled over on his side, the bottle somehow still upright in his clutching fist. After a moment's alarm August registers the relaxed eyelids, the even breath of sleep. The fire is dying, but the night is mild—surely not the first the poor man's spent alone outdoors. August rises joyfully and sets off, dead certain of the direction in which St. Mary's lies.

My God, Christ lamented on the Cross, *my God, why hast Thou forsaken me?* August grins, fairly skipping through the shadows. God hadn't, of course. Nor had He forsaken Saint Agatha, nor any other who had the courage to be martyred in His name. This is what August has forgotten. Earthly suffering is not merely to be weathered. It is to be welcomed, celebrated even, proof positive of the special attention of the Lord.

He can feel himself mending, each step the setting of some tiny but indispensable bone. When the switches strike him, he finds they have no sting. Untouchable now, he takes in a lungful of spring, pictures himself drawing back every curtain at the rectory, throwing every window open wide.

Deeply grateful for the new lease on his spiritual life, August goes about setting things to rights. After thankfully forcing down every scrap Mrs. Stitchen's set out for him, he carries his breakfast plate and teacup in to the sink. She looks up shocked from the far counter, the rolling pin stalled in her floury hands.

"I'm off on my rounds, Mrs. Stitchen," he announces, feeling his shrunken stomach buck. "Thought it best to get an early start, I'm terribly overdue."

She nods speechlessly.

"I'm looking forward to visiting the Chartrands. Those children are such—" He gags a little. "—such a joy."

"Yes, Father."

He smiles tightly. "Tell me, Mrs. Stitchen, have you any family of your own?"

Caught off guard, she betrays herself, her eyes leaving him to fix on her ragged circle of dough. "Mr. Stitchen passed away young," she says softly, "not two months after we were married."

August feels his heart swell. He takes three jerking steps and curves a skeletal hand over hers. "There now," he says, "you're a member of Christ's family, aren't you?" She nods, looking up at him. "Remember," he murmurs, "no one is alone who knows God."

The sentence acts like a tonic, its effect instantly evident in her eyes. He carries this small triumph like a trophy around the parish, repeating the winning words at some opportune moment during each of his stops. Only after the last visit, when he's back in his office making notes, does he recall the question that first necessitated his fine pronouncement. *Have you any family of your own?*

And now, as though the old desk were suddenly made of glass, August looks down through three drawers to the little pile of letters he's stuffed away.

Why hast Thou forsaken me?

He draws the bottom drawer open slowly, shutting his eyes to reach inside, as a child shuts his eyes to enter a darkened room. There are four in all, about one every other month since he put the first away. He arranges the letters by date stamp—peach sent in late October, powder blue in January, mint in March. The latest arrived a week ago, stamped two weeks before that. He turns it gently, petal pink in his hands.

No. Begin at the beginning. He'll answer every one of them line for line and mail the whole thing off in one of those cards that reads, *Sorry I haven't written in so long.*

Waving the oldest letter under his nose, he finds its fragrance distinctly changed—old-womanly rather than womanly—having taken on the back-corner mustiness of the drawer. He slits the top edge with Father Rock's opener, a small tarnished sword.

Dear Son,

No way to say this but to say it. You know how I like a soak in the tub. Well that's where I was when I found this lump. It's

181

been there a while I guess but how is a body to know when the damn things feel like a couple of sacks of tapioca in the first place? Anyhow it's there and a fair size too. Doctor Soames says I have to go in to Brandon for the operation. I asked him why can't you do it but it's complicated or so he says. Father Felix will give me a ride in so don't you worry about that. I will be sure and keep you posted.

Your ever loving mother,
Aggie

August breathes hard, but the air is suddenly thin. He reaches for the blue letter with rattling hands.

Dear Son,

      Wouldn't you know it. They lop the whole thing off and a good piece of the chest muscle under it and sew in a nice long scar. Then just when I'm starting to get a little strength back in my arm they find another one over on the other side. This one is smaller but I guess once you have a big one they don't like to take any chances. So that's that. The next time you see me I will be a whole lot flatter. I know you are busy but maybe you could get a break and come see me once I get home.

Your ever loving mother,
Aggie

Dark balls of sweat fall one after the other from August's brow, spotting the third envelope forest green.

Dear Son,

      I am back some weeks now with two purple stripes and a couple of craters on my chest. I understand if you can't visit but the thing is I could use some money. I have a little put by but I

182

can't say who will last longer me or it. There might have been a few willing to pay when I still had the one good breast but now— well I guess they are all after a mother in the end. Anyhow, I know they don't pay you much. Anything you can spare.

Your ever loving mother,

Aggie

He's dizzy now, his gut cramping, the final letter wilting in his slippery hands. He forgets the little sword and rips the envelope with his fingers, tearing it open in an unholy mess.

Dear Son,

I can guess why you don't visit or send money or even write. Well I am still writing. I am writing to tell you they didn't get it. Two good-sized tits and they still didn't get it all. So I guess that's that. I want to write something else August. I want you to know that I know you don't want me for your mother because I am a whore. Plain and simple. Only it's not. Your father said he would marry me. He said that right up until the night he ran off. After that I had you in my belly and exactly three and a half dollars to my name. Who gives a job to a girl in trouble? Same person who marries a slut. Nobody. What would you do August? You know what I did. Fine. Just so long as you also know that every time I lay down under a man or bent over for him or what have you it was for survival. And not just my own either. You might remember I had a child.

That's all I guess.

Your ever loving mother,

Aggie

August palms his eyes, pressing hard on the balls so they spread in their sockets. He feels a knocking in his chest cavity, his skull and finally his ears, where he recognizes the

183

sound of knuckles at the office door.

"Father?" Mrs. Stitchen asks in a quiet, troubled voice. "Are you in there, Father Day?"

He lowers his hands. "Hmm."

Mrs. Stitchen's face, gentle as a cow's, in the crack of the door. Her wide-set, curious eyes. "Here you are. I thought you'd've been in for your supper by now. I've been calling all over town—"

"What is it?" he asks hollowly.

"Oh, Father, I'm so sorry. A Father Felix telephoned—"

Whatever else she has to report, whatever details she may know, it's all lost in the howl that escapes August's mouth. He leaps from behind the desk as though caught in a criminal act, pushes past her and tears away down the hall.

21

HIS LIKENESS

The first contraction peals like a warning through Mathilda's lower back, its echo a dreaded question. *What if it looks like him?* She's a definite redhead, Thomas a dirty blond. What if its head comes out plastered with black hair? What if it has rings in its eyes? The Catholic Church skivvy with a kid the spitting image of the priest. Thomas will stand brokenly by her, Father Day will be sent away, and she'll be saddled with a little replica to tug at what's left of her heart.

After a time, another contraction. She says nothing of them when Thomas appears in the doorway with a steaming kidney pie.

"I'm tired," she tells him. "Let me sleep."

He bows a little, like a footman. Sets the pie down and backs out quietly, leaving the door ajar.

"Close it, please."

"But what if you need me?"

"You think I can't make myself heard through a door?"

"Okay, honey. Sweet dreams." He pulls the door shut, squeezing out his face, narrowing the hallway light to an eerie line.

For the first time in months Mathilda sits up in answer to something other than her bladder or bowels. Her feet are sacks of sand, but she stands on them all the same. Somewhere else, she thinks feverishly, have it somewhere else. Then what? See what it looks like? Give it away? It doesn't matter. The words revolve like a rosary in her skull—*somewhere-else-somewhere-else-somewhere-else.*

She unhooks the fly screen from the window and lifts it out. Looking down, she finds the Virginia creeper has already made it to the second storey. Hooked a leaf up over the sill like a hand.

SMALL GAME: SKINNING

The parlour sofa wasn't built for so substantial a man. Nonetheless, Thomas has been exiled to it for the past two weeks, Mathilda huge under the sheet, complaining of the heat his body gives off, his incessant snoring and over-powering smell. She's delicate, he tells himself. Besides, she's softening toward him, needing him more every day.

He sits up to unkink his massive back. He can't sleep, and it's been far too long since he dismantled that slicer and gave it a proper going-over. Truth be known, the shop's not half so clean as it was when Thomas was on his own. Stealing downstairs, he smiles to himself. Who cares? He's got better things to do, now he's practically a family man.

Amid the clatter of parts, he hears nothing of Mathilda's escape. Not her desperate clambering through the window, not even her lumbering descent—swollen feet and hands grappling down the lattice, tearing the glossy vine. There's no sound of a motor. Even with all her wits about her, Mathilda wouldn't know how to start Thomas's truck, let alone clunk it into gear. Which leaves the old bicycle the butcher Ross left behind.

Thomas is deaf to his wife's fat, gravel-spitting tires, the squeak of her seat springs as she pedals insanely away.

The slicer's blade shines like an eye. He's gone on to organize and wipe out the fridges, polish the display case, scrub down the blocks and mop the checkered floor. Instead of tiring him, the work has filled him with beans. It's in the name of preparation, after all, everything just so for the arrival. The idea of the baby halts the white cloth in his hand. He secretly hopes not for a son but for a little Mathilda, gazing out at him through blue-black eyes.

A gift. The baby should have a gift from its father, something to welcome it into the world. Sure, there's the sheepskin, but he needs something more solid than that, something the child can hold.

Of course. He brings an open hand down on his knee. The rabbits.

THE DOCTOR'S DANGLING EAR

One minute Castor's wailing one of his daddy's shanties, the next he hoists his bottle and the wandering eye has its way. The curtain goes up on a bloody scene. He looks out from a stethoscope's silver plate, dangling like a medallion from Doctor Albright's neck. Before him a woman's

187

straining thighs, her sex a yellow-bearded face beaten to a pulp and bellowing. Castor swings in close then back, settling against the doctor's lambswool chest.

Who? Castor runs down a list of Mercy's natural blondes, looking for one with strong, heavily fleshed legs. Elsa. But it can't be—Renny would've told him, even with things the way they are. Surely he would've told the uncle-to-be.

Doctor Albright stands, and for a moment Castor glimpses the head of the bed. The woman's face is turned aside, but the braid gives it away. It's long, impossibly glossy and thick, twitching bluntly on the pillow like a cut snake.

Castor comes back to himself as though falling down a hole. That blasted braid. It was what got her Renny in the first place, he's sure of it. That and the berry-spattered cleavage she made sure the poor sucker caught sight of whenever she stopped by the station on her way home from work. Castor should've scented trouble the day Renny came home smelling of preserves. Still, she's having his brother's baby. Things are bound to be different now.

Castor staggers to his feet, stuffs the bottle down his pants, licks his palms to smooth the greasy black pelt of his hair.

HIS LOSS

Mathilda's water breaks several miles up the north road out of town, soaking the seat, running warmly down her thick, pumping thighs. She gasps at its fluid tickle, then pedals backwards hard to brake, planting her feet and bracing herself for another wave of pain. Even through the steamy jungle of her mind the contractions are getting harder to ignore. This one doubles her up over the handlebars, bringing her nose to nose with the black rubber bulb of the horn.

Her face would be ashen if the moon weren't buried so deep in cloud. She can scarcely tell road from shoulder, shoulder from knobby-topped trees. All the same, the moment the pain subsides, she remounts and wobbles on.

One thick-ankled foot after the other, Mathilda shoves the pedals down. The road shifts and rears beneath her until, countless contractions later, she finds herself at the mouth of a rutted track. Away down its tail end there's a twinkle of light. She's got just enough sense to take the turn.

The glimmer leads her on to an enormous stony-faced house. She's close enough to make out the carved lilies on its doors when the bicycle betrays her. Feeling it slide out from beneath her, she gives vent to a terrible scream.

THE CLAN

Castor hears the screams long before he can make out Renny's house. Shrill and murderous—it's Elsa, all right.

"Uncle Castor," he says giddily, trying it on for size, then goes shaky, remembering his sister-in-law's words, her lips pink and poisonous at his ear. *Look, it's Uncle Castor. Run!*

He stops dead in his tracks. Almost turns back but for the whiskey's liquid hope. Start all over, he thinks fuzzily, just one big happy clan. He'll hold the baby in his arms, safe as can be, the way he held Renny the night he caught him from the sky.

He enters the yard now, reeling past the garden, moonlight down the rows and not a solitary weed to be seen. He breaks off a sprig of mint for his breath.

Renny's house is nothing like the tinderbox they were both born in. It's nothing like the series of yellow-papered boarding-house rooms the kid grew up in either, or the original shack Castor knocked together when they first arrived to claim their mother's boggy land. His brother's house is solid. The Devil himself couldn't blow it down.

The front door's hard under Castor's fist. He hammers twice, but the sound gets swallowed up in Elsa's hollering, so he tries the handle, finding it unlocked. Renny's pacing by the hearth, almost running, tearing tiny laps around the braided rug.

"Little man!" Castor shouts, and Renny freezes, eyes lifting, jaw dropping down.

"Castor, what the—"

"Nnnnnaaaaagh!" Elsa bellows from somewhere down the hall, behind a bedroom door. Renny winces, lunging at Castor and spinning him on the spot, pushing him like a wheelbarrow out the gaping front door. He shuts it quickly after them, his eyes fixing on Castor's ragged pant legs and bog-pickled boots. A roll-your-own twitches in his fingers, smoked halfway. He holds it out without speaking.

Castor takes the smoke shyly. "Little nipper, eh?"

"Ren-nnny!" Elsa's voice rattles the windows. "Nnn-GAAAAAAHHH!"

Renny shrinks in the frame of the door. "How'd you know?" he asks finally, still not looking up.

"How'd I know?" Castor tries out a laugh. "You know me, little brother. How do you think?"

"RENNY!" Elsa's voice could cut timber. "Is somebody there? Who's there?!"

Renny reaches behind him to open the door a crack. "Nobody!" he shouts over his shoulder.

Castor lowers his gaze, Renny laying his overtop, so the two sightlines cross somewhere around their knees.

"Little man a daddy." Castor chuckles, the sound falling all over itself in his throat. Then he zeroes in on Renny's hand, the way it's holding the door almost closed, with such a grip on the knob it looks as though the knuckles are in danger of breaking through.

"It's all right, Ren." Castor turns slowly. He stumbles on the first step but catches himself. It's suddenly terribly important that he keep his feet, that he not let his little brother see him fall.

Renny catches up with him at the foot of the gravel drive. He's got his hands behind his back like they're tied there, a half-crazy smile on his pointed face. He pulls the left hand first, holds out a fat bottle of brandy, three-quarters full. "It's all we got in the house," he says sheepishly. "You know, *medicinal.*"

"Thanks." Castor takes it with a shaky hand.

"There's an old bur oak just outside the back fence," Renny says quickly. "You check it on Fridays. I'll hang a little something up there, not too high. Fridays, okay?"

Castor nods.

Renny swings out the other hand. Dangling from his

fingers, a pair of tiny yellow boots. Castor's eyes fill up and swim. "Elsa knitted 'em," says Renny. "You keep 'em. A keepsake, like."

Castor holds out a crooked finger. Renny hangs the booties there by their laces, then turns to the house, letting out a strangled little laugh. "She'll have a bird when she finds 'em missing."

That boy could always run like the wind. By the time Castor can lift his head, Renny's gone.

HIS CHILD

Mathilda comes to on an iron cot, surrounded by shrouded forms. *The orphanage.* The rest of her life never happened. She's a child again, miserable in her narrow bed. "Not wanted," she whimpers to the shadow who mops her brow.

"Nonsense," the shadow replies. "All God's children are wanted."

Then pain. Mathilda panics, struggling against a dozen wiry arms.

"Lie back!" a superior voice commands, and she does, collapsing into a stupor of tears. The straw mattress jabs her, and for the briefest of moments Mathilda understands. She's having the baby, the shadows are nuns. Her blood runs cold. They're a different order—simple veils instead of bonnet-like coifs, brown habits girded with rope—but in the end it's all the same. A circle of staring virgins watching her open wide. They'll see the child come out, undeniable proof that she let it climb in. She tries in vain to close her legs, all clarity washed away in a breaker of pain.

"Forgive me, Reverend Mother," says a gentle voice. "I've seen her before, in Mercy. I believe she's the butcher's wife."

Mathilda howls.

"That's it," says the Superior, "push. *Push!*"

Her eyes wild and uncomprehending, Mathilda clenches her teeth and bears down.

"Is that true, now?" The old nun cups her hands over Mathilda's bare knees. "Are you the butcher's wife?"

Mathilda's eyes bug out huge in her crimson face. "AAAARRRRGH!" she bellows as the baby crowns. "Father Day!" she screams, passing the head, and with the next breath, "AUGUST!"

The Reverend Mother's face pops up dark and knowing from between Mathilda's legs. "Good girl. Head's out now. Shoulders next."

Mathilda strains hard, feels it slip from her body and relaxes, spiralling into space. The old nun clears the mouth and cuts the cord, then lays the bloodied newborn in a waiting towel.

"Keep the child warm," she says briskly, "the mother quiet." She wads a towel up between Mathilda's legs, then washes her knotted hands with alarming speed, drying them in her habit's folds. "Pray," she instructs her charges. "I'll be back just as soon as I can."

22

Only when he's back in Mercy—when he's pulled up and braked out front of the rectory he calls home, cut the lights to let in the dark and cut the engine to let in the quiet—only then does August fully realize his mother is dead. It's as though the past days' events have been following him in a convoy, and are now piling into his back end with impact after impact—screaming rubber, wailing steel, exploding glass.

Wreckage.

The night drive there along poorly kept roads, this time feeling more than one furred body flatten beneath his wheels—seeing no deer, though, not a single, solitary deer. He hadn't returned Father Felix's call, knowing just how the old priest would put it—not a word of reproach, just the simple truth—*she's gone.*

The top half of the casket stood open to display a powdery, cotton-packed approximation of her face. The once full lips were painted candy-floss pink, a little-girl shade Aggie wouldn't have been caught dead in—except she was. August never got a look at the space where her breasts had been. The funeral parlour had fitted her up with a stuffed bra.

Father Felix departed from tradition, choosing to read first from Judges—Samson eating honey from the lion's carcass—*out of the strong came forth sweetness*. Next came the Gospel of Saint Luke, how Christ let the woman who was a sinner cry on His feet and dry them with her hair, then kiss and anoint them with salve from an alabaster box. "'Many sins are forgiven her,'" read the old priest, "'because she hath loved much.'" The final passage came from Saint John, Christ saving the adulterous woman who was to be stoned. The Saviour stooping to write with His finger in the dust, then straightening, saying, *He that is without sin among you, let him first cast a stone at her*. Then, almost casually, stooping to write again.

Father Felix spoke the service softly, as there was only August to hear. Even the organist had begged off with a headache, so when the two priests sang Aggie's favourite hymn, their voices rose unaccompanied to the vault.

Stabat Mater dolorosa

Juxta crucem lacrimosa—

August knew the English well—*at the Cross her station keeping, stood the mournful mother weeping*—but translating it to himself didn't help. The sound was all he could understand. Stabat Mater. *Stabat.*

He bashes his forehead three times hard against the steering wheel, then slumps against it and finally weeps, crying first like a man, each sob something broken or torn, then like a child, surrendering, letting it rattle him like a window in a storm.

He wakes to a muted hammering, lifts his sore head slowly, orienting it toward the sound. Through the passenger-side window he can make out the glow of the flagstone path. Beyond the last stone, a slight figure, arms up over its head, pounding hard on the rectory door. A moment more and a panicked Mrs. Stitchen yanks it open wide, flooding the front stoop with light. A covered head, dark cloth falling in folds to the ground. August leans out across the empty seat beside him and rolls down the window for a better look, as though the glass was affecting his vision, somehow warping a normal human silhouette into the shape of a nun.

He sits back, confused. It is, of course, one of the Poor Clares from the monastery just south of St. Antoine. But their visiting chaplain is Father Beaubien. Perhaps something's happened to the old Franciscan, or perhaps an extraordinary confessor is required. Either way, August has no choice but to step out of the car.

Mrs. Stitchen points over the nun's shoulder, singling him out like a suspect in a lineup. "Oh, Father," she calls anxiously, "you're back—"

The nun whirls, her veil flying out to flap in Mrs. Stitchen's face. "Father Day." Her voice carries like the tolling of a bell. She hurries forward to meet him halfway on the path, each of them landing on a flagstone like a frog on a pad. "Father," she says in a low voice, "there is a woman come to us at the cloister."

"Yes?"

"A woman with child." She looks up into his face, her eyes sweeping left to right, as if over a printed page.

His mouth works hard to make a sound.

"I delivered the infant," says the Reverend Mother. "A healthy girl." She hesitates before adding, "The mother is asking for you."

The sound he finally manages approximates no known word.

She reaches up for his shoulder with a hooklike hand. "She's in danger, Father." Any doubt she may have had dissolves in the look on his face. "Take the northbound road out of town, it's the first turnoff on the right once you're through the bog."

"The bog?" he stammers. "But what—how will I know—"

"The trees change." She fixes him with a loaded stare. "They start looking as though they're getting enough to eat."

He nods dumbly.

Her hand turning him now. "I'll send the doctor on after you." Looking down at her sandals, she releases her grip. "I'll give you a head start, Father, fifteen minutes before I go to the husband."

August breaks for the car, no thought for what might be required of him—holy water, holy oil, holy bread. He goes empty-handed, an ordinary man.

✝

The baby mews softly, bandaged to Mathilda's belly with a length of torn and knotted sheet. She can't trust the bicycle—it's a wild animal beneath her, her blood darkening its spindly back. Besides, she can see headlights down the long lick of road. They're coming for her. She dumps the bike in the rushes and lumbers into the raggedy trees.

✝

August brakes late, spraying gravel up the monastery doors. He leaps from the car, hauls on the bell rope and hauls again, then mashes his face to the carved emblem, his eye too close to comprehend its form. He falls in when the door opens, a young sister half-catching him, softening the blow his knees receive.

"Oh, Father," she wails, "I only went for more towels, she was bleeding so, and—oh, oh, she's got the baby—oh, Father, I can't see how she could have ridden it, but the bicycle's gone!"

August doesn't waste time answering. He struggles to his feet, takes the steps at a leap, hits the ground at a run. The Plymouth is too cumbersome, too unfeeling—he'll use his own two legs to chase her down. When the cassock cuts into his stride, he tears it off, hammering on in T-shirt and trousers while it soaks up filmy water in the ditch.

He almost misses the bike. But for a glint from the roadside cattails he could easily have passed it by. She's trampled a wake through the sedge. He tracks her into the trees, where springy moss and the dark eliminate any sign of her trail. "Mathilda!" he yells. When the bog offers no answer, he plunges on.

‡

Time and again Mathilda stumbles, thrusts her hands out to clutch blindly for a branch or take the brunt of another fall. This time she hits moss, wet and cool about her fiery wrists. Accustomed to being belly-heavy, she remembers the baby only because it squeaks. Her brain simmers in its juice. She could've crushed it, the poor thing, gone lurching on with it bound to her, smothered and still.

She can't be trusted. Struggling to her feet, she tears at the knotted bedsheet, worrying the little bundle free. It whimpers, and as if in answer the cloud cover parts to reveal a full-faced moon. The baby lights up. For the first time Mathilda really looks at it, finding no trace of its father, only a shadowy resemblance to herself. It's practically bald, its eyes anonymous, a milky, newborn blue.

Mathilda looks up as though somebody's spoken her name. Not ten paces away, a tall, hairy evergreen stands slightly apart. Halfway up its trunk, a branch beckons like a human arm.

‡

It's mostly pines up here, higher, drier ground. Castor stands on unsteady legs, gazing down on the shaggy, sway-backed expanse of the bog. Black spruce dog, he thinks, grinning at the idea.

"Ya miss me?" he shouts. "Been waitin' for ol' Castor to come home?" Then stumbles forward into a bald spot, slips on the long, slick needles and falls flat on his ass. He's not hurt. Truth be told, he can't even feel his behind, like when you pass out sitting up in a car.

"Sonofabitch." He giggles, tipping the brandy to his mouth. The sky's dirty with clouds, but just now there's a fair wedge of moon showing through. It glints in the slosh-ing amber, flashes in the glass, and before Castor can blink, his eye has broken away.

It lands in a drop of sap, opens on a timber wolf up on its hind legs against a tree. There's something above it in the branches, but the angle's bad—a blob of white is all Castor can make out. The wolf drops to all fours. It's a loner, a stranger to the local pack, and therefore skittish, snout lifting, ears pricked to the threat of its own kind. The moss under its feet is pale. The wolf lowers its nose to a dark patch, sniffs, then snuffles. Draws its lips back and licks.

Castor's eye snaps back. He slumps forward, hanging his head. Run up a tree, he thinks mournfully. Trapped.

He knows the tamarack—it's one of several with deformed tops, the mark of the sawfly grub. This one like a slender, headless woman, arms raised as though she's looking to dance. But where? He searches his brain, squinting inwardly through a yellow, soupy mist.

‡

Thomas faces the killing-room wall, where a dozen headless domestic rabbits hang by their right hind legs. He cuts off twenty-four small front feet at the first joint, moving rapidly down the row. Carves off their tails on the way back, then scores around the hooked feet, leaving each a fuzzy white sock. One by one he slits all twelve pelts along the inner legs. The first comes loose with a tug, pulling free of the rabbit to hang flaccid in Thomas's hand.

Chances are the Varguses will be glad to let him keep a couple of pelts in lieu of pay. He smiles, picturing little arms circling a fluffy grey neck. How hard can it be to make a bear? He's a fair hand with a needle and thread, having practised on hundreds of roasts. He'll sew two arms, two legs, a belly, a furry-eared head. For stuffing, he can tear up a few old cloths, ones that are stringy or stained.

A sudden racket sounds next door in the shop, someone hammering hard on the storefront glass. It irks him. He pictures Mathilda upstairs, perhaps startled from a heavy sleep.

"Hold your water," he mutters, tossing the pelt on the table and wiping his hands. He steps out of his high slaughter boots at the threshold of the shop and pads quickly to the glass door, still shaking under some idiot's fist. He yanks on the blind, sending it flying up wildly around the roll.

It's a nun. A goddamn, honest-to-god nun.

Thomas holds a finger to his lips, fumbling with the lock while she gestures at him through the glass. The bell jangles wildly as he hauls open the door.

"Sister," he begins, "uh, Mother, please, my wife isn't well upstairs."

"She's not upstairs."

"What?"

The story comes apart in his ears. Bicycle. Convent. Baby. He takes leave of his senses. Takes the old nun by the shoulders, lifting her like a goose-down pillow. For several seconds he can neither hear nor see.

The nun's sandalled feet dangle in the air. Thomas lets her down easy but doesn't let go, sagging forward as though her sinewy frame is all that's holding him up. "I'm sorry," he croaks. "Where is she?"

✝

That's it, all right. That's the tree. Slim and curvy with a missing crown, uppermost branches held high. No sign of the wolf, but Castor's no fool. It will have heard him and slipped away between the trees. He yanks his knife from its sheath—it's no small thing to come between a wolf and its food. It's probably watching him right now. Or else he's too late. What about that? What if the wolf and whatever it was after are already gone?

He's well and truly loaded. With only the moonlight, and that coming off and on, he should be flat on his face by now. Thank the Lord for bog legs. He's a sailor on a mossy sea.

He makes the tamarack, holds a hand out to steady himself against its trunk. After that it's a good minute before he remembers why he's there and looks up, startled to find neither animal nor bird after all. It's more like the cocoon of a giant moth. He reaches for it, rises up on his tiptoes, even jumps, half a dozen jester leaps before he falls. The knife grazes his numbed belly. Another mark to find in the morning, run his finger wonderingly down its length.

He pulls himself up by a low branch, spots the soiled knife in his hand and, forgetting the wolf, shoves the blade peevishly away. Climbing's not really his strong point. The first branch is a picnic, but the next is a stretch. His fingers aren't up to it. They clasp too soon and clutch the air, unbalancing him so he teeters and tips. His face meets trunk. It hurts him bluntly, somewhere distant, the bridge of someone else's nose.

Another near fall, and then it's third time lucky and his scabby hands catch hold. It's darker among the boughs, but the thing gives off an eerie glow. Hauling himself up level with it, he suddenly feels unsure. What if it *is* a cocoon? What the hell kind of bug spins itself a basket like that?

The thing lets out a sound, halfway between a gurgle and a squeak, which in turn rings a bell in his head—Renny beside him on the mattress, waving his little fists.

"Jesus," Castor breathes. He lifts the swollen bundle from its crook. Another squeak, a splutter, and it lets loose with a hair-raising wail. Castor lets out a yelp of his own, presses it to his chest and somehow monkeys his way down.

Back on land, he parts the mess of cloth for a peek at its face. A howling mouth, the rest still red and pruney. The little beggar's brand new—still used to a belly, and God only knows how long it's been wedged in that tree.

A splotch on the white startles him. Then another, spreading and merging with the first. Blood? *Blood!* He panics, fumbles and almost drops it, horrified by what's seeping through. Then a breeze touches his face. Nosebleed. He laughs out loud. Dammit, he ought to know the feel of one by now.

The cloth's no good anyway. It's too thin, all lumps and loose threads, and it must be wound around the poor mite a dozen times. He lays the screaming parcel on the moss and struggles out of his mangy fur vest. It might be old, a little grubby even, but it's the softest thing he's got.

He unwraps the newborn slowly, loop after loop, the over-careful hands of a habitual drunk. She's flawless. He gazes at her—all that tiny, unbridled rage—then folds her in the vest, lifts and holds her close, feeling her quiet against him.

His nose is bleeding freely now. He wipes it on one end of the knotted sheet, then reaches up into a nearby spruce for a hunk of old man's beard. Shoving it up his nostrils, he gives his baby a gentle squeeze. Gets his bearings and heads for home.

‡

Hell-bent for the monastery, Thomas hits a washboard on a turn, foot to the floor. No time to correct—the tires slip sideways in their ruts, meet the dirt shoulder, spin out of control. A sickening lurch, a squeal, and the truck's belly up in the ditch.

He crawls from the wreck and hauls himself up through the cattails, miraculously unharmed. A little disoriented, maybe. Stars in his skull and overhead, marring the country dark. He looks right, then left. The road exactly the same both ways.

‡

"Heavenly Father," August pants, but the word cracks open inside him. *Father.* His own left before August was born, so the one memory he has can't be real. It's like a picture taken through the bars of his crib. It could be any man, except that August *knows.* His father has jet-black hair and a narrow back. A red plaid shirt, long arms hanging from its rolled-up sleeves.

And hasn't August been the same—no earthly good, just a stick man turning his back? He stops, hands braced on his knees, bent gasping, almost retching, for air. His shoes and socks are gone, sucked off his feet by the bog.

Who's my daddy? He asked it only once. The boys at school had told him it was like when a stray bitch had a litter—so many dogs got at her, sometimes even a coyote, there was no way to know for sure.

Aggie pointed up through the water-stained ceiling. *God's your daddy now.* So that was him. Sometimes a checkered back through wooden bars, more often whatever lay on the other side of that enormous airy dome, staring down at him through its ever-changing eye.

August lifts his head, still panting. Which way?

He closes his eyes briefly, sees himself in full vestments, stationed at the baptismal font. *In nomine Patris.* Holy water thrice-poured, the baby's tears, then the mother's— yes, the mother's tears, for close beside him stands Mathilda, her face flushed and happy in the red waves of her hair. Looking at her, August suddenly realizes, not just any baby, *my* baby, and he hugs it closer, bending his face to its innocent breath. All at once the rushing weight, the sweet burden of fatherhood. *Claim her.*

The ground is resilient for a few steps, then rotten, the sphagnum nothing but a surface to break through. Over and over he goes down, moss slapping him in the face like a sour sponge, and still he rises and slogs on, taking as straight a course as the trees allow, until even the trees won't hold still. He freezes, watching them shudder in a spreading black circle, those closest leaning into him and away. This is it, he thinks numbly, this is what it is to be mad.

It's not the deformed tree that catches his attention so much as the length of mottled cloth at its feet. Looped and wavy, it scrawls a long, indecipherable word across the moss. At its tail, in place of a period, the bloody approximation of a paw. Like a dog's, only worse. August recognizes *wolf* in some ancient chamber of his brain.

He shuts his eyes. Sways on the spot, listening hard with his whole body, sounding the depths of the bog.

Nothing.

It's what he should have expected. Both dead. Both in a state of sin—the baby unbaptized, the mother unabsolved.

He stoops to take up one end of the cloth, holds a dark patch to his nose and breathes deeply, the odour a downward pull, a pure opposite to the heady lift of wine. Slowly, ceremoniously, he feels his way along its knotted length, feeding it blotched and spattered through his hands. The far end is spotless but for a few clinging shreds of moss. Here he imagines he can smell traces of the baby's skin, impossibly fresh. He straightens. Loops the tail back on itself in a noose.

August shins up the tree with ease, a kind of animal joy even, his body remembering how. He picks a dependable limb, glancing down to confirm that the height exceeds his own.

He sees all three of them during the short drop—his mother, Mathilda, the daughter he'll never know. His neck snaps mercifully. His naked feet kick and swing.

‡

Safe in the bottle house, Castor uses what little energy he has left to empty the dregs of Renny's gift down his throat. The kerosene lamp flickers beside him, licking up through the last of the brandy, sending his eye bouncing off through the night. Not much out there. A host of trees. A dangling shadow, black and white.

He curls down over the blue-eyed infant in his lap. His breath hollows out, and soon boozy bubbles are slapping against his lips. Extra-proof drool falls in long, glossy drops. Tainted and sweet, they splash softly on her delicate skull.

‡

Mathilda staggers through endless underbrush, her nightgown a soggy tangle, part bog water, part fever, part blood. The wolf follows at a discreet distance, hanging back whenever she falls.

Nothing but trees. They're inside her now, humped and shaggy, spreading roots in her belly, swaying crowns in the vault of her brain. If only it would cry. She could retrace her steps then, follow the thread of its plaintive noise. "Cry, baby," she whispers. "Come on, cry."

Out of nowhere, a clearing. She stumbles into its near-perfect circle, a subtle depression in the endless carpet of moss. "BABY!" she screams. *"BAY-BEEE!"*

What seemed solid beneath her is not. There's nothing to grab hold of when the bog opens and swallows her whole.

NOW

✢

(one June night, 2003)

I

AN OPENING
(clare)

It's after ten, but the teacher says nothing of bed. Instead, she follows my lead, sitting beside me with a second pair of scissors, cutting blank paper while I dismantle my drawings one by one. My precision frightens her. After all, I'm only three.

Seeing the care she takes with her empty pages, I fish out a drawing and pass it her way. She's a quick study. Her blades mimic mine, parting the black borders that traverse the page, rendering five unique fragments, each with its own dark frame.

Every picture tells a story, true, but these are not pictures. Not yet.

OUR LADY OF REFUGE

The man on Mary's bed is beautiful, in spite of his wounds. He's still out cold, so for the time being she turns her attention to his clothes, rolling him deftly out of his shirt, slipping off his shoes and socks, tugging down his pants. A muddy fragrance rises from his skin. His legs are long and firm, his chest smooth but for a diamond of gold and silver hair. Late forties, she estimates, younger than her, but not by much—she'll be fifty-four come midnight. She stands back for a moment, staring. Then draws the blanket up his length and turns away.

She carries his wet things to the table, hanging his shirt and socks over a chair back to dry before invading the pockets of his pants. His wallet surfaces first, the leather damp like living skin. She turns it in the lamp's low glare. No need to look inside—she knows perfectly well who he is, what he's doing here in her bog.

She fishes out a ring of keys, then a rectangular electronic device, brushed metal and glass, cool against her palm. Upon closer inspection the number pad gives it away. She's seen people talking into them in town—a teenage girl outside Harlen's Pharmacy, throwing her head back to laugh, an older man scowling, steering his truck with the heel of his free hand. Mary holds the little box to her ear, then hunts for an *off* button to render it mute.

Last of all, she draws a broken compass from the right back pocket. He must have landed on it when he fell—its face has been damaged beyond repair.

After draping the pants over a second, mismatched chair, she takes up the lamp and crosses the room to gaze at him again. He looks much the same as he did when she found him, only then his head rested not on her pillow but on the corded roots of a spruce.

She bends over him for a closer look. His scalp has stopped bleeding, the fist-sized blotch no longer spreading through his gleaming hair. Both his eyes are swollen shut, turning a glossy indigo-black. Like giant, blood-encrusted sutures, six deep scratches hold his eyelids closed. The two that cross over his pupils are longest, slashing down through his eyebrows and cresting the tops of his cheeks.

She's never been one to flinch at the sight of broken skin. Castor was always scraping or gouging himself on something—her earliest memories include washing and binding his wounds. He never fussed. Even when she had to stitch him up, he just closed his eyes and nodded, as though she were telling him a story instead of leading a needle through his flesh. He was a lamb of a man. The only man she'd ever laid hands on, until now.

GREAT GREY OWL
(strix nebulosa)

The Reverend Carl Mann drifts awake in darkness, tries to open his eyes and finds he can't. "My eyes." He struggles to sit up.

"Whoa," comes a woman's voice, "it's okay, Reverend, you're safe."

"Who's there?!" Half rolling out of bed, he lurches to a stand, upsetting something knee-height and wooden, sending whatever was on it smashing to the floor. Hot liquid scalds his bare feet. He dances and slips, crashing hard on something hairy and damp.

"Lie still," the woman barks.

The pulse hammers in his ears. "Where am I?"

"Where do you think."

It comes back to him in patches—driving north out of Mercy, leaving the car at the roadside, striding into the trees. "Are you—?"

"Bog Mary?" A smile creeps into her voice. "I am indeed."

"What's wrong with my eyes?" His hands seek them out.

"Don't touch!"

He freezes. "What happened to them?"

"You tell me. They were like that when I found you. Lucky thing you went down close by—I had to drag you back here on that hide."

He touches the bristling skin beneath him, feels his own crawl slightly in response. Then a sudden chill as he realizes she's removed everything but his briefs.

"Your clothes were soaked," she says, as if in answer to his thoughts.

He sits up carefully, the motion causing his face to throb. "I need a doctor."

"No you don't."

"Yes I do. I've got to get back to town."

She lets out a snort. "Ever been in a bog at night, Reverend? You got pretty messed up in the twilight, never mind the dark."

The twilight. It all happened so fast—a rift in the forest before him, a sudden, gliding shade. He took three, perhaps four stumbling steps back, snagged his ankle in the undergrowth and fell. Blackness came with the blow to his head, overlaid with an impression, the faintest suggestion of wings.

"Besides," she goes on, "for the time being, you're blind."

He feels gingerly for his swollen eyes.

"I said don't touch." Her fingers clamp tightly around his wrists, relaxing only when he lowers his hands.

214

"They'll be all right so long as you do what I tell you. Okay?"

He nods, taken aback by her strength.

"Good. Now get back up on the bed and lie still." She gives him a hand up. "That's it, now lie back. There."

Her scent is overwhelming, a musky freshness, like lowering the car window beside a lake. It confuses him. Given what he's been told, he would've expected her to smell unpleasant, even foul. She pulls a coarse blanket up over his legs, her knuckles barely grazing his thigh.

"My phone," he says, remembering. "I had a cellphone in my pants pocket."

"Well, it's not there now. You going to tell me what happened out there?"

He hesitates, unsure whether she'll believe him, whether he fully believes it himself. "I tripped."

"Face first onto a set of claws?"

His heart skips a beat. If it marked him, it must have been real. "I thought I saw something. Before I fell. Something was—coming at me through the trees."

"Something?"

"Like a bird. Only huge."

She says nothing for a moment. Then, "What colour?"

"The same colour as everything else. It was dusk."

"Smart time for a stroll in the peatlands. Let me guess, you grew up in the city."

He bristles. "There was plenty of light when I set out. And no, actually, on a farm."

"Uh-huh. Did you hear it coming?"

He remembers the hush, more threatening than any cry or call. "Not a sound."

215

"Great grey."

"What?"

"Great grey owl. Silent flyer. Predators can't hear it and neither can prey. It hears better that way, too—voles in the leaf litter, even down under the snow."

"You think that's what it was? A grey owl?"

"*Great* grey."

"Are they dangerous?"

"Dangerous?" She laughs. "Shit, Reverend, not half so dangerous as you."

A PETAL SEA
(clare)

The teacher's living room makes a fine studio. There's little on the walls, little furniture even, to distract us from the task at hand. The plain dark rug is big enough for the both of us—the teacher cross-legged, I in my standard crouch. Above us on the bookshelf sits a small ticking chalet.

My scissor tips cross over a previous cut, freeing a crayoned fragment from the page. Shaped like a crude porthole, it shows a terrible scene—the barest of isles rising up from a troubled red sea.

Victoria General Hospital, south Winnipeg. Jenny Mann in a bed of roses and me in the white mound of her inside. Or not roses—something else, spreading crimson through the mint green sheet. Men and women, also green, masked panic and feet scudding like clouds.

I was the small self she hid inside, the one she couldn't

live without. I howled when they pried me from her, and then, as though I were the stopper, my mother flowed out after me, dyeing the bed, the floor, red lapping at their cloudy blue feet. How could she have given rise to such a flood? One small blonde woman, lovely the way birds are when the cat leaves them curled at the door.

Where were you, Preacher? Were you praying for us, down on your knees in the Church of the Water of Life, that flesh-toned eyesore down the road?

No.

Shall I tell you where you were? Offer even a hint of how much I know?

You were fitting yourself into a hospital closet, with just enough room for the nurse you'd locked eyes with in the hall. She was dead on her feet, fresh from sixteen emergency hours—overdoses, a miscarriage, the inevitable nameless pains. Her hair was a dark twist to hold on to. You were heady with disinfectant, humming tunelessly to yourself—*hmm, hmm*—thrusting deep into her promising dark.

Twelve doors down, they'd torn me from your wife. What was left of her flowed wordlessly away.

BLACK SPRUCE
(*picea mariana*)

"Let's have a look." Mary's weight at the edge of the bed pulls the blanket taut across Carl's belly. Her breath is warm on his face. "Hold still, I won't bite." She begins at his temples, pressing a slow, careful circle around each of his eyes. Then withdraws her hands. "I'll be back in a minute." She stands and moves away.

"Mary, wait—"

A door closes behind her. He stares into his own inflamed flesh. It's not a total dark—now and then a flicker comes through, making his head feel empty, like an abandoned cave.

Something rustles. From across the room there comes a low, definite scritching. A rat? Are there rats out here? Where is she, anyway? How long has it been? He sits up a little, begins silently to count. At seventy-five the door creaks open, her scent riding in on the night air—that and kerosene, as she brings the lamp close, expanding its red influence in his head. After a moment's hesitation he reaches out, groping across a low table until his fingers enter the circle of the lamp's heat.

"Careful," she says. "I've got a knife here."

His hand jumps back. She's harmless by all accounts, but how can you ever be certain with the mentally ill? He catches a whiff of something new. "What's that smell?"

"Guess."

He draws a long breath through his nostrils, feels a ripple of longing, of loss. "It smells like—Christmas."

"Close. Lie still, okay, dead still." She makes a spitting sound.

He flinches. "What was that?"

"Hold still."

"What are you doing?"

"You want to keep your eyes?"

"Yes, but—"

"Then shut your mouth."

He takes a breath and holds it. Something brushes his

218

left eye. A shadow crosses his featureless crimson screen, repeating itself in soft, sticky strokes.

"What—?"

"Keep still." She sighs. "It's resin. Black spruce sapling."

Her touch is feather light on his tender lids. It's bewildering—not pain exactly, more like a gentle reminder of his wounds.

"You split the twigs," she says, "warm them till they bleed, mix the sap with a little spit. It's the best thing for banged-up eyes."

"Oh." Sweet astringency settles like a wreath about his neck. He relaxes a little. "Okay."

A SILVER TONGUE
(clare)

Preacher, that small pink muscle was the strongest you had. You were exceedingly fond of it, resting intimate in the rounds of your mouth. Did you think no one could see you, those times you stood at the mirror folding it between your teeth to show the underneath vulnerable veins?

I saw, Preacher. You wouldn't believe what I've seen.

I remember the day you hit your evangelical stride. The words came up silver, riding your breath like an underground stream, leaping muscle and scale into air. They multiplied for you as they had for your Master, fanning out over the pews in great slippery shoals. The women turned hungry and shameless as seals, clapping their hands, rolling their wide sea eyes.

"'They shall have the gift of tongues,'" you promised,

talking of believers to those desperate to believe. *Yes,* the men nodded, and their wives sighed *yes* inside. Oh, for the gift of that tongue, thrust into their mouths, lapping endlessly between their thighs.

"'Think how small a flame can set fire to a huge forest,'" you quoted liquidly from the Epistle of James. "'The tongue is a flame like that. Among all the parts of the body, the tongue is a whole wicked world unto itself.'"

The widowed organist thundered wildly through a hymn, after which you turned to the Old Testament, a bodice-ripper of a tale. Boaz, drunk in the barley, awakened to find Ruth at his feet. "'I am Ruth,'" you announced, your voice softening to tell it, "'your maidservant. Spread the skirt of your cloak over your servant, for you have the right of redemption over me.'"

The men smiled smugly, picturing girls curled like dogs at their feet. The women grew flushed and faint. Oh, to be mounted in the barley, in the barn. You spreading your cloak, shafting light and manure, the animal romance of it all.

LAVINIA'S FOOT

Passing the halfway point on her circuit of town, Lavinia Wylie maintains her target pace in spite of the pain. Sometimes it eases when she runs, but tonight it's rooted deep in her heel, branching up through her well-muscled calf.

It's worst in the morning. She's just as glad Carl has held on to his room at the motel, returning there every night for the sake of appearances. It's humiliating enough hobbling out of bed when she's on her own—she doesn't need him seeing her like that. Not yet, anyway. Not when the two of them are so new.

First-step pain, Doctor Briggs called it when she went in to see him last week. "Plantar fasciitis," he said bluntly. "Tough band of tissue runs along the sole, attached to the heel and the toes. Loses elasticity, gets irritated. All part of the joy of aging." He pointed at her high-heeled pumps on the floor. "You'll have to get off those things, get into some sensible shoes."

"Not a chance."

"Lay off the running, too."

"Oh, *come on.*"

"I mean it, Lavinia. Go swimming. Ride a bicycle."

"I already swim. And I hate bicycles. Can you imagine a woman in my position wheeling around town like a little girl?"

Wheeling around town.

Lavinia feels herself lagging and pushes a sprint. It's been twenty years since she pushed Mama around Mercy in that chair, and the shame of it still burns. *It's all in her head,* the doctors advised, as though Lavinia should take comfort in the fact that her mother's legs were in perfect working order—that only her mind was no longer sound.

All through Lavinia's teens and twenties, Mama demanded to be taken out in all weather and rolled around town. *Train Street!* she would shout, or, *Left here, left!* The dementia grew steadily worse, and by the time Lavinia turned thirty, she could no longer cope on her own. Then came a miracle of sorts. Shortly after entering the Mercy

Retirement Lodge, Mama lost all interest in the outside world. Lavinia drove to the dump with the radio on loud and the wheelchair in the trunk of her car.

Try stealing a man's heart when you're shoving a witless wonder down the road. It wasn't that they took no notice of her—she often felt the heat of a male gaze on her firm brown legs as she bent to wipe Mama's mouth or to pull a twig from between the spokes. But there was a world of difference between being watched and being wanted for a wife.

She sees herself running now, as if from one of the picture windows she races past—her burgundy windbreaker and little black shorts, the flash of her runners, the gleam of her freshly bobbed hair. Her stride is formidable, her breath even, controlled. *There goes Mayor Wylie. Doesn't she ever get tired?*

The road veers right, becoming patched and potholed as it enters the northernmost section of town. It's her least favourite stretch. The sad-sack houses with their scrubby little yards, half of them littered with toys. Not a mile beyond their rooftops, the menacing silhouette of the bog.

He's out there. She's told herself she won't worry, but why else is she running at this hour when she normally goes at first light? He left over three hours ago, driving off after an early dinner with her compass in the pocket of his pants. She warned him it wasn't safe, wasn't worth it in any case, but he remained adamant about the need for action. The spread in today's *Globe and Mail* was proof—that woman could cause them no end of trouble if she wasn't made to see sense.

At an empty lot between houses, Lavinia jogs on the spot, facing the bog with her eyes shut tight, imagining it ripped away. Finally, a clean horizon, a chance to develop her town. Heartened, she sets off on her bad foot. He'll be back soon. She'd better get home and showered, get into that teddy he likes.

A CLAIMING HAND
(clare)

I was riding the red horse—mane of yellow yarn, yellow yarn—rocking. The Sunday school teacher was brand new, and already she was following you like a lamb. The two of you paid me no mind.

"She gets upset during my sermons," you confided, explaining me in so few words. "Can't sit still, it seems."

But I could, Preacher. We both knew I could sit still without blinking far longer than any normal child.

"You'd be doing me a favour," you told her, "a very personal favour, if you could sort of, well, *take her on*."

Doing you a favour. She was clearly taken with the idea, but you went further, bowing your head, your voice softening like chocolate in the sun. "Since my wife died, Clare's mother, well, it's been hard." You looked up suddenly, gathering her in your eyes. "Very hard."

"Of course," she murmured.

You closed the net. "Well, Cathy, what do you say?"

Already she was Cathy. Catherine on her church membership form, where you'd first learned she was once a nurse, Catherine to the congregation, but Cathy to you. Said slowly, achingly, so she could feel herself rolling over in your throat.

"Of course," she blurted. "Yes, of course."

Your hand found her waist, outrageous yet expected, as natural as life and death. It rested there a moment before lifting away. At the door your voice thinned out, strained through a boyish grin. "You'll find she's a bit fussy about touching. She doesn't really like to be held."

OUR LADY OF PEACE

Wide awake in her armchair, Mary listens to the night beyond her walls. Sound travels erratically in the bog— glancing off standing water or smothering in moss, angling a thin course through the trees. Because of this, she can only guess at the wolf's proximity to the house.

It looses a second echoing wail, and this time the Reverend hears it too. He claws at the blanket, lets out a restive, whimpering snore.

"Hush." She leans out to quiet his hand with her own. It's a natural enough fear. She herself suffered a particular terror of wolves as a small child, until Castor cured her with an elixir of words.

At the age of five she was well accustomed to being left on her own. Normally she felt safe inside the bottle house, but that night the moon was huge, the bog resounding with howls. She tried everything—singing to herself, even pushing dried mushrooms into her ears—but nothing blocked out the sound. By the time Castor made it home, she'd taken refuge beneath her bed.

He didn't try to lure her out. Instead, he turned the wick up in the lamp and lay down where she could see him on the floor.

"There's this town, see," he began, folding his arms behind his head, "and they're gettin' terrorized by a big old wolf. One by one he's pickin' 'em off, and you can bet the ones he hasn't got a hold of are shittin' their pants. Nobody can kill it. Anybody stupid enough to try gets found with not enough meat left on 'em to feed a cat. That's when Francis shows. He's got no gun, no knife even, but you think that stops him? No sir. He marches barefoot straight through town and out the other side into the woods, and nobody gets in his way, 'cause every one of 'em's thinkin', thank Christ, the poor bastard'll fill up that wolf's belly for another day. Shows what they know. Francis finds the wolf in no time, and it's a big bugger, make no mistake. He walks up to it and starts talkin', and before long the wolf's got a grin on its face. Francis heads back to town, blows 'em all away just by not being dead. You gotta feed him, he tells the crowd. Put meat out for him every day and he won't harm another soul. He's not bad, says Francis. He's hungry."

2

A PALLID SOLE
(clare)

High up on the bookshelf, the time-bird rockets out the chalet's front door. "Cuckoo!" it reports, the first of eleven identical cries. The teacher smiles wistfully at the sound, forcing me to look away.

There's nothing so treacherous as a human face. I keep my own a determined blank, decline to meet others' head-on. Newborns know—they refuse to focus no matter how people long for their gaze. Parents and perfect strangers holding them close or at arm's length, even shaking them a little. *Look at me, baby, look!*

I sneak another glance, watch the teacher's smile sag over the drawing in her hand.

"Hello, Cathy." You flooded the schoolroom, climbing the walls until they swelled and cracked. The teacher was ready for you. You'd left her ripening in that room full of parables and toys, let her watch you from too far back to spot a single flaw.

She was ready when you cupped your knuckled hand beneath her breast. She was willing, even eager, when you eased one foot and then the other out of your tasselled shoes. Bending, she pulled pins from her hair until it sprang down like a leopard from a tree. Tresses on your ankle as she pressed her fine lips to your toes.

PITCHER PLANT
(sarracenia purpurea)

For as long as he can remember, Carl has woken as though shocked, sitting bolt upright seconds before the alarm. Now he mooches along the underside of sleep, becoming gradually aware of a sound—the bubble and sigh of something on the boil.

"Mary?" he asks the dark.

"Good," she says, "you're awake. I've made you more tea."

He props himself up against the head of the bed. "That's kind of you, but—"

"I'm not being kind. It's what you need."

"Tea?"

"This tea." She crosses the room, guides his hand to the steaming cup. "Try not to knock it over this time. I've only got so many cups."

He lowers his nose into the fragrant steam before taking a hesitant sip. The taste is wholly unfamiliar. "Exactly what kind of tea is this?"

The pot hisses on the stove.

"I told you, Reverend, it's what you need."

His head lolls to one side, rousing him to a light, rhythmic scraping, the floorboards squeaking under Mary's weight.

"What did you put in that tea?" he says. "I can barely hold up my head."

"That's because you hit it on a tree. Besides, it's night. You're tired."

To and fro, to and fro, as though she's swaying a solo waltz.

"What are you doing?"

"Sweeping." The scraping stops. "Feel that." She lays something brushy in his lap. His hands respond instinctively, discerning a bundle of slender, warty twigs. "Bog birch. Nothing makes a better broom." She lifts it away and the scratching begins again. "Shin-tangle's another name for it. Probably what tripped you up."

"Shin-tangle," he repeats like a student.

Her footfalls move away. "Over here's what I call the pantry, shelves all down the wall, a bit of everything put away." She lets out a small, reaching grunt. Glass meets glass. The grind of a lid as she returns.

"Hold out your hand," she says, and without thinking, he does. She places an object on his palm—hard and fibrous, a large hairy bullet with bumps. He holds it gingerly to his nose, smells things rustling and normally unseen.

"What is it?" he says finally.

"Owl pellet."

"Ugh!" He drops it on the blanket.

She laughs. "It's not shit, Reverend. A great grey swallows a vole in one gulp. Inside him, he takes what he can use, then rolls up whatever's left into one of these. Spits it up just like that. Fur, teeth, claws—what you've got there is a vole minus the meat."

"Really?"

"Really."

She plucks the pellet up just as he's thinking he might feel for it, hold it again. Another twist of metal on glass, and he finds himself extending his hand.

"Careful," she warns. "It's fragile."

This time she gives him something like a dried flower or leaf—only hairy, slightly sticky, emitting the faintest waft of acrid dust.

"Sundew," she murmurs.

He hesitates. "A plant?"

"Mostly."

"Mostly? Mostly what?"

"It's a meat-eater. Bugs get trapped in the sticky little hairs."

"Charming."

"That too. Sundew's a love charm. Makes women crazy for it, so they say."

"Oh?"

"Not just women, either. Cows and sheep, makes them bellow for it, even the littlest taste."

"You don't say."

"I do say. Not that you'd ever need it."

He smiles. "No?"

"A big golden-haired bastard like yourself." Her tone darkens. "Fire and brimstone, and all those God-fearing church ladies with coals in their pants."

"I beg your pardon?"

"I bet you've had half of them. Am I right?"

His stomach pinches. "I don't know what you're talking about."

"Your followers, Reverend. Your flock."

The sundew clings to his palm. "I don't have to listen to this." He rubs his hands together, crushing it to a powder. "Just who the hell—" He catches himself.

"Uh-oh." She chuckles. "Reverend said a bad word."

He clenches his fists. "Take me to town."

"Nope."

"Take me to town, dammit!"

"Take it easy, killer," she says mildly. "I'll take you."

"You will?"

"In the morning. You'll be better by then anyway. You won't need help."

"Yeah, *right*."

"Well, maybe not with that attitude."

He clamps his mouth shut. Laces his fingers together and bows his head. *Dear Lord*, he thinks forcefully, *look down upon your humble servant—*

"Sundew's not the only meat-eater we've got around here, in case you're wondering." She crosses back to her jars. "There's the pitcher plant too. I've got some fresh here. Want to feel?"

He sighs angrily through his nose. *Look down upon your servant and—*

"Okay, I'll tell you. The leaves are kind of rubbery, green with purple veins. They're hollow—that's the pitcher part—with a big, flared-out lip."

—give me strength in the face of—

"Inside, it's all slippery, with these stiff little hairs leading down. Some fly spots that pretty purple lip and lands, starts exploring, and before you know it, he's in the throat of it, losing his grip."

He drops the thread of the prayer.

"He's scrambling now, sliding sideways or backwards or headfirst, only there's nowhere to go but down, into the pitcher's little pool." She claps her hands. "Splash. He

drowns in there. Rots. And that pitcher soaks up everything he's got."

It's Carl's turn to speak. And he would, if only he could
force his tongue to move.

"Special plant, this," Mary tells him. "Cree used it for
the very, very sick. You'll see. I put a little in your tea."

A LYING HOLE
(clare)

Yellow in my glass, like the yellow in the window-Jesus.
The juice leapt when I tilted it, tasted pretty. Away down
the long shine of wood, you clucked your tongue.

"Put it down, chicken. Not until we thank the Lord."

Behind you a framed Christ, darkly unctuous, back to
the wall. You bent your head to release a glittering stream
of grace.

I stopped my ears to you. Then, as children will, I
made swinging shutters of my hands, chopping passages
into words, words into syllables of sound. It helped, but
there was still the sight of you, the sermonizing hole in
your face.

Just as the ears could grow flaps, so the eyes came
equipped with blinds. I blinked you, cut you up so you
were easy to carry, easier still to leave behind. Better yet—
hearing the tree made it fall, so maybe looking at you made
you lie. Instead of holding you in my beams, I inclined
them to the table's design.

It worked. *Amen.*

The swollen backs of the cook's hands, her metal ring

cutting deep. Suddenly I wasn't hungry. There was green on my plate, the same green that grows in plush over a grave.

OUR LADY OF THE ASSUMPTION

It's hard to tell whether he's sleeping again or just lying there in a sulk. "Reverend?" Mary says softly.

He lets out a long, exasperated sigh. "What?"

"Want me to read to you?"

"What I want is for you to take me back to town."

She crouches down before a silvered wooden crate. "I've got some great books here, the Bible even—or maybe you're sick of that one."

He says nothing. Turns his face away.

"Suit yourself." Delving in with both hands, she releases a cloud of mildew, old leather and ink.

Who'd a believed it? A whole crate full of books.

It was one of Castor's most precious finds—he told of it as though he were recounting a miracle. "The bears were like flies on the dead that night, but I waded in there and snagged it all the same. The stuff people chuck away. So what if some of the titles were rubbed so thin you couldn't read 'em. Doesn't matter what book you pick up, every one of 'em's got a story inside."

He read aloud to her when he was sober enough to manage it. Mostly the same few books over and over, but she never got sick of them, not a one—probably because she didn't know any real-life people besides him, just Mowgli and Anne Shirley and Heathcliff, little baby Moses in his basket, floating around in the reeds.

Anne of Green Gables made her chest hurt when she was small. The first time Castor read it to her, she stopped him partway into the second chapter, just after Matthew loaded Anne into his buggy to take her home.

"Castor," she asked, peering over his hairy forearm at the incomprehensible page, "are you my daddy?"

He looked at her strangely for a moment. "Mary, you know I am."

"And a mother?" she blurted. "Do I have a mother too?"

"Well now." He let the book fall shut on his hand. "Most of us do. Even ol' Castor did for a time. But every so often there comes a special one. See, Mary, you weren't born of a woman."

"I wasn't?"

"Nope. You were grown." He laid the book down then, losing the page. "Like an apple, see. You were grown on a tree."

A FINGER, A LIP
(clare)

It was a game we played, Preacher. You called me with the tip of your finger to the lip of the glass, and I came out from wherever I was crouching, drawn to your circling sound. I couldn't help myself. It was sweeter than any church song, every lap of your finger a rosy ring.

Until you ruined it by opening your mouth.

"You like that?"

The hand dismantled itself, fingers falling away. Beside it, the tail of a loosened tie. I followed its paisley trail to where your face loomed, lips parting to swallow me whole.

"You like that, chicken?"

The pet name was my escape, a red-crested bird scattering white feathers in my mind.

"You like when Daddy plays the glass?"

You were so human, sunk in your recliner, nursing your nightly Scotch. The house was dark, the cook gone home. We were alone, Preacher. I'd have come closer, but you were lit up like a fuse. If I'd set foot in your field, you'd have blown my little body sky-high.

SWEET GALE
(myrica gale)

Carl half dozes, Mary motionless, somewhere to his right. He imagines her in a filthy armchair, the stuff spilling out from its sides.

"I've been trying to figure you, Reverend," she says suddenly.

"Oh?"

"Maybe you think nothing lives here, just some underfed trees and a loony in a shack made of glass. Like this is some kind of wasteland. Some place you and that sad bitch of a mayor can just raze to the ground."

He clears his throat. "I certainly wouldn't put it like that."

"No, you wouldn't. But that's how it is." She stirs. Footsteps and the creak of a door.

"Hey—" His voice comes out higher than planned. "Where are you going?"

"To smoke. Sit out awhile."

"To smoke?"

"Yep, dead baby hair." She laughs. "Christ, tobacco. Ever heard of it?"

"Mary, you need to get me some help."

"You've got help."

"I mean *medical* help."

"You've got that."

"I need proper—" He pauses to sweeten his tone. "Look, I'm asking you, please take me back to town."

"Nope."

"You're keeping me here against my will?"

"The door's right here."

"You know what I mean."

"What I know is you probably would've croaked out there if I hadn't found you. People have, you know." She shuts the door firmly, leaving him alone in his dark.

Let her go, he thinks, I'm fine here on my own.

Less than a minute passes before he's drawing the rough blanket around his bare shoulders and rolling off the bed onto his knees. He crawls toward the memory of the slamming door, feels slat boards on his smarting forehead, gropes for the handle overhead. Before he can find it, the door swings out into her strange-smelling smoke.

"What's this, Reverend? You coming to propose?"

He feels for the door jamb and hauls himself up.

"There's a chair there for you," she tells him. "One step forward and two to the right."

He edges forward.

"I meant man-steps. If you're going to walk like a weasel, I'll have to figure it again. That's it. Reach out to your right now. Bingo."

He lowers himself into the seat.

"Want me to roll you one?" she asks.

"I don't smoke. And that doesn't smell like tobacco, either."

"That's the sweet gale. It grows in the bog here. A pinch in the paper keeps the biters at bay."

The hum of insects intensifies in his ears. They begin to land on his ankles, his neck, and he slaps himself, making her chuckle. The blanket's scratchy, but he doesn't dare expose more skin. They're dive-bombing now, the air around his head is alive.

"Sure you don't want one?"

He shakes his head. But maybe he does. After all, he smoked a little in college. For a while he even bought the odd pack of Sportsman's, wore them in his chest pocket like a badge.

Down the bare board porch Mary rustles. Then a scraping, the feet of her chair pulling close. "Maybe my smoke'll do us both, eh?"

The bugs back off and despite himself Carl feels thankful.

"You wondering what's out here?" she asks. "Want me to tell you what I see?"

"If you like."

"Well, behind us there's the house, and it's made out of bottles, all right, that part of the legend is true. It's dark right now, but in the daylight it looks kind of like a hill covered over with flowers." She pauses for a drag. "There's a lamp hanging up over our heads, moths dancing around it, chucking themselves at the glass. A few of them at our feet here, too. Singed wings. One of them fluttering its last."

He sits forward. Hears a powdery twitching, a delicate, dying thud. *Moths.* As a boy he collected their silver bodies, until his mother found a paper bag full of them at the back of his bottom drawer. It didn't matter how he pleaded, she held the bag up high where he couldn't reach it, stalked wordlessly down the stairs and dumped them in the crackling stove.

"We're in a clearing," Mary goes on. "Fairly dry, lots of hummocky moss. There's a patch of Labrador tea dead ahead, moonshine lichen around some of the stems, glowing so you can see it from here. Over to your left there's a big knot of tamarack roots I hauled back here for decoration. I guess I felt like putting my mark on the place after Castor died."

"Castor?"

"Don't tell me Her Worship hasn't told you about Castor."

"No."

"He was my daddy. You know, the crazy bugger who built this place. Drank up all those bottles. That part's true too." She shifts on her chair, the old wood releasing a groan. "Just past the roots there's what's left of the old shack, and in behind that there's the owl tree."

"Owl tree?"

"Ravens built a nest up there a few years ago, abandoned it after a season. A couple of great greys came to check it out, but they didn't like it enough to stay, so I shinned up there and did a little work—wove in some new twigs, bolstered up the base, left some vole fur lying around so they could see it was good hunting. It did the trick. There's a pair and three chicks up there now."

"Now?" He draws the blanket tighter. "Where, exactly? Where are they?"

Her smoky fingers take hold of his chin, manoeuvring it gently until he's staring up into the dark mass of the nest— or would be, if only he could see.

LAVINIA'S HAIR

Her hair twisted up in a red cone of towel, Lavinia limps naked into her bedroom, coming face to face with the closet's mirrored door. She looks good. Better than good. Amazing, really, for a woman of—hell, for a woman of any age. She runs her hands up the flat of her belly, takes hold of her B-cup breasts. Still firm, still exactly where they ought to be. She smiles, picturing all those saggy-titted moms and grandmas down at the pool.

She bends forward and loosens the towel, shaking out her chin-length ash blonde hair. It's a cut many women get but few can truly wear. Lavinia has the face for it—high cheekbones and Egyptian eyes, the kind of skin that holds a tan. Her contacts are a bold shade of green—again, something she pulls off where so many others fail.

Taking up the hand mirror from the vanity, she swivels to check herself out from behind. What are they thinking, those women who let themselves run to fat the minute the man coughs up a ring? She's worked hard for this ass. It's obvious how much Carl appreciates the effort, the way his hands seek it out in bed.

The idea of his touch makes her miss him. Surely he must have found Mary by now. Talk about letting yourself go—that one still wears her hair like a black bramble down her back, only now it's smudged all over with grey. It's hard to tell what kind of shape she's in under that pile of rags, but Lavinia can well imagine the mess. A lifetime of not bathing or wearing a bra, legs that have never seen a razor, let alone a professional wax.

It was Constable Chartrand who spotted Mary nailing up those pathetic scrolls. Lavinia hasn't laid eyes on her in months, not since she drove down Leila Street and passed her shovelling snow. She idled at the stop sign for a full minute, staring. There was something so animal in the way that woman moved—something *Indian*, Mama would say.

A FILTHY BEAST
(clare)

Sunday best was torture—lace slitting my throat and wrists, tourniquet tights, a petticoat of spiralling wire. I should have been safe in the schoolroom, but you sounded off at me through the door. Lovesick, the teacher kept it ajar. Time and again her soul slipped out the crack, crawling up the aisle to take refuge in your gospelling mouth.

Your sermon washed over me like all the others, streams of nonsense with nouns leaping out. Fishes and loaves, baskets and grass, swineherds and blood and bulls. At times a scrap of story made it ashore—the baby to be cut in two, the fig tree blasted by Christ's forgiving hand.

The teacher's fur coat hung limp by the door, no animal left except you, Preacher, who'd offered it as proof of your wilderness ways. "Lynx," you'd told her proudly. "Big cat for the Reverend's little kitten."

I stalked it, slunk for it where it hung. The moment I made contact, the petticoat had to go. I scratched myself, howled and stamped, the others drawing back, the teacher kneeling, one hand shielding her face.

"What is it, Clare, what's wrong?" She asked with words, never once having heard me speak. "Are you hurt? Show me where."

I hauled at the petticoat.

"It hurts? The petticoat? Is it too tight? Too—scratchy?"

I froze, quivering in my skin.

"Is it scratchy, Clare?"

She wanted a word, a nod, even a look, but I couldn't— it would've been like picking up a power line to offer the answer she craved.

She took a chance. Her hands under my skirt, digging fingers, and the petticoat fell frothing to my feet. It was nowhere near enough. I clawed at my neck, tore frantically at my chubby legs. The teacher panicked, began fumbling with zippers and snaps, undoing me until I stood shaking in cotton panties and nothing else. After a moment I reached out and stroked the coat.

"You like it?" she asked.

I grabbed a handful, burying my face in its camouflage blur.

"You want to wear it, Clare?" She slipped it free—clash and tangle of hangers overhead. "Here. It's okay. You can wear it."

I gathered it jealously, fur-side-in to my tenderized skin. Then scurried to my corner, grasped a grey crayon and began to draw. Bliss. The others whispered about me over cookies and juice. The teacher drifted back to her doorway and the strains of your voice.

I slipped out of the panties. I needed all of me touching, the guard hairs piercing me so the *Clare* could leak out and soak deep into the tufted fuzz. Then there would be no teacher, no children, no church. Nothing but field after field of fur.

That was how you found me, Preacher, your shadow falling across my back.

"What's this? What's she supposed to be, a caveman?" You lifted me out of the coat only to find I'd left something of myself behind. "Christ!" you yelled, and the teacher gasped—the smear, the stink, you dirtying the Lord's name in your mouth. "Cathy!" You turned on her. "What were you thinking?!"

"I—she needed it," the teacher cried. "She needed something soft."

3

A FEATHERED BREAST

(*clare*)

The teacher's cat comes stretching into the room, his pupils diminishing to slits. He marks me for his own, then the teacher, then cuts a long-bodied path through our work to sit waiting beneath the clock.

"Yahoo." The time-bird comes out fighting. "Yahoo, yahoo, yahoo—" It hurls a dozen fast insults, the cat hunching and cackling his desire.

"Easy, boy," the teacher murmurs, distracted by the image she's just cut free. She holds it at arm's length for perspective. Tilts it, plumed and wounded, to the light.

I opened the bird—took scissors from the craft box and pushed them in, snipped up the belly and laid it wide. Gizzard and guts. I hunted for its love, the egg-tenderness, inner mirror to the feathers it would've closed over a brood. Then fanned out a wing, held flight in the palm of my hand. Made a perch of my finger so it could hang bloody-breasted from its claws.

I felt the others draw close, then wailing and tears. The teacher grabbed and shook me, terror rending her face.

Why hers and not the bird's? So peaceful. Dead on its glinting breast.

"She cut it open, Carl. With scissors."

"So?" Hearing yourself, you softened your tone. "Cathy, kids dissect stuff. I did it. My friends did it. It's normal."

"At three?"

You brushed the back of your hand down her breast.

"It's *not* normal." The teacher tore herself from your gaze, staring past you to a doll on the floor. "She won't look me in the eye, won't speak—"

"I told you before," you said evenly, "she's quiet."

"It's more than that, you know it is." Her voice sped up. "She won't listen either. No, not *won't*. It's like she can't, like she's deaf, but only sometimes—" The light came on. "Only to human speech!"

You took a step back, your hand falling away from her side.

"It's not healthy, Carl," she insisted. "I've never seen a child play the way she does."

Your dual focus on me was too much. The charge began coursing, forcing me to run circles up on my toes. It flowed into my hands, making me shake them, flap them hard to release a shower of sparks.

"See that?" The teacher pointed. "See what she's doing? She'll do that for an hour at a time."

You gave her your shiniest, most settling smile. "She's just being a bird, aren't you, chicken? Just flapping her little wings."

"Carl—"

243

"Come on, chicken." Your hand looped out and tightened on my arm. "You come back down now. You know chickens can't fly."

Later, you nodded to where I hunched scribbling on the floor, my face close to the paper, as close as I could get it without colouring my nose. "See there? That's a happy kid. She'd be happy doing that all day."

The teacher stiffened in your arms. "But that's what I mean, Carl. It's not right to be happy with one thing for so long."

"Oh, now."

"See how she screams if you interrupt her. Go on."

"She's quiet, Cathy, that's all. She's a child of God." You slipped the top button of her blouse from its hole.

"Carl!"

"We're alone, sugar. Empty church." Another button. The teacher cast me a glance. "Cathy," you moaned, licking a finger and tucking it inside her bra. She melted, the spine sliding out of her to clatter on the floor. You pulled her after you into the storeroom, drawing shut the door.

Empty church.

Except for me, Preacher. Had you forgotten about me?

GREY JAY

(*perisoreus canadensis*)

Back in Mary's bed, Carl tries lying on his side, but finds the increase in pressure to his left eye unbearable. Besides, the mattress is too soft, with a definite central sag. He rolls onto his back and sighs.

244

"Ever seen a grey jay?" Mary asks.

"I wouldn't know. Why?"

"He looks like a blue jay, only grey, and no crest on his head." She pauses. "Used to have one, though."

"One what?"

"Crest. He's greedy, see. Steals scraps from the other birds, animals too, even humans, snatching them right off the plate. Then one day he eats so much he can't move. That's how he gets himself caught. This woman grabs him and lays him down on a stump while her man hoists up his axe. He's not such a good aim, though, lops off grey jay's crest instead of his head. Ever since then grey jay makes the softest nest, even uses the silk from old cocoons."

It takes Carl a moment to realize she's finished. "The softest nest? Is that supposed to be some kind of moral?"

"If you want."

"I thought this was a story about greed."

"Greed's tricky. Some seem greedy when the truth is they just need a lot to keep going. You take shrews—if they're awake, they're eating, everything from ants to whatever they can manage to drag down. They're like little furnaces. They've got the heat up so high it's all they can do to get enough fuel. Weasel's the same."

Carl says nothing, a memory playing across the backs of his eyes. For years he rose early to gather the eggs, crawling up the ramp into the shadowy coop, sliding his hand under the sighing birds. He heard scuttling beneath the floorboards from time to time but said nothing, knowing Papa would make him go after whatever it was, down on his belly in the dark. He caught sight of the weasel only once, streaking away from the coop with a white feather in its fur.

245

Papa gave him a dozen of the best with the strap, one for every mangled bird.

"Why don't you spill it, Reverend."

"What?"

"You wanted to talk to me, right? I can't see what else you'd be doing bumbling around out here."

"Well, yes, actually. I thought we could discuss all this—fuss that's been going on. See if maybe we couldn't work something out."

"Not if that something includes you levelling this bog."

He holds up a hand. "Now look, I'm not sure where you got that idea—"

"From you. You know, a couple of weeks ago, you and Mayor Lavinia and the guy with all the equipment. 'Pulp trees, horticulture grade peat.'" She mimics the forestry consultant's deadpan tone. "That guy."

Carl gapes at her blindly, stunned. "You were there?"

"You never heard how the trees have ears? That's some sweet deal you've got going, Reverend. The town tears out the bog and sells it off, then they turn around and invest in your little project. You get cheap land and the money to build with, Mercy gets hundreds of kids and their families passing through every summer, and Lavinia—well, she's the real winner here, let's face it—Lavinia gets shut of me and everything I remind her of, gets shut of this messy old bog, *and* gets to keep a certain preacher close at hand."

He smiles tightly. "You're mistaken, Mary. What you witnessed was simply an information-gathering exercise."

"Horseshit."

"I assure you, Mayor Wylie and I are—"

"Screwing like rabbits?"

"W-what?" He forces a laugh. "For your information, Lavinia Wylie—"

"There's nothing you can tell me about Lavinia I don't already know. Anyway, that's not the point. The point is, you came out here to get me to stop stirring up the shit, only you thought you'd find some old girl gone soft in the head. Isn't that what Lavinia told you?"

He searches for a half-truth, coming up dry.

"You thought you'd just come out here and sweet-talk me or scare me, or whatever it took to get your way. Well, now you've met me, what do you think? You think you're going to get me to stop nailing up those scrolls? No way, Reverend, no matter how many kids you hire to rip them down. You think I'm going to quit writing to the papers?" She chuckles. "Stroke of genius signing myself Mother Nature, eh? Nothing like birchbark to make them sit up and take notice. That's the thing, see—they open those scrolls in their little offices and the smell of the forest hits them square in the face. Once they get a whiff of that, they don't need anybody to tell them how much it matters."

"Of course it matters," Carl says evenly. "But we must remember to worship the Creator, Mary, not His creation." For a moment he imagines his words have hit home. Until she speaks.

"You know something, Reverend, I never met Castor's mother—she was long dead by the time I came along—but she was called Mary too. This was her land. Breed land, Castor called it. I guess most of what got parcelled out to the Metis was land the whites couldn't use." She pauses. "Until now, that is. Anyway, it was her land, and Castor's, and now I guess it's mine. It's only a little corner of what you're after, but I'll be damned if it's any use to me with the bog torn out." Her voice swoops in close. "It's not happening, Reverend. You can kiss your blessed camp goodbye."

LAVINIA'S THIGHS

The teddy's a thin secret between Lavinia and her sheets. She squirms a little, feels a naughty scratch of lace. The colour suits her—*apricot glow* according to the catalogue, and for once they got it just right. Carl called her a peach the first time she wore it for him. Threatened to peel her and suck up the juice.

She reaches for the bedside clock. A quarter after twelve. Maybe he's gone straight back to the motel for some reason. Or maybe something's happened to him. He could be lost out there, or hurt. He could be— *Stop it*. He'd phone if there was a problem, she made sure he took his phone. He's probably turning up the street right now. She'll hear his car any minute, then the back door deadbolt as he lets himself in with her spare key.

She could pretend to be asleep. That way he could gaze at her from the bedroom doorway, take in her mussed-up hair, her glossy parted lips. Her thighs prickle with impatience. Surely they can't still be talking. Even a preacher can only talk for so long, and as for Mary—well, really, what on earth could crazy Mary have to say?

Lavinia feels her heart contract.

It was rarely spoken of at home, and never when Mama was within earshot. The few times Daddy dared bring it up were when he came in to kiss Lavinia goodnight.

"You're a lucky girl, Lovey, you know that? I never had a daddy to tuck me in, all I had was a brother." That was usually the end of it—he'd kiss her on the forehead and leave her lying alone in the dark. One night, though, he took a deep breath and went on. "He was a good brother. Saved my life when I was just a few weeks old."

Lavinia wanted to ask how, and why, and where the brother was now, but she was silenced by Mama's dark shape in the door. "Time to go to sleep, Lavinia. Renny, let her sleep."

Daddy sat perfectly still on the edge of the bed.

"Renny," Mama said again, and he rose stiffly and followed her out of the room.

Lavinia caught snippets of the argument that ensued. *Elsa, he's my flesh and blood. You swore to me, Renny, you swore!* Then came a terrible sound, the report of the slamming front door. Lavinia lay trembling. Heard Mama let out a loud, racking sob.

Daddy must've heard it too. He couldn't have made it far, must have been standing shocked and wretched on the stoop. He shut the door carefully on his way back in. Lavinia closed her eyes during the charged silence that followed, drifted off to the familiar rhythmic creaking of their bed.

All mention of the brother ceased. A couple of years later Lavinia got wind of the family shame at school. She fought her own battles, knowing better than to bring the matter home.

The teacher had seen one of my drawings. After nearly two months of hugging them to my chest and sidling past her with teeth bared, I'd marched right up to her, waved one like a flag, watched her eyes open wide.

She hovered as the last of your flock took their reluctant leave, then dragged you to the schoolroom, where the drawing lay in wait on her desk. I was rocking. Riding the red horse with its whinnying face to the wall.

"It's Clare's, can you believe it? And no doubt there are hundreds like it. She smuggles a bunch of them out of here every week."

"Hmm." An innocent sound, enough to show you were listening, nothing more.

"It's almost expressionistic," she rushed on. "Can you believe the composition, the precision? It'd be incredible for a twelve-year-old—but for three?"

"Hm."

Confused by your lack of enthusiasm, she tried again. "The images are so compelling, especially that middle one. I almost feel as though I've seen it before."

Like all of them, the page was divided into five. Each black border enclosed an image somehow incomplete, cut to size by the absolute line. The centre block showed a waning moon, blue and glassy in a pinkish sky.

"These are not a child's drawings, Carl." She swept a hand toward the crude scribbles she kept tacked to the wall. "See any difference?"

Of course there was a difference. I held my crayons like I

meant it. I bore down hard, wore my tools down long before the others did, with their vague ideas and even vaguer hands.

"Carl?"

Something was troubling you, Preacher, comprehension just below the horizon, the rusty birdsong before the dawn. It was that thin, icy slip of a moon. You'd never seen it, but you knew it all the same—the knowing somehow shameful, almost incestuous—the way it hung as though hooked into that fleshy sky. It was a very particular blue, that moon, like a surfacing vein—a little milk, a little rose.

It would come to you. Later, when you were alone, it would come with an ulcerous twinge, your gut taking a bite of you from inside. You'd turn your back to the mirror, drop your pants and find it gleaming on your own behind.

And then you'd remember.

Wild Bill. He was your papa's prize coloured German, a shit-brown billy goat with a little black smile, black trails beneath his eyes and a bristling black ridge along his spine. Eel-backed, they called it. His coat was like long sick grass, as if he'd grown up out of the dead corner where your papa dumped turpentine and old motor oil, any poison he could find.

He was the scourge of your tender years—his sideways yellow eyes, the way he stood up like a man to tear leaves from your mother's fruit trees, the stink of him.

He pissed in his own mouth to stroke it through his coat when the neighbours brought their nanny goats round. She-goat after she-goat, Wild Bill circling, lips drawn to show his ochre teeth. He mounted them like they were boulders. Raising himself up like a conqueror on the last thrust, planting his front hooves on their backs.

His chain-link tether was too long, your papa forever uprooting and moving the peg before you could be sure of its reach. Thinking he was still penned up for the night, you crept into the yard. A low bleat was the one warning you got. You took to your heels, kicking up chicken feed, shinning up the old ash tree seconds too late. Wild Bill reared up on his flinty hooves, goring you with a dirty horn.

Maybe it wouldn't have scarred so mirrored and blue if your papa hadn't heard you scream. *Yellow*. He bent you over his knee, spoke it slow and broken to the beat of the strap—*yel-low, yel-low*—while your mother stood watching, unconcerned. The wound opened wide, took a month to stop weeping and heal.

Recognizing the scar, you realized I'd seen it. You couldn't begin to understand how—all you knew was that I'd caught sight of your bare backside and the Lord only knows what else. So quiet, so caught up in my drawing. You'd never dreamt I had eyes for you.

What would I draw next? What had I already drawn, stashed away like ammunition, so many charges and rounds? The teacher was right. It wasn't healthy to be happy doing one thing.

You took my crayons. Hid every last one of them away.

OUR LADY OF THE VISITATION

The Reverend hasn't spoken since Mary put him in his place. She imagines touching the hard line of his mouth, insisting with her fingers until it buckles into a genuine smile. She could almost feel sorry for the poor mayor. Imagine looking to a mouth like that for love.

Not that Lavinia deserves much sympathy. Mary can scarcely believe the same blood runs in their veins. Their encounters may have been few and far between, but the first set an unforgettable tone.

At seven years of age Mary had never even heard tell of her cousin. Normally loose-lipped to a fault about the inhabitants of Mercy, Castor had kept mum on the subject of his little brother's family, knowing Mary would be curious, and that her curiosity could only lead to pain.

What he failed to understand was how lonely she was, how badly she needed a friend. Even when he was home, he was often too worn out or too wasted to play. On the day in question he lay fully dressed on his bed, tipping a bottle to his lips and staring up through his vault of mortared glass. Mary tugged at his sleeve, even whined a little, then gave up and went looking for somebody her own size.

She took nothing with her. Heading south on one of Castor's many trails, she followed it further than ever before, breaking branches to mark her passage, losing all sense of time. Eventually spruce gave way to poplars, poplars to swaying grass. Beyond lay the shape of a town. She had long known of Mercy's existence but was still shocked to see so many houses crowded together, and not one of them glittering like home.

She approached stealthily, pushing her way into a bank of snowberries that bordered the grounds of a huge red house. At the time she paid little attention to the building that was the Mercy United Church—she was too busy watching the girls who were playing in its yard. All three had on pale, frothy dresses and shiny black shoes. The short, yellow-haired one was running the show, riding around in a make-believe coach while the other two shouldered its weight. "Gee-up!" she kept screaming at them. "Geeee-up!"

Mary caught a whiff of them when they circled close—flowers held too tightly and too long. The smell made her anxious, but she'd come too far to turn around and go home. On their next pass she steeled herself and stepped out from the hedge. The three of them stopped dead and stared.

In the heat of their combined gaze Mary caught an unflattering glimpse of herself from the outside. She was wearing one of Castor's old shirts for a dress, chopped at the sleeves and cinched with a strip of hide at the waist. Her feet were bare. Her hair hung to her elbows in dark, tangled skeins.

The leader wore hers in two tight, shiny braids, each with a red ribbon at its tail. They fluttered defiantly as she stepped forward between the other two. "Who are you?"

It was a bewildering question, one Mary had never heard. She gave the only answer she could think of. "Mary."

"*Mary?* That's it? No surname?"

Mary stood motionless, unsure. The horse-girls giggled.

"I guess we'll have to give you one." Yellow-braids thought about it for a moment and smiled. "*Contrary.* That's it. Mary. Quite. Contrary."

More giggling. Mary was the wild kid among the townies—she knew that—but somehow it seemed as though she were the tame one, brought up soft while they'd been sharpening their claws. "Okay," she said finally.

"Okay? Mary *Contrary? Okay?*" Yellow-braids turned to her horses and they started whinnying for her, holding their bellies and rolling their eyes. Mary took a step back.

"Hey!" said Yellow-braids, spitting almost, then abruptly sweet. "You wanna play?"

Mary was powerless in the face of such an invitation. "Okay," she heard herself say. "Sure."

"Good." Yellow-braids gave her a smile. "Franny," she said to one of the horses, "gimme your scarf." Franny untied the pink band that was holding back her hair. Yellow-braids circled behind Mary. "Shut your eyes," she ordered, and just like Franny, Mary wordlessly obeyed. She felt the scarf drop down over her eyes, then sharp little knuckles knotting it at the back of her head.

"Can you see?" Yellow-braids demanded. "And don't you dare lie."

"No."

Mary felt hands on her back. "We're playing Blind," Yellow-braids said in her ear. "You have to trust me. I'm your guide."

Mary could hear the horses stifling themselves.

"Get back, Franny," Yellow-braids barked. "You too, Paula, get out of Mary Contrary's way." She said the name differently that time, her tone protective, as though she were speaking of someone she loved. The last of Mary's misgivings dissolved. She melted back into those hands and allowed herself to be pushed around.

Yellow-braids went slowly at first, telling her when to lift up her feet. "There's a rock here, Mary, step over it, that's right." After a while she sped up and started taking sharper turns, but Mary was too elated to mind. Running without her eyes was like flying. She let her arms rise up in their sockets, placing her faith in the air.

The tree trunk caught her full in the face. Sheet lightning flooded her skull, then blackness, until a tugging at the blindfold dragged her back. Yellow-braids stood over her, the scarf hanging limp in her hand. Franny was blubbering, Paula blinking, stunned.

"You shouldn't have," Franny wailed, "you shouldn't have."

"I never meant it!" Yellow-braids turned on her and shrieked. "It was her hair, her filthy hair blew back in my eyes!"

Mary rolled over onto her side, somehow found her feet and stood. Her nose was streaming. Franny screamed and ran for it, then Paula, with Yellow-braids bringing up the rear. "She asked for it!" Mary could hear her yelling after them. "She did it to herself!"

Mary didn't let herself cry the whole way home. Not until Castor was washing her face with rain from the barrel.

"She got small bones, this girl?" he asked, dipping the cloth. "Pointy little face, quick on her feet?"

She nodded.

"Black hair?"

She shook her head. He seemed relieved, until she told him how bright the girl's hair was, except for a dark line down the middle where the two halves came apart.

"Christ," he said, "you mean to tell me she's already bleachin' the kid's hair? It was black as pitch when she was born. And not the kind that falls out, either, the real thing."

"When she was born?" Mary asked, sniffling. "Did you see it?"

256

He didn't answer.

"Do you know her, Castor?"

He stroked her forehead where it was starting to turn blue. "You keep your distance from that one, Mary," he said finally. "You keep to the bog."

FOOL HEN
(dendragapus canadensis)

It should be easy to ignore somebody you can't see, but Carl finds the opposite to be true. Every rustle, every creak Mary makes commands his attention. Her presence looms large, spawning questions in his darkened mind.

She coughs, small and dry like a cat, and he finds he can no longer hold his tongue. "This father of yours," he says, "how did he feed you?"

"The world's full of food, Reverend. Somebody chucks out a sack of potatoes because the eyes have sprouted, but that just means they're ready to grow."

He flashes on the black towers in his mother's garden, each one six tires high, packed with swelling tubers and dirt. It was a trick she knew, a way to choke twenty pounds from a single plant. "You lived on potatoes," he says, the words bitter in his mouth.

"Not only. Castor was a crackerjack slingshot. Squirrels and hares, platefuls of wood frogs in spring. Not to mention fool hens. The bog was still crawling with them back then, you could just stroll up to one with a stick in your hand and nail it between the eyes. He got stuff in town too, a soup bone from the butcher, a bag of soft apples. He had the kind of face people gave to, ugly but soft, not too proud. Even pissed, he was harmless to everybody but himself."

"Sounds like the ideal parent."

Her silence is disconcerting, impossible to gauge. "You got kids?" she says finally.

He opens his mouth to find it empty. For a moment the girl's face hangs before him, devoid of expression, framed in her mother's fine hair.

"Well?"

"One. A—daughter."

"Yeah? Well, I don't see her. You keeping a close eye on her, Reverend?"

"She's in good hands," he says quickly. "She's only three. I can hardly take her with me on business—"

"Business? You and Lavinia?" Mary clucks her tongue. "Wait, don't tell me, your little girl's at home with the wife. The two of them praying for you, counting the days till you're home."

A chill runs through his body, a ruthless current of control. "For your information, my wife is dead."

"Oh."

"Satisfied?"

"I'm sorry."

"I bet."

"I mean it, Reverend. I never knew my mother. Never even knew who she was." She pauses. "Where is she?"

"My wife? What kind of a question—"

"Your daughter, I meant your daughter. Where is she?"

"I told you," he says through his teeth, "she's in very good hands."

A PADDED FIST
(clare)

Deprived of a creative outlet, the charge rained, flash-flooding me until it welled in my useless hands. My eyes were ground-level windows stuck open in a storm. No choice but to hammer them closed. Three strikes left and three strikes right—I kept at them until they swelled, until there was nothing but endorphin green, pain like springtime in the blood.

You caught me at it, grabbed hold of my little fists. You must have recognized them, Preacher—surprisingly powerful, sized to the socket of a three-year-old eye. You'd carried them all your life, curled like code on a twisted gene. They were your gift at my conception, the glint in your paternal eye.

You could've comforted me with crayons. Instead, you taped your thick winter mitts over my hands and smuggled me out to the car.

You drove clear across town, from Winnipeg's suburban south to its alien north end, far from the family doctor, in the hope that you wouldn't be known. One hand on the wheel, the other barring me like a door, you careened into the hospital's lot.

The intern was wary, he'd seen black-eyed children before. To save you from suspicion, I socked myself as hard as the mitt would allow. A shadow came down over his face. A beaten child was one thing—the diagnosis simple, if sad. Another can of worms altogether, the child who beat on herself. He excused himself, a white beard returning in his place.

"What have we here?" the new doctor asked. "Hello there."

My eyes were overripe plums weeping through slits in their skins. He peered into them and watched the pupils roll away.

He took a step back, waved and watched my padded hands lie limp, pulled faces to my waxy smile. His hand crawled along my arm, feeling me shrink. Finally, he feigned stubbing his toe, yelped aloud and looked up to find me unconcerned. When he turned to you, his face was impenetrable. "Does she speak?"

"She's pretty quiet."

"Does she say any words?"

"She—used to. A little."

"When?"

"When? I'm not certain. When she was a baby. One, maybe one and a half."

"And she stopped?"

"She's quiet, yes."

"You've said that already, Mr. Mann."

"Yes," you admitted finally. "I suppose she did at some point. Stop."

I pawed at my forehead. The doctor watched me out the corner of his eye. "Does she like routine? Get upset over change?"

"Don't all children?"

"Some more than others. How does she play?"

"Pardon me?"

"Does she play well with other kids?"

"Well, she's—"

"I know, she's quiet." He paused. "Does she play with one toy for a long time? Do the same thing over and over?"

"I—I don't know, really. She draws."

A light came on in the doctor's wire-rimmed eyes. "Any good?" Faced with the idiot, he hoped for the elusive savant.

"How do you mean?" you asked, stalling.

"Does she draw well? Unusually for her age?"

"Oh. I don't think so." *Liar.* "Not that I've noticed, anyway." *Liar, liar.*

The doctor fished in the white pocket of his coat, drawing out a thin red pen. I reached for it, but by the time he'd found paper, you'd already snatched it away.

"It makes her nervous," you explained, eyes on the door.

"Drawing?"

I croaked, and when the pen didn't come, I rained blows on my temples and wailed.

"See?" you said. "I don't know why, but sometimes it gets her all riled up."

"Okay." He took the pen from your fingers, hesitated, then slipped it away. "What about rocking? Flapping her hands? Ever seen her do this?" He stretched up on tiptoe, fluttered his hands and began stepping gingerly about. Your jaw dropped, followed by your gaze.

"Well?" He stopped short, letting his hands fall.

You couldn't look up. "Yes. Something like that. Now and then."

"Uh-huh." He leaned in close to my ear. "Clare? Can you hear me? Would you like a treat, Clare? Would you like some candy?"

I was humming, swaying on the steel table, slapping the hard shell of my skull. Calling the hand to home base reaffirmed the skeleton's ties. Otherwise the neck bone connected to the thigh bone or, even worse, to nothing at all.

Tinkling. Tweezers in a test tube. I froze, then leaned forward into their crystalline tone.

"Mr. Mann," the doctor said gently, "I think you'd better sit down."

Autism. He said the word—said it was possible, probable even, but not certain. Further testing required, and even then no hard proof, only diagnostic criteria based on the behaviour of the child. Bewildered, you asked how it could have happened, assured him you were a healthy, God-fearing man.

"Better God-loving, Mr. Mann," he answered quietly, "if you want to come through this in one piece." With that, he handed you a slip of paper, the specialist's number and name.

You took the road out of town rather than home, unwilling to return to our lives. Cowed by the everlasting Trans-Canada, you kept to the Perimeter, four blacktop lines that box the city in, a detour for those who would rather pass it by.

"George, George, George of the jun-gle," you sang suddenly, "strong as he can be!" You glanced at me. "Remember, chicken, you used to laugh when Daddy sang that song."

Your hands were shaking so violently, you began to mistrust your ability to steer. You pulled onto the shoulder beside a furrowed field. Slowed to a standstill and stared.

To think I'd been the kind of baby you could leave waiting forever. Once, in my car seat, I watched you through the windshield—the waitress leaning close to pour your coffee, you squeezing the Styrofoam, breathing her fragrant steam. Your sunglasses glinted on the seat beside me. I reached for them, slid their golden arms down the sides of my fragile skull. They were on the floor when you got back. It frightened me, Preacher, looking out through your dark.

4

A CIRCLE OF TEETH
(clare)

The heart of this page startles me, it's so real. Isolated, under no influence, I'm the naive impulse, the unadulterated eye. *Draw what you see, not what you know.* This is how most learn a nose is not a nose but a collection of darkness and light. But what if there were never any breach, never any knowing beyond what is perceived? We'd all be gifted if we took the world on faith. *Art?* Like the carvers of totems, we'd have no need of the word.

"Too-true," says the time-bird, and nothing more. The teacher yawns. I close my scissors boldly, capturing the central image entire.

You dreamt me a leech, Preacher, anchored to your neck, sucking what little you had left over from your ladies and the Lord. I'd latched on hard, my mouth bloodied and round, a hundred tiny teeth taking hold. *Demon.* A single word as you woke shaking, fingering the dream hole in your throat.

"Demon." You spoke it aloud.

Pale and wakeful in the room down the hallway from yours, I ran a mitt over my quilt, touching the moon where it lit upon the pattern of dancing bears.

You rolled heavily from your covers and dropped to your knees. "Lord—" You wrung your hands. "Lord?"

No answer.

"Help me," you pleaded. "Speak to me, Lord."

Nothing.

"Jesus," you whimpered, "give me a sign."

Your hands delved beneath the pillow to find the Good Book where it lay. You raised your eyes to the bed-head Cross, let the pages fall open, and pointed. Your fingertip stuck lightly to the passage it found. *Anyone who prefers son or daughter to me is not worthy of me.*

God wished you to place Him before me. It was a good start, but you needed more. A path. A runway, even, cleared for speed.

Ask and ye shall receive. The scene unrolled like a canvas in your mind—top-heavy evergreens, a patchwork of flowers and moss. In the midst of it all stood your dead wife, Jenny, lovely in a long green gown. She bowed her flaxen head, and with that small movement the movement all around her began. Children took shape gradually, almost magically, among the trees. As they gathered about her, Jenny raised and opened her arms. She was a queen to them—no, you realized with a jolt, *a Christ*. In that instant your mission became clear.

RUSTY PEAT MOSS
(*sphagnum fuscum*)

"What do you know about this bog, anyway?" Mary asks, her voice dispersing the murky first scenes of a dream.

265

"Hmm?" Carl shakes off his drowsiness, answering before he has time to think. "The bog? Nothing."

"Ever heard of a kettle lake?"

"No."

"This one started when a meteor hit and left a big smoking hole to fill up little by little with rain."

"I see. And you know this how?"

She goes on as though he hasn't spoken. "No rivers in or out means not much flow, so the lake just lies there, turning all vinegary and sour. Only the tough trees can handle it, so they're the ones to take hold in the banks— around here it's black spruce mostly, some tamarack. After a while the banks get crowded, so those nearest the edge start dipping their roots and easing in. Moss creeps out along the roots, and one day there's enough of a mat for some leatherleaf or crowberry to take hold. It takes forever, but in the end you get a forest, with everything woven so tight sometimes the trees can't even fall when they die."

"But—" He hesitates. "What about the lake?"

"What about it?"

"What happened to it?"

"That's the beauty part, Reverend. It's still there."

"Where?"

"Here. Underneath us, underneath the whole bog. You can feel it in some places, like walking on somebody's gut. Some spots, the trees wobble when you jump."

"What? Come on."

"It's true, Reverend, this forest is floating."

"Okay." He swings his feet out from beneath the covers, planting them on the floor. "Whatever you say."

"Going somewhere?"

"I need a bathroom."

"What for?"

"What do you mean, what for?"

She laughs. "I mean, will you be standing or sitting down?"

"Oh. Standing."

"In that case, just go off the porch."

"What?"

"I'll get you into position."

He feels a wash of shame, recalling how his mother looked over his shoulder the first dozen times he tried it standing up. She said nothing to guide him, only clucked her tongue in disgust, swiping the rim with her cloth whenever he spilled so much as a drop. "I don't think so," he mutters.

"Why not? Castor did it enough times. The moss doesn't seem to mind."

"No, I mean about getting me into position."

"Suit yourself."

He stands slowly, extends his arms and starts shuffling in the direction of the door.

"A little to the left."

His fingers meet the door and search out the handle.

"The porch is about six feet deep."

"Thanks." He hangs back, the night air on his face giving him second thoughts.

"Don't just stand there letting the bugs in, Reverend."

"Okay, okay." He steps out quickly, pushing the door shut behind him. Once out of her sight, he drops again to his hands and knees. A sliver jams into his palm, and after that he lifts his hands rather than sliding them, setting them down cautiously, like an injured cat. When one of them meets empty air, he suffers a sudden, dark vertigo, as though he's come to the edge of a great bluff. Unwilling to stand, he rises up shakily on his knees.

His ears are ringing, insects coming at him from all sides. Waving them away with his free hand, he looses himself hurriedly from his briefs, releasing hours' worth of urine in a hissing, splattering stream. The sound comforts him a little, along with the spreading sensation of relief. Before him, the night is vast. He shakes his penis gently before tucking it away.

A LECTERN OF FLESH
(clare)

There was to be no schoolroom for me that Sunday. No sweet teacher worrying, watching me where I crouched. That Sunday you kept hold of me, fingers clamped to my shoulder, digging in.

The congregation was ill at ease, but you stared them down, singing loud enough to make up for those who had trouble belting out praise in the face of my discoloured eyes. You raised your free arm as the hymn crested to its end, held it aloft in the ensuing hush.

"Brothers and sisters," you began softly, "some things are out of our hands."

A murmur of assent, heads nodding, front pews first, the movement rippling back. It was your special genius, Preacher, that gift for intimacy from afar. I saw them through your eyes now—women and men, small children, even teens—all of them hungry, ready to swallow anything you saw fit to share.

You let the arm drop. "Many of you will remember when I lost my darling wife."

Again came the murmur, reaching higher, dying back to a moan.

"Those of you who knew Jenny will remember her as a gentle soul. She was delicate, like this child. Fair." You lifted two fingers from your grip, flicked the white-blonde curl that dangled from behind my ear. Then bowed your head. Let them hold their breath until the weaker ones began to feel faint.

"When I lost her," you went on, raising your eyes, "I told myself the same thing I tell each and every one of you who comes to me in the shadow of grief. God never gives you more than you can handle, I told myself. He never gives you more than you can hold."

The teacher's face appeared at the far end of the room, wedged in the schoolroom door. Her bloodless lips were a crack like the crack where she stood, half in, half out, as though she wished to come forward but didn't dare. As though she wished to speak.

You cleared your throat before beginning again. "I thought that was the worst I'd have to bear." You stepped out from the pulpit and knelt down behind me. Both hands on my shoulders now, you held me out like a shield, bracing yourself against the small bones of my back. "You see this child before you?" you demanded. "This poor, afflicted child?"

The mothers surged in their pews, fighting the urge to

rush the aisle, to thunder up the stairs, and fold me—or was it you?—to their breasts.

"Maybe you've noticed her before. Noticed she was different, a little too quiet. Or maybe you've seen her throw a tantrum. Something wrong there, you might've thought. Something not quite right."

As if on cue I balled up a fist and slammed it into my eye. The congregation recoiled. You caught hold of my wrists, binding them with a hand behind my back. The teacher swayed forward, then withdrew.

"I've taken her to the doctor," you soldiered on, "and she is indeed afflicted. The details don't matter. What matters, good people, is that the Lord is testing me, the Lord is laying on another Cross. Now why should I be surprised? Didn't He test Abraham to see what he was made of? Didn't He test a man called Job? Isn't this very life one long test to see if we have what it takes to live forever in the glory of God?" You paused, your face working hard. "Still, you find yourself asking why. Not even, Why me, Lord? but, Why? To what purpose? What is it You want me to see? I asked these questions. Over and over I asked. And last night, brothers and sisters, the Lord answered."

A squeal of delight sounded from halfway back.

"We have spoken often of the Godless world. Those who cannot see. Those who refuse to see. Worst of all, those who refuse to let their children see. We have spoken time and again of these lost sheep, fretted over them until we are sick to our very hearts. What can we do, Lord? we ask. How can we save them? Help them save themselves? Well, I don't know about you, but when I have a question, there's only one reference book for me."

You didn't need the Book. You'd long ago learned the effect of the memorized Word, how the Saviour Himself seemed to speak through your lips when your eyes remained free to caress the crowd.

"'Let the little children come to me; do not stop them, for it is to such as these that the Kingdom of God belongs.'" You paused to let the passage sink in. "It's right there in the Good Book—the Kingdom of God belongs to the children. The children are our future, not just in this life but in the next, and if that's the case—" You rolled your eyes heavenward. "Look around you, good people. Look at the newspapers, look at your neighbours, open your eyes to the plight of the Godless children of today!"

You swept your gaze over a sea of helpless stares.

"Brothers and sisters, I have done just that, and that's what I'm here to tell you today. By blighting this child, this *only* child of mine, the Lord Jesus has opened my eyes, opened my heart to *all* children. He has shown me that they are in need of something, in dire and desperate need." You lowered your voice. "Today's children need the Lord Jesus Christ. It's that simple."

Quantity over quality, Preacher. All that talk of children and you'd forgotten your own. I'd taken the shape of a lectern, wooden in your spirited grasp.

"Simple? you ask yourselves. Here, in the city? In this Babylon of modern life? Why, you can't turn around without meeting temptation." You shook your head. "So where does that leave us? Nowhere? Or does it *lead* us? Does it in fact lead us somewhere very special, somewhere holy, even, somewhere where Jesus is waiting for all those lost little children, waiting with wide open arms?" You began gently to nod. "I spoke earlier of an answer. Well, it was more of a vision, really, a picture set before me by the Lord."

They yearned forward in their seats. What could it be? A flood? Angelic revolution? The longed-for Day of Judgment at last?

"A camp."

The church was all sighs. The Apocalypse was well and good, just not quite yet.

"That's right, brothers and sisters, the Church of the Water of Life must found a camp, a sanctuary where today's children can come to know the teachings of Jesus Christ, where today's youth can learn to take up the Cross and follow in His path!"

The congregation began to buzz. You stood up, your grip still firm, and they lifted their adoring eyes. "And what's more, I know just the place. The Lord has shown me."

More than shown, Preacher—He'd taken you there the previous fall. The rural tour was nothing all that serious, mostly a lot of fishing and taking local ladies for long rides in your car. You'd planned to bypass Mercy—Jenny had spoken of it rarely, and always with regret—but in the end curiosity won out. Good thing, too. It turned out your late wife's hometown had a fine-looking woman for a mayor.

You couldn't see it, could you, Preacher? The same slight hips and wrists, the glowing hair and eyes. Only my mother's flesh had lain softly on her bones, and those had been her true colours—blonde and new-leaf green. The mayor resembled her as only a golem could. You gave her life by blurring your eyes.

"Mercy," you called out suddenly, your voice booming through the nave. "Believe it or not, brothers and sisters,

the town is called Mercy, and it's surrounded by some of
the prettiest country you've ever seen." You smiled broadly.
"Can you picture it? Can you see the children, the little
lambs of God?"

The women were dewy-eyed, hearts in their throats, a
maternal turn-on warming their laps. The men shifted on
their wallet wadges, intuiting your call for funds. As if by
magic, the collection plates appeared.

"Remember the words of the Lord Jesus." Your tone
was Mafia-gentle. "'Anyone who is an obstacle to bring
down one of these little ones who would have faith in me
would be better drowned in the sea with a great millstone
around his neck.'"

LAVINIA'S NECK

Unable to lie waiting any longer, Lavinia's wrapped a short,
matching robe around the teddy and slipped an apron on
over that. She stands at the kitchen counter now, one knee
propped on a chair to keep the weight off her aching heel.

The butter's too hard, so she microwaves it for a minute
on low before dumping it into the bowl. She wouldn't even
have it in the house, but Mama's cookies call for a full cup of
unsalted, and there's no point making them if she doesn't
do it right. She squashes the beaters into the yellow mess
and switches them on, adding sugar in a gradual stream.

She has the recipe firmly by heart. It stands to reason
Mama demands them every visit. Doesn't know her own
name, but knows she wants those cookies, and won't be
fooled by store-bought, or even bakery-fresh.

It's the first time Lavinia's been moved to bake them for a lover. Late start or no, she's had a fair number of men in her bed—in her life, even, for a few months at a time—but none she's been tempted to spoil.

She cracks and adds two large eggs, watches them whirl and disperse. Fighting the urge to lick the beaters, she sets the mixer aside and begins folding in flour, soda and salt.

The thing is, Carl isn't just *any* man. She knew it the moment he set foot in her office last fall. He was on a tour of Manitoba towns, he explained, scouting possible locations for a satellite church. She'd never heard anyone speak with such passion. He went on at glorious length about the Water of Life, his desire to pour it like a healing balm all over her town. Raised United, Lavinia had rarely missed a Sunday service in her life. It was a detail that played well during elections, but the truth was, she hadn't felt a thing for Jesus in years. Until Carl. The way he talked that day, she felt some part of her rise up joyfully, as if in recognition of its spiritual home.

Hugging the mixing bowl to her belly, she tips in a cup of slivered almonds, then two cups of semi-sweet chocolate broken into jagged chunks.

They both knew there was nothing spiritual about the invitation she issued—dinner at her place, a couple of T-bones and a good bottle of wine—yet he accepted without batting an eye. He wasn't a generous lover. He didn't kiss her fingers or stroke her neck, didn't deliberately please her in any way. Just backed her up against the china cabinet and made her come harder than ever before.

He was gone when she woke at six. She went for her usual run, held off phoning the Mercy Motor Inn until shortly before lunch. Only then did she learn he'd checked out before coming over. Packed his bags and had them waiting in the car.

A glob of ready dough bristles on her wooden spoon. She eyes it steadily, considers gobbling it down, then takes a deep breath and scrapes it loose with the rubber spatula, letting it drop to the Teflon sheet.

Despite her prior experience with casual encounters, Carl's wordless departure caught Lavinia by surprise. Wounded her, even. For months she expected to hear from him—she simply couldn't believe there wasn't more. It turned out she was right. Three weeks ago to the day, she glanced up from her Powerbook to find the prodigal lover returned.

OUR LADY OF HUMILITY

It seems a body's demons inevitably humiliate its flesh— even a magnificent body like the Reverend's. Having watched him stumble back across the room and lower himself clumsily into bed, Mary can't help but compare him with the only other man in her life. It was a good night when Castor found his way between the covers. Many a morning she awoke to find him splayed out on the floor.

She got hold of a bottle herself once, when she was all of nine years old. It had nothing to do with getting drunk. She wanted to see things the way Castor did, even though the visions left him weak as a kitten—as if he'd run the whole way there and back instead of slipping through space. The rye looked sweet, but it went down fiery and sour. She managed half a quart, didn't see a thing but the floor flying up to meet her.

Castor never let her forget how he saved her life that day. He must have told the story a thousand times—not as a reminder of how much she owed him, but as a testament to the depth of his love.

"So in I come and there you lie, dead to the world with a dead soldier leakin' beside. I look down on your skinny back and I think, No. No way in hell is my Mary dead. So I lift up my hands. I can barely stand, but I lift 'em and I say, Arise. You don't, so I cross my fingers, both hands, mind, and this time I yell it—Arise! Arise and live!"

Here her own memory kicks in—the moment when, in response to his bellowed command, she let out a groan, rolled over on her side and started chucking it all up. Castor fell down on his knees beside her and gathered her hair in his hands, holding it back from the mess.

When she was all emptied out, he took her by the shoulders and shook her, then pulled her against him, holding her so she could scarcely breathe. "Christ, girl, what in hell do you want with that poison? You wanna end up like ol' Castor? Wanna rot yourself clean through?"

Later, he put the kettle on to boil and made her drink a whole pot of Labrador tea. From then on he kept liquor out of her way whenever he had the wits to think of it. He needn't have bothered. That once was all it took to put her off the taste of it for life.

After the service your followers lingered to mingle and swarm, each of them vying for your hand, your constantly shifting gaze. Still captive at your side, I slipped beneath the canopy of their talk to the jungle of sense—squawks and snapping jaws, a chorus of possessive growls.

After a show like that you had your pick. The women said long goodbyes, pressing your hands, so grateful for a man who could move them to tears. It was more than your way with words. You were tall and clear-eyed, with the chest of a warrior and a lover's loping gait. Just the man to do battle with their demons, take them on like so many Trojans or hairy, fur-clad Celts.

You chose the organist. She'd waited so long, hammering out hymns in the corner of your eye. That morning she'd pounded so hard it had seemed she would crack the keys. She was a little old but still pinkly attractive from afar, and so pent up she was almost panting. You'd had them like that before. They'd do anything.

She fussed with her sheet music while you pawned me off on the teacher, promising to return within the hour.

"Can I offer you a ride, Mrs. Winters?" You helped her on with her coat, escorting her out the back door.

She was too thrilled to speak, in danger of choking on her own good luck. She said nothing when you drove past her street and across the old bridge to an abandoned lot. Nothing still when you coasted to its willowed corner and buried the car's nose in the weeds.

"Oh!" was all she could manage when, without further ado, you unzipped your pants. "Oh," she said sadly when your broad hand closed on the back of her neck and you began steadily to lever her down. She resisted a little, never having taken a man in her mouth.

"Hearken to the Word of the Lord," you whispered, removing her rose-coloured beret. "'As I, who am sent by the living Father, myself draw life from the Father, so whoever eats me shall draw life from me.'" You laughed softy. "What do you think of that, sugar?"

Her reply was muffled, too muffled for you to understand.

LAVINIA'S MOUTH

Inside Lavinia's oven the blobs sweat butter and begin to spread. As chunks forfeit their shapes, she switches on the oven light and draws up a chair to watch. Already the smell is enchanting—Carl will start slavering the moment he walks in that door. And he *will* walk in. He came back last time, didn't he? It may have taken him the better part of a year, but in the end he couldn't stay away.

He caught her off guard, showing up like that after she'd made herself stop believing he would. She had the home advantage, though, and she played it, staying put behind her desk instead of rising to shake his hand.

"Reverend Mann," she said coolly.

"Mayor Wylie," he replied, "I come in the name of God."

He wasn't two minutes into his proposal when she thought of the bog. By the time he was on to dormitories and tennis courts, there were chainsaws roaring to life in her mind. She let him finish, though, thrilling inwardly to the timbre of his scriptural warning, something about children and obstacles, a millstone around some poor sap's neck.

"Sold." She flashed him a winning smile. "I've got the perfect site."

They brainstormed beautifully together. It was all settled in under an hour—she would convene a special meeting of the town council later that week, and in the meantime they could hire a consultant to work up some figures on the bog.

"Don't worry about the council." She walked up behind him where he stood at her office window. "It's as good as passed."

"God willing." He turned to face her.

"Oh, He's willing, all right." She walked a hand down the front of his Dockers. "I can feel it."

The timer shrills eleven minutes. Lavinia takes down her oven mitts—two quilted rainbow trout—and pushes her hands in at their finny tails. She yanks open the door, releasing a blast of redolent heat. The first batch is flawless.

She knows perfectly well they're not for her, just as she knows the molten chocolate will stick to the roof of her mouth and burn. Still, the padded fish snatches up a cookie and holds it to her lips. She stares into its painted eye. "All right," she tells it evenly. "But just the one."

Would you leave me then, Preacher? Pluck me from your side and drop me, lock me away while you remade the rotting world?

The three of us were gathered in the teacher's kitchen. It was the first time you'd brought me with you to her stark little home.

"You're the only one I trust her with, Cathy," you murmured, caressing her inner arm. "She likes you."

"But why do you have to go now?" she said miserably.

"Cathy, look at me. When Jesus calls, you pack your bags and go. You know that, now, don't you?"

Her face crumpled around the edges.

"It won't be for long. I'll be sending for you before you know it." You reached around behind her, applying pressure to the small of her spine. "I'll need you beside me down there."

"You will?"

"Uh-huh." You pulled her close. "Beside me, beneath me, on top of me—"

"Uhnnn," she said low.

You trapped her small pearl earring between your teeth. "You'll take her then?"

"Mmm."

"Just until I've got things settled." You stroked her behind, lifting it in your hands. "Then we'll see about— things."

The teacher opened her eyes. "What things?"

"Well, help. Getting her the help she needs."

"What kind of help?"

"I don't know. There are places."

"Places?" She took a step back, a step closer to me. "You mean—putting her away?"

"Not for good, Cathy." You looked hurt, and maybe you were, coming face to face with what had been swimming around in your brain. "What do you think I am, a monster?"

She bit her lip.

"Just until we're set up," you said soothingly. "We'll have a lot on our plates, you know. As soon as the camp is up and running, we'll see what we can work out."

She was still a little rigid when you reached for her again, so you laid the trump card, the one you'd been guarding in your hand. "Maybe we'll have a child of our own one day, Cathy. Ever think of that?"

She caved. It was no wonder, a woman like her—not yet forty, in no way pretty, nearly striking but falling somehow short of the mark. A nurse turned Sunday schoolmarm. Always a caregiver, never to one of her own.

"Yes, Carl," she sighed, nuzzling your chest. "I do."

"Good." You smiled. "That's settled. Now, you remember what I told you?"

"Hmm?"

"No more drawing. No crayons, no pencils, nothing."

"But Carl—"

"No buts, now, I told you, it upsets her."

She looked doubtful.

"Doctor's orders, Cathy. She mustn't get agitated, understand?"

"Which doctor?" she said quickly. "Maybe I could get a second opinion, maybe some tests—"

You stopped her mouth with your hand. "No. No doc-tors. I don't want you worrying yourself. I'll take care of all that when I get back."

Her mouth worked silently against your palm.

"Cathy," you murmured, "we've been over this. I'm leaving first thing in the morning. You don't really want to spend the night arguing, do you?"

You peeled your hand away to find her mute. Knowing full well what she wanted, you punished her a little, made her wait. Her eyes filled up with tears. You smiled indul-gently, lifted a finger and pushed it softly between her lips.

In the morning you left a trail, a long tail dragging, growing a mile for every mile you drove. The teacher stood waving on her front stoop, watching the space where you'd been. After a time she remembered me.

"Hi, Clare." She held out a hand and I flapped my giant mitts in reply. She nodded sadly and withdrew, leaving me to walk in on my own.

5

A BLOOD-BROWN FRAME
(clare)

I'm hungry." The teacher sets down her scissors and stands. "You hungry, Clare?" She jumps to a bare spot on the rug. "I'll get us some crackers and cheese."

I carry on without her, dividing two drawings into ten but holding off on a third until she returns. The time-bird greets her with a brief announcement. "You-knew," it tells her, "you-knew." She looks down at the page I've kept waiting. Nods mournfully as I execute the first cut.

You'd been gone a full week, Preacher, when you finally bothered to call. The teacher pounced on the phone, holding it pressed to her ear even after you'd hung up. How I longed to draw her, lay her down in glossy wax. The sad, sea-green ellipses of her eyes.

Come nighttime I was glowing, overflowing with the charge. While the teacher slept lonely and fretful in the next room, I gnawed doggedly at my wrist, worrying until the tape began to fray. I took the end in my teeth and tugged, unwound the white snake, whipped the fat mitt across the floor. The hand came out spindly, like a plant growing blanched in the dark.

There wasn't a pen, wasn't the stub of a pencil left
loose—she'd seen to it, feeling your eyes on her from afar.
Undaunted, the hand offered itself, index finger volun-
teering separate and straight. I let it hang, felt ink well at
the ready tip. Then bit. Delicately, persistently, I nibbled
until the print whirled open and colour began to flow.

But how to evoke sea green with nothing but red? And
where?

The wall loomed up beside me, blank but for a Cross of
woven reeds. With no black for borders, I had to make do.
The lines weren't as thick as I would've liked, but the nib kept
running dry, forcing me to pause and chew it open afresh.

"Clare!" The teacher scooped me up, wriggling, then
rigid in her arms. She ran madly down the hall. Brightness
and tiles, cold comfort to my small bare feet. "Oh God,"
she wailed, "oh God, oh God." Then my hand under the
tap, falling water, flashing chrome.

"Why, Clare?" She fumbled for a roll of gauze. "Why
did you do this?" I allowed my finger to be wrapped, but
grabbed it back when she reached for the sticky white tape.
"No tape?" Her voice shook. "Okay. It's all right. I'll just
tie it. There, like that."

She followed me back to the spare room, watched me
slump to where she'd found me on the floor. Then lifted her
gaze, staring straight into my empty frame. Her lips moved
silently for a time, then hung open as though she were listening for a reply. When she looked down again, her face was
white. She lunged at me, grabbed my still-bound hand and
tore at the tape, ripping the mitt off and hurling it away.

I was blinking, the whole too great—her knowing me,
enough at least to set me free. She rose and disappeared,

284

returning with a blue bucket and a fluttering sheaf. She papered the floor. Dumped the bucket end up, crayons scattering like rainbow hail.

LEAST WEASEL
(mustela nivalis)

Having traversed it twice now, Carl finds himself charting the bottle house in his mind. From what he can tell, there's only the one room. The bed beneath him backs onto a wall and juts into open space. To its right sits the side table he knocked over, the one where she later set the lamp and warmed the spruce. Beyond the small table, the drying hide and Mary's chair. Then perhaps a dozen feet further to the door.

Her kitchen, such as it is, lies directly across the room. There's a stove—he imagines it like the one he grew up with, pot-bellied with a glowing grate—probably a table or counter of some kind, and row upon row of jars. He can hear Mary fiddling with them, a concert of glassy clinks.

"Mary," he asks, "what else have you got?"

"Hmm?"

"In your—pantry. What else is there?"

"All kinds of things. I told you, there's a whole wall."

"Well, tell me some of it. Tell me a shelf."

"Okay. Let's see. Horsehair lichen, old man's beard— Don't worry, the guy was dead when I found him, all I did was cut it off."

"What?"

She snorts. "Easy, Reverend, it's that woolly stuff you see hanging on trees. Jesus, you really are ignorant."

"About some things."

"About this forest you want to knock down."

"Okay." He holds up his hands. "What else?"

"Coltsfoot, thrush feathers, crowberry jelly—too bad you can't see the colour." Something rattles. "Teeth. Looks like least weasel, but I can't be sure."

He shakes his head. "I don't get it. Why do you keep all these—things in your house?"

"Same reason you keep things in your house. Either they've got some use, or else you like them. Take this cloud-berry leaf—great tobacco stretcher. Tamarack fat—draws out poison and closes up wounds. Or this—a shrew's skull, so tiny, so perfect. Used to be home to a hungry little brain. What's the line, Reverend—all creatures great and small?"

"Yes, all right."

"I got all these jars when the jam factory shut down. There was already enough empty glass around this place, so I figured I might as well fill a few up. The thing is, once you start looking, there's no end to what you can find. Oh, hey." Her voice softens. "This one's a little different—special, you might say. Been a while since you felt the air, eh?" She addresses the jar's contents tenderly, the floor-boards creaking as she draws near. "Here."

He holds out his hands. It's two objects, really, or two halves of one, tied together with greasy string. Each is coarse on top and smooth below. His thumbs locate iden-tical openings, a pair of woven mouths.

"My baby booties," she says proudly.

"Yes." He smiles. "Of course."

"They used to be yellow, but you wouldn't know that now. I guess I came across them one day when I was two or so. It took me a few hundred tries at shoving my feet in before I gave up and started carrying them around. I kept them with me while I ate, played with them, took them to bed." She lifts the booties away, leaving him coddling a handful of air. "Castor even had to let me hold them while he washed me in the basin."

Carl swallows hard. The baby bath was one of a hundred pastel items Jenny brought home in the months before she died. He put off the first bath longer than he should have, waiting until the newborn stranger began to smell distinctly sour. Then poured the shallowest of tepid puddles and lowered her into it, grasping her stiff, slippery body, making her scream.

LAVINIA'S EAR

It's dark in the den, the loveseat less than comfortable, chosen solely for its pleasing lines. Lavinia's head pulses with a sugar comedown. So she ate a few cookies, so what?

Her hand seeks the remote, bringing the wide-screen flashing to life. She mutes it instantly, flicking down through countless silent channels until her eye fastens on a head of golden hair. *Charlie's Angels.* It's one of the later ones, where Farrah's gone off to drive race cars and Cheryl Ladd plays her little sister, Chris.

The angels are at a disco, probably trying to crack some kind of ring. Lavinia could turn the sound on and find out more, but it's better this way, watching them without caring what they say.

Kate sweet-talks one of the bad guys at the bar, distracting him while Sabrina jimmies the lock on the club's office door. The brunettes may be necessary, but Chris is clearly the one to watch. She's out on the dance floor, shaking her frilly red halter top and white hip-hugger jeans, plus a sweet slice of midriff between. Lavinia pokes an accusing finger deep into her own bloated middle. A *few* cookies? Try two dozen. And she nearly didn't stop there—it had taken everything she had to leave the second batch cooling and come away.

Chris is doing the hustle on a pair of impossibly high-heeled strappies. Lavinia stares mournfully at the skeletal shoes, the feet inside them so supple, so *young*. Her thumb jumps to the power button and flicks it off.

Did you happen to know Jenny Swann? The question hangs in the dark, just as it hung over the bed when Carl posed it the night before.

"Jenny Swann?" Lavinia rolled over to face him. "You mean Fran and Ted's girl?"

He cleared his throat. "I believe so, yes."

"Sure. She moved to Winnipeg after her mom died. Franny was never very strong—you know the kind of kid, always crying, always telling tales—" She halted, realizing she was dating herself. "How do you know Jenny?"

"What?" He was miles away. "Oh, she—she was a member of my congregation for a time."

Lavinia's mouth tastes suddenly sour. Pretty little Jenny Swann, *a member of his congregation*. And he just happens to want to build his dream camp outside her hometown? She nibbles a thumbnail. The VCR clock shows 2:23, but it doesn't matter—Paula hardly ever sleeps. Lavinia gropes for the phone, hitting four on the speed-dial.

"Hello?" Paula answers after a single ring. She has the shopping channel on loud.

"Hi, it's me."

"Madame Mayor? Don't you have to be up and running in a couple of hours?"

"Ha ha."

"Hey, what's all this I hear about a man?"

"What man?"

"Big shoulders, blond. Don't play the innocent with me, Lavinia, I've known you too long."

"Oh, him. He's a colleague."

"That what they're calling it now?"

Lavinia controls herself. "Listen, Paula, what do you know about Jenny Swann?"

"Franny's girl? She moved to Winnipeg."

"I know that. What else?" No answer, save the babble of Paula's set. "Paula?"

"Sorry, I had to write down a purchase number."

"Paula—"

"Okay, okay. Jenny. Well, she was going to the university there, but I think she dropped out. Ted stopped talking to her when she joined some new church, but I guess she married a new daddy pretty quick. Might've even been the minister—I seem to remember something like that."

"She's—married?" Lavinia says softly.

"So I heard. That was a few years ago, though, so who knows. She didn't make it home for Ted's funeral, I know that. What's all this about, anyway? Lavinia? Hello?"

Lavinia drops the receiver into its plastic depression. Begins worrying her blistered palate with her tongue.

(clare)

The teacher had no idea how much her hands gave away, hanging orphaned between every pulled weed. The cordless phone lay beside her on the grass, bleached and silent as a bone.

Three dry days and the garden had cracked to show the lines along which it was made. Her hands on the hose, hairline fractures on their backs, too fine for detection by any but a caring eye. Fissures and faults. She was coming apart at the seams.

"He's busy," she whispered to herself. "He's thinking of us," she assured me. "We're in his prayers."

But it wasn't nearly enough. She had to do something— anything—to take her mind off the phone.

So many words. The teacher had checked out an armload, her table swam with coloured books. She laid one open, then the next, pouring herself out over the text. Meanwhile, I drew feverishly, no longer obscuring my work with a jealous arm.

She was learning me. Reading a passage and glancing up, threading the printed line to my face. She knew the term for it now. Her face clouded over with case histories— the hopeless ones, those lost in a walking death, those given up on, locked away. Then brightness. Occupational therapy. Speech therapy. Results. I watched the tug-of-war play across her face.

—You have to catch them young.

—He said no doctors, he'll take care of it.

—When? Time is of the essence, it says so right here.

—She's not your child.

—But she needs help. You have to get started when they're young, while their brains are still soft. Break new ground, sow heavily. If nothing grows, go back and break ground again.

—No doctors.

—That's right, no doctors. But he didn't say anything about a washed-up nurse.

She lowered herself to my level, reaching out to cup and capture my chin. It hurt, that tender insistence, her leading my gaze, lifting me to meet her eyes.

"Clare, look at me. Look at me, Clare. That's good. No, look at me."

Child overboard. Her irises expanded to meet the horizon. Everything she'd ever survived went bobbing past— casks and timber, floating chests. Her monsters brushed past me on their way up from the deep. I shut down. Flipped one eye inward, the other out. Hummed like a transformer until her grip slackened and fell away.

SMALL RED PEAT MOSS
(sphagnum capillifolium)

Sitting up in bed, Carl stretches his arms out and back, his fingertips grazing a bottle's cool mouth. Startled, he twists and explores the wall further, finding rough mortar collars around neck after glassy neck.

"Castor set them like that for insulation," Mary explains, drawing near. "Every bottle holds a little pocket of air."

He nods, withdrawing his hand.

"It took him over a year to finish the place, but it's still solid today. It gets a crack now and then, but nothing a chunk of moss can't take care of. The red stuff works best. It looks nice, too, like the walls are smiling at you."

"Sounds very—unique."

"He liked to follow a line of bottles with his finger, listing them off—Empire aqua pints, Brandon Brewing green. Over here he made a flower, amber quarts for the petals, suncast for the centre, green for the stem. Up over your head there's a dark green star. Those are Melcher's Red Cross Gin."

Carl does a quick calculation, figuring nine bottles of beer, four of spirits to an average square foot of wall. "He really drank them all?"

"Except for the patch over the door, they were his mother's. I guess she kept her medicines in them, tonics and teas. The bottles were all different shapes back then. Castor drew pictures of them for me, taught me the names. Here." She takes hold of his wrist and turns it, begins tracing an outline on the inside of his arm. "Shoo-fly flask," she says slowly, her fingernail describing its corners and curves.

He holds dead still. She pauses for a moment between drawings, but it doesn't help—he's too distracted to follow a straight line, let alone discern one profile from the next.

"Pumpkin seed."

Her overlapping trails begin to tickle, even to itch.

"Jo Jo."

He finds himself imagining the shape of her, wondering how well she's built.

A CHOCOLATE CURL
(clare)

A second week had passed, Preacher, and this time you hadn't phoned. Artists have known longest—the body is nothing more than a collection of basic forms. Your absence was affecting my cohesion. I was in danger of disintegrating, of degenerating into cylinders and spheres.

I'd felt it before, that urge to be held in one piece.

The living-room rug was cocoa brown, the largest block of colour in the teacher's house. I lay down and took up a corner, rolled myself snug as a bug.

The pressure was pure comfort, so much simpler than a circle of arms. I grew calm, began quietly to hum. Hm hm *hmmm* hmm, hm hm *hmm*. I chose your favourite, Preacher. *Rock of aaaaa-ges, cleft for me. Let me hide myself in theeeeee.*

OUR LADY OF SORROWS

Mary might have gone on to say more, if only the Reverend hadn't become so unnervingly still. Before the change in him made her lay down his arm and retreat wordlessly to her chair, she'd been on the verge of telling the story behind those old bottles—how Castor had to sift through smouldering wreckage to retrieve them, singeing his fingers on the few that had somehow survived the blaze.

Fifteen years old and your parents charred to coal. It would've been enough to drive any boy to drink, but there was more—the burden of mixed blood, an infant brother to raise. Castor got a job running so-called prescriptions for the Roseville Pharmacy and took to sipping along the way. That led to driving temperance beer into Saskatchewan, only most of it was the real thing dressed up pretty for church. Before long he was running cheap whiskey down south.

It kept Renny in food and clothes, even if they moved around too much to keep him in school. Kept Castor in liquor, too. By the time Prohibition ended, he was a hopeless drunk. There was only one thing to do. The two of them found their way to Mercy and claimed what their mother had always told them was unlivable land.

Maybe, if Mary could tell it just right, the Reverend would listen, maybe even understand. He's had losses of his own, after all—a dead wife and God knows what else he has locked behind those bars on his eyes. Men are good at secrets. It took a third untimely death, a blind stupor of mourning, to get Castor to share his pain.

Mary was eleven years old, frying up supper with him drinking quietly by her side, sitting close to the stove to keep warm.

"Ren," he said suddenly. *"Renny."*

She looked up to find him staring deep into the bottle in his hand. Shoving the pan to the back of the stove, she knelt down beside him and laid a hand on his trembling knee. He began muttering, recounting the vision as he watched it unfold.

The whole thing took less than a minute. Renny swung down from the shunting train and hit the ground at a run, tearing a beeline alongside the rail. He flew past car after car, then leapt for a ladder to mount the train again. The rung was slick with ice. It ran through his fingers like sand, his body hurtling beyond its purpose, twisting and slipping down between the cars.

Castor came back to himself with a terrible howl, leaping to his feet, nearly knocking Mary over on his way out the door. She went after him with his coat, but he was deep into the snowy bush before she even set foot on the porch.

What followed remained a puzzle for days, Mary coaxing the story out of him in babbled fragments and reassembling it in her mind. It seemed she had an uncle—or didn't have one, not any more.

Castor knew there was nothing he could do for Renny—he'd watched the train wheels pinch his little brother in half—which was why he headed not to the tracks but to Renny's house. Elsa made him knock until his knuckles bled. When she finally came to the door, she didn't say a word, just stuck her face in the crack as though she was worried he might be carrying the plague.

"Elsa—" He could barely speak, he was panting so hard.

She brought a hand out to cover her nose.

"Mama?" the girl called from somewhere inside the house.

"Go to your room, Lavinia, and stay there till I say." Elsa stepped out a little. "You get out of here now, you hear me?"

"It's Renny," Castor gasped.

She crossed her arms. "He's at work."

"I know." He began to cry. "He slipped."

"You're drunk."

"Renny slipped, Elsa," he said, sobbing. "He's dead."

Her eyes opened wide. "Liar."

"I'm not, I'm not."

"Liar!" She began walking at him, saying a word for every step. "Filthy. Drunken. LIAR!"

By then she'd backed him down the stairs. "I seen it," he pleaded.

"Where, in a bottle? You're *the Seer*, isn't that right? You *see* things?!"

"Yes," he said, helpless.

"You're CRAZY!" she screamed. "You get out of here now and maybe I won't tell him what you said!"

She turned and took the stairs at a run, slamming the door so it shook in its frame. Castor looked up in time to catch a glimpse of the girl's face at the window, then Elsa's hand, yanking the curtain shut.

He was a good way down the road by the time the Mounties showed. Sinking to his knees on the icy shoulder, he watched their headlights disappear up his brother's drive.

LAVINIA'S EYES

Out in the carport, Lavinia skirts the Land Rover and presses her hand to the deep-freeze, feeling it purr. The lid makes an unsealing sound as she lifts it, and she opens her sore mouth in response, letting it hang slack over the escaping cold. The freezer's close to full, dozens of triple-wrapped packages stacked in tidy piles. She bends to read a few of the nearest labels—*Rib Chops*, *Top Sirloin*, *Grade A Boneless Breasts*.

Never mind her stomach, Lavinia's eyes are bigger than her deep-freeze. No matter how much she already has at home, she can never seem to pass the meat counter by. She chooses the family pack more often than not, seduced not by the better deal but by the fresh promise of all those portions in a row. Even with Carl to cook for, she hasn't thawed a single thing. Triple-wrapped or no, it'll all be freezer-burnt before she gets the chance.

Maybe she should chuck a block of something in the microwave now, defrost it and broil or brown it up, mask that lovely nut-and-chocolate smell with something a little more serious. Why not? Break out the fancy linen and a nice Cabernet. *What's the occasion?* he'll ask. Assuming he ever shows.

No occasion. Not unless it's some occasion of his he hasn't mentioned. A wedding anniversary, maybe. Or maybe his wife's birthday. What would Jenny be now— twenty-five? twenty-six? God knows it's not Lavinia's birthday. It would be, only she stopped having them years ago, when she realized not celebrating meant not having to count.

Normally a source of comfort, the frozen parcels seem suddenly obscene. There are too many for a whole family, never mind for a woman on her own. What if there's a blackout, not just a little one, one that lasts? What will she do then—haul it all out by the box load and bury it in her treeless yard? Daddy would spin in his grave.

Never waste meat, Lovey.

They were all three in their usual chairs, Lavinia's with a fat book on the seat. "Come on, now." Daddy pointed his knife at the abandoned bacon on her plate. "Somebody died to give you that."

"Nonsense," said Mama. "That's what animals are for." She covered Lavinia's small hand with her own. "You don't have to finish if you're full, honey. Are you full?"

Lavinia nodded.

"They're not *for* that," said Daddy.

"What's that, dear?"

"Animals. Just because we eat them doesn't mean that's what they're *for*."

Mama flinched and took back her hand. "I wish you wouldn't talk that way, Renny."

He glared at the pepper and salt. "What way?"

"You know *what way*." She stood abruptly and began clearing away dishes. "Lavinia, you may be excused."

A TORRENT OF WHITE
(clare)

They were waiting, Preacher—the women sullen and faithful, fantasizing your return, their men shifty beside them, suddenly unsure in their belief. You'd chosen your stand-in well. He was mottled like a sausage, entirely uninspired. You'd be welcomed back to the fold like a saint.

The replacement's sermons were watery, lapping monotonously at the Sunday school door. The teacher never so much as peeked at him. She let me draw, let the others do whatever they pleased. Freed from Bible lessons, they ran amok, high on cookies, spilling juice down their giggling chests.

At home, the teacher gave me milk, the white cascade hitting bottom and bubbling up the glass. "Want milk?" She phrased the question simply, the way the books advised. "Clare?" Her fingers were cold with it, soft on my chin bone, guiding me to meet her gaze. "Want milk?"

6

A FELINE LINE
(clare)

This time the cat sits with his back to the bookshelf, casually tonguing a paw. "Yoo-hoo," the time-bird calls, "yoo-hoo, *yoo-hoo*." But the cat ignores him, save for the instinctive swivel of an ear. Watching him, the teacher lets her scissors dangle. Her thumb hovers over the corner image on a page.

The teacher's pet wore his insides out, nerves diverging from his spine in a barred black map. White marked where he was vulnerable—the belly, the narrow throat. Grey told where he felt most keenly—whisker puffs, tail tip, feet.

He found me in the garden, wound an elaborate knot around my legs. I knelt down to face him, sliding a finger along his foreleg, nudging the tip into the pink secrets of his paw. A white curl of claw slipped its sheath.

I buried my nose in his fur. His back smelled sleekly of rain, his belly of dust. Smoke and blood under the claws, the ears bitter inside but sweet in the fine fuzz at their backs. Both ends gave off darkness—dusk in the mouth and a musky behind, violence and traces of waste.

His needs were simple, clear. I reached out carefully to stroke his length—bridge of nose to slope of skull, sway-back valley to tail's incline. Time and again my hand travelled his form, feeling him resist and receive.

SNOWSHOE HARE
(lepus americanus)

Mary comes close again, stroking a second coat of sap along the damaged lids of Carl's eyes. Her proximity calls up his blood.

"Is that your finger? It's so soft."

"I could wish for fingers like this." She touches a hard finger pad briefly to his cheek. "That's my finger. *This*," she says, stroking again, "is a feather."

"Oh." He contemplates reaching for her.

"That ought to do it." She stands, withdrawing her body's warmth. "Does it sting?"

"A little."

"Good."

"Mary?"

"Hmm?"

"Come back. Sit close to me again."

She says nothing.

"Mary?"

"I don't think so, Reverend."

"Why not?"

She takes a moment to respond. "Maybe you think you've got something to teach me."

He smiles. "Maybe I do."

"Maybe I've got something to teach you, Reverend, ever think of that?"

"Okay." He reaches out in the direction of her voice. "Come here and teach me."

She lets his hands float expectantly, then fall. "Ever heard the expression 'mad as a March hare'?"

"Sure."

"Know where it comes from?"

"No." He pats the bed. "Come and tell me."

"It comes from mating. A male snowshoe hare hops up to a female, jumps in the air, takes a piss on her, and takes off. Then another one comes along. Same thing—jump, piss, run. Sometimes they just fly past her, pissing the whole way. Sometimes she leads a whole train of them around, all of them leaping and pissing and drumming the ground. All that song and dance goes on forever, but it only takes a few seconds once they finally get down to brass tacks. A couple of squeals and that's it. The male follows the female around for a while, but only to fight off any others that might swamp his seed."

Carl can feel his lust evaporating, a low-level queasiness rising in its place. "Is this really all you want to do?" he says impatiently. "Talk?"

"Short-tailed shrew gets himself stuck in there. She drags him around by it after, ten minutes or more."

"Okay." He laces his hands behind his head. "I know what this is about."

"You do?"

"Look, if I *had* been with a lot of women, and I'm not saying I have—"

"You don't have to, it's obvious."

"As I was saying, *if* I had, I'd have to suppose those women got something they wanted from the experience."

"Uh-huh. Like what?"

"Why are you so curious, Mary?" He smiles unpleasantly. "Hmm? What is it about this particular subject?"

"You going to answer my question?"

"Which question is that?"

"What did they get, the women?"

"Well, they would've gotten a little excitement in their lives. A little release."

"Love?"

"I beg your pardon?"

"Love. Did any of them get a little of that?"

"I don't—" He feels a wave of true nausea. "This is all hypothetical anyway."

"Bullshit. You've got to change the way you think about women, you know that? Your daughter'll be one someday."

"Leave her out of this." He pushes himself up into a sitting position, the movement making his stomach churn.

"Why? That's what little girls grow up to be, you know." One hand on his belly, he shifts to the edge of the bed.

"You want somebody like you to bed her?"

"Shut up." His voice cracks. "I told you to leave her out of this—"

"It hurts, huh, Reverend, to think about her that way?" He shakes his head violently. "You don't know what you're talking about."

"If I don't know, tell me. Why shouldn't your daughter grow up to be a notch on some hypocrite's Cross?"

"Shut up!" he cries, heaving to his feet. "Goddamnit, woman, shut your filthy mouth!" He lists dangerously.

"She's not growing up to be anything, okay?! I don't even know if she's growing up!"

"What do you mean? Hey—" Mary's powerful hands catch hold of him by the shoulders, and he strikes out with a balled-up fist, feeling it glance sharply off skin and bone. She staggers back a step, keeping her grip, not letting out a sound.

He begins to shake, his arms like rags now, pinned to his sides. "Let me go," he says brokenly, but she won't.

"What's wrong with her?"

He stands speechless, gulping the air.

"Is she sick?"

"She's—yes," he blurts, "she's sick."

Her grip softens. "I'm sorry."

"I'm sure." His mouth twists bitterly. "You probably think I deserve it. Reap what ye sow, an eye for an eye." His voice rises to a hysterical pitch. "Divine retribution, that's what you think!"

"No," she says quietly. "That's your God, Reverend, not mine."

He pulls away from her. "Jesus, I hit you. I've never hit a woman."

"It's okay."

"I'm so sorry—*nnnngh*." He doubles over.

"What is it?"

He grits his teeth. "Nothing."

"Is it your gut?"

"Ulcer," he says tightly. "It's nothing. I just don't have my medication with me."

She moves swiftly to her shelves and back. "Open your mouth."

"It's okay now—*nnngaaaah*—it's passing." He straightens
a little.

"Jesus, Reverend, trust me."

"It's not that I don't—"

She sprinkles something in his open mouth. Powdery,
earthy, it coats the length of his tongue. "Swallow," she says
firmly.

"Ggg—kkk—kk—"

"Swallow, Reverend. Have a little faith."

He salivates and, as if by reflex, swallows the mouthful of
mud. Almost immediately the attack begins to ebb.

"Good stuff, eh?"

He uncurls himself. "What—?" he asks in wonder.

"Peat. You know, *horticultural grade*." Her jar lid tightens
down. "Come on, now, back in bed."

A TORTURER'S WHEEL
(clare)

The teacher had hung a swing. Her palms singed the small of
my back, such pendulum joy to leave her and risk a return.
She pushed higher, higher, spurred on by the squeals I
couldn't help but let out.

The world blurred. Letting go the ropes, I leapt into it,
open-mouthed. I gave no thought to landing, hit grace-
lessly, like a sack of grain. The teacher cried out for me.
She was at my side in an instant, breathing hard.

Later she made a wheel of her body, long, spoked limbs
turning circles on the glimmering green. "Cartwheels,
Clare." She smoothed her blouse. "Catherine wheels,

actually. Maybe that's why I'm so good at them, hmm?"
She turned two more.

I surprised her. Stuck my hands up and tipped sideways,
felt their heels sink into the grass, felt a split-second thrill
of inversion before I collapsed.

"Clare!" The teacher gaped. "Good try, Clare! What a
clever, clever—" She halted mid-breath. I was dead to her
approval, a spiritless heap. Her face was my full-length
mirror. I stole a look, just long enough to watch it crack.

LAVINIA'S GUTS

The duvet drawn up tight around her neck, Lavinia con-
centrates on keeping her stomach perfectly still.

It all happened so fast. Passing through the kitchen on
her way back from the carport, she caught sight of the second batch. She only meant to put them away. She even
brought down the Tupperware, even peeled back its cloudy
lid, but by then the first cookie had found its way past her
teeth. After that it was a single frantic act, never about the
one in her mouth—never tasting, not even feeling it
there—always the next one, the next one, the next.

There was no such thing when Mama made them. The
cookies were Daddy's special favourite, and Lavinia was
never allowed more than one. Well, not *never*. The trick
was to stick close while Daddy stood at the counter with the
lid off the jar, wolfing seven or eight in a row. Then if she
was lucky and Mama happened to turn her back, he'd slip
her the crumby seconds she craved.

There's no way she'll sleep now, sick to her stomach,

jumpy with sugar and caffeine. She blinks rapidly in an effort to wear out her eyes.

He's fucked her.

The thought flashes like a cheap sign. It's simple. That's why Carl hasn't come back, why he hasn't even bothered to phone. He's fucked the crazy hag. Hell, he's probably fucking her right now. Isn't that what they're all after in the end—a roll in the hay with some dirty, uninhibited bitch?

Lavinia yanks the duvet up over her head, trapping herself in a cloud of his cologne.

"Fuck!" She flings back the covers, yelping aloud when her heel hits the floor. "Fucking, fucking, FUCK!" Hopping on one foot, she wrestles the duvet out of its flowery bag.

"Bastard," she mutters, digging for the undersheet's elastic edge. "Bible-thumping *prick*." She's not buying it any more, not a word. What kind of God would dangle a man in front of her like that, then go and drop him in that bog?

Dumping her pillow from its case, she knocks a small orange bottle off the bedside table. It bounces on the broadloom, rolls up and rests against her toes. She stoops for it. *Zantac, 300 mg.* So he's out there without it. Good. Maybe his gut feels even sicker and sorrier than her own. She rattles his prescription, watching the tablets jump and collide.

Two to help her sleep, and one whenever she gets upset.

Doctor Albright was close to retirement when Daddy died. His hands were ice-cold when they folded the little bottle up in hers. "No more than eight a day." He drew his white eyebrows into one. "You've got to be strong now, Lavinia. Your mother's taking it bad."

307

"Yes, sir."

He lowered his voice, as though he were letting her in on something good. "Sometimes the hard ones are the easiest to fold."

She squared her thin shoulders. "Yes, sir."

As soon as he was gone, she set to work scouring the house. By the time the neighbours came calling with their casseroles and advice, she had everything under control.

A JAGGED BOLT
(clare)

The charge had built to where it was splitting the sky. I was balled up at the head of the bed, certain it would find me, fork back into the ground where it had grown.

"Clare?" The teacher formed a cut-out in the open door. "Are you scared of the storm?"

She crossed the floor in a sheet of light, turned dark again as she perched on the bed. "Okay, Clare," she told me. "Clare safe."

She was such a gentle slope. I was tumbling—I could feel myself, Preacher—rolling toward the half-dug hole you'd abandoned in her chest.

She knew enough to fold back the covers and let me climb in on my own, but I could see how she ached to lay her cheek against mine, to stroke my small hands where they laced tightly across my chest.

I rocked myself after she'd gone. Made my three-year-old form newborn.

Too restless even to doze, Mary sits forward in her armchair and watches the Reverend dream. His bruises shim-
mer, the scratches rippling with the shift of his eyes. God
only knows what he's seeing. It could be any corner of
Creation, any moment in time. Castor taught her that.
The year she turned fourteen, he caught his only glimpse
of the future—not in a vision, but in a dream.

"It was you," he told her upon waking. His face was a
misery. "You were painted all over with blood."

She caught him staring at her throughout the day.
"Strong as any vision," he kept saying. "Stronger." Later,
he looked up between two bites of supper and told her
she'd better stay home until he could be certain whatever it
was had passed her by.

"Sure, Castor," she said lightly, never dreaming he meant
what he said. She was happy enough keeping to the bog, but
there'd never been any talk about locking her up inside.

That night the dream returned. He kept at her about it
the whole next day, begging her to stay in, ordering her,
shadowing her whenever she set foot out the door. She
laughed at him until he fell quiet, told him he was out of
his tree.

The next morning she awoke to find a rope tied around
her ankle. Following its length with her eyes, she found the
other end fastened to a leg of the stove. At first she thought
it was a joke, but only until she tried to untie Castor's
knots. His daddy had been a sailor, and it showed.

Castor's bed was empty, and there was no sound of him
moving around outside. Mary felt for the hunting knife

she kept under the mattress. Gone. She stood up and began searching to the limits of her tether. The cooking knife, his straight razor—he'd taken everything sharp in the place. She could have burned through the rope, only he'd thought of that too. There wasn't a match to be found.

She sat down heavily on her bed and before long she was wishing evil on him, the leash making her think terrible things. Then it dawned on her—the walls, the ceiling, everything around her was made of glass. The cast iron pan was in its usual spot on the stove. She lifted it like a club and swung a vicious arc down the wall, snapping twenty bottle necks or more. The floorboards glittered. She dropped into a crouch, selected a jagged shard and started sawing.

She didn't stop to pack, not even to change, just flung open the door and headed deep into the bog. Her mind blurry with rage, she ran an erratic course. One moment she was going to climb a tree and stay there for good, the next she was going to push through to the road and hitch a ride to who knows where.

After crashing through the bush for a good hour, she sat down on a hummock to get herself in hand. That was when she felt it—a nasty sliding sensation in her belly, oozing down to something sticky between her legs. She eased up her skirt and let out a yelp. There was blood leaking out of her insides.

She clutched at the moss to steady herself, then tore up two handfuls and stuffed them in her underwear. Her heart thundering, she stood up slow and easy. So far so good, except for the feeling in her gut, sick and fearful, coming in waves. She took a deep breath, and with it a shaky step.

Castor was home when she got there. She hauled open the door to find him pale as a ghost, standing in the pool of smashed glass.

"Mary!" he cried.

"You were right!" She lifted her nightgown and yanked out the moss, throwing it down at his feet. "I'm bleeding!"

She expected him to panic, grab hold of her, bellow and sob—do anything but break out in smiles.

"Christ, Castor!" She burst into tears.

"How old are you now, girl?" he said gently. "Twelve?"

"Fourteen!" she wailed. "I'm fourteen!"

He stepped toward her, glass grinding under his heels. "Fourteen, eh?" He took hold of her trembling hands. "Where does the time go?"

HERMIT THRUSH
(catharus guttatus)

Carl starts awake to a night sound, an outdoor sound—only it's coming from across the room. A single soft hoot. Ghostly, tentative, it lifts his neck stubble at its roots.

"Mary? Are you there?"

She shifts in the armchair. "Right here."

"I heard something," he whispers urgently. "There's something inside the house."

It sounds again, the same inquisitive note.

"There!" He points sightlessly across the room.

Mary chuckles. "That's Junior. She fell out of the owl tree last year, broke a wing. I made her a nest over by the window."

311

"*What?*"

"I know. I would've snapped her neck if it wasn't for the way she went all limp when I picked her up. At least they're day hunters, so most of the time she lets me sleep through the night."

"A nest," he says a little too loudly. "You mean inside a cage."

"A cage? What kind of a sick bastard keeps a bird in a cage?"

"Okay, but it stays there, right? In the nest?"

"Well, she hops around now and then. Sometimes she comes out on the porch with me. She's chicken, though, hightails it inside at the smallest sound."

"So it won't come near me?"

"Huh? Don't tell me you're scared of a little owl with a bum wing."

"*Little?* Not if it's anything like the one that came at me out there. Great grey, isn't that what you said? I don't imagine they call them that because they're small."

"Well, no, not for an owl. They're mostly feathers, though. You wouldn't believe how light Junior is."

"I'll take your word on it."

She stands and moves away. The familiar scrape of a jar lid, more footfalls, and she takes hold of his hand, turning it palm up in hers. "Here."

His thumb follows a smooth arc to where it breaks in a seam. It's like the top half of a baseball, only hollow, almost weightless. He curls up his fingers. Something sharp presses into the pad at the base of the middle one, while the index and ring follow the rims of two vacant holes.

312

"That's the skull of an adult male," she says. "That's as big as they get under all that show."

As if in protest, Junior hoots long and low. Mary clears her throat and returns a perfect echo.

"Hey, that was good." Carl feels the brush of Mary's fingers as she retrieves the skull from his hand. "My mother could do a house sparrow. I used to sit in the peony bush under the kitchen window and listen."

"How come?"

"Hmm?"

"Why did you sit in the bush?"

"Oh." He flashes a pained smile. "No reason." Except that it was the only way to hear her—she always stopped dead the moment he or Papa came anywhere near. "Any house sparrows in the bog?"

"No. Lincoln's sparrow, though. Want to hear?"

"Okay."

"Chip—chip—chip chip chip chipchipchipchip—" She builds to a frenzied tempo, transporting him to the depths of a wet thicket in spring. After a brief pause she breaks into joyous, burbling song. His mouth falls open. In his mind she sprouts feathers, her mouth curving out bright and hard.

"You like it?" she asks.

He grins openly. "I can't believe it."

"Here's another one, listen." She begins as though striking two small stones, then digs a hole of random notes, finishing with an unmusical, spiralling trill. "Know it?"

He shakes his head.

"Sedge wren."

"Do another."

"Okay, one more." She falls quiet. Holds her tongue for so long he nearly speaks—only there's a pregnancy to her silence, a preparing. She opens with a long low note of almost unbearable sweetness. What follows is unearthly, phrase upon phrase, the flowering of endless bells. He feels the swell of it in his chest, grows heartsick in the stream of her sound.

"Hermit thrush," she says simply. "Sings at nightfall in a standing dead tree."

"How—?" His voice comes out feather-thin. "Who taught you?"

"Who taught me?" She laughs. "The birds did."

A GLITTERING CACHE
(clare)

I was a hush in the teacher's closet, scissors flashing in my hand. One after another I cut them away—glassy discs from her lambswool vest, golden domes from her coat, rolling pearls from her billowing blouse—each fraught with her current, imparting a tiny shock. They smouldered in my pockets, but I kept on until everything hung open, unable to close. Emerging from the shadows, I turned dark and light, patched like a thieving bird.

I laid the buttons out beneath my bed, sorting them by colour, by shape, by size. With each reordering came a little relief. The charge abated. I peeked out from the overhang blanket, watched it retreat like the tail of a storm.

7

A HANDFUL OF HAIR

(clare)

The teacher's crawled to the sofa and fallen fast asleep. She's hugging herself. Try as I might, I can't help but pause between pages and stare. "You-two," says the time-bird. I shift my gaze as the teacher wakens. "You-two, you-two, you-two."

"Mmmm." She sits up, opening her arms in a stretch. I grab the next drawing, snip hastily down the first of its lines.

I was still hitting myself, the blows more inevitable than deliberate. The teacher consulted her books, then dug in her closet and produced a round of pale bristles on a long wooden arm. Keeping her distance, she reached out to brush my elbows, my forearms, the backs of my rigid hands.

I sang to her strokes. I couldn't help it—my blood thronged to the surface like minnows to the water's skin. There had been no retribution, no mention even of ruined clothes. When she stopped, I laid my hand on her shadow, a dark bust on the table's face. Her hair slipped forward. Burnished by the lamp, it curtained her eyes. It wouldn't kill me. It was dead, after all. Rooted in her, true. A conductor, no doubt, but nothing like living flesh.

My fingers climbed. Closed. I held a hank of it in my trembling fist. The teacher didn't breathe. Her hair crackled, and I let go. Felt the lack of it unfold in my hand.

TIMBER WOLF
(canis lupus)

Carl can't get over the idea of it—Mary and her father stuck out here all on their own, with nobody but each other, year after year. Until the father passed on, that is. After that, Mary would've had nobody but herself.

"Mary," he asks, before he has time to think better of it, "how old were you when your father died?"

"Eighteen. I came home with a bucket of cloudberries and found him curled up around a bottle on the floor."

"I'm sorry." The words seem feeble, inadequate to the sorrow in her voice. "Where was he—I mean, did you—?"

"Bury him? Sure."

"Where?"

After a moment it dawns on him what her silence means.

"Out there?"

"What do you think I did, call in a doctor to tell me he was dead? Or a preacher maybe, or maybe the Mounties? Of course he's out there. Probably all in one piece, too, still got that look on his face."

"What did you tell people?"

"What people? Nobody ever visited him. A few of them noticed he was gone once I showed up in town, but even then all I said was that he'd disappeared. The Mounties asked me a couple of questions when they got wind of it, but you couldn't help feeling it was just for the books."

"Surely they looked for him?"

"You got any idea how many ways an old drunk can die in the woods? How fast a body gets picked clean and scattered?"

"Scattered?"

"That's what I said." Her voice is suddenly at mattress level.

"What are you—" He's silenced by a dragging sound from beneath the bed.

"Hold out your hands. Both of them."

She lays something across his palms like a sceptre. His hands seek each other instinctively, walking inward along its gently arching shaft. They meet, then separate in search of its ends, the left tracing a gradual thickening to twin porous knobs, the right stumbling over a skewed and bumpy spool, an abrupt narrowing, and finally a ball like the bed knob on the four-poster he slept in as a child.

"Human?" he asks softly, his spine thrilling.

"I told you people have died out here. Know where it fits?"

Without a word he rotates the femur, laying it carefully atop his own.

"Bingo. Must've been a tall bugger. It sticks out a good inch past your knee."

He gropes for the distal end.

"Seems skinny, too," she adds, "even for a bone. Feel here." She guides his fingers to a series of indentations around the centre of the shaft. "Teeth marks. God knows how far it was carried—it was the only piece Castor found."

Carl worries the deepest pit with his thumb. "He found it?"

"Uh-huh." She pulls the long bone gently from his grasp, shoving it away beneath him, slapping the dust from her hands. "A few weeks after I was born."

A TREE'S PALE SKIN
(clare)

The teacher was seated at the table, staring dry-eyed and desperate at the photograph you'd left behind. She possessed no couple shots, had to content herself with a portrait of you alone.

I gleaned certain drawings from my pile, crept up beside her and laid them out. Bits and pieces of you, Preacher— the pipe of an organ with a fleshy pink head, a slippery, sickle-shaped scar. She knew them in her fingers, if not in her eyes. It troubled her. Gazing deep into my wax mystery, she struggled to place your parts.

The morning paper lay unread atop the stack in the front hall—three weeks of news delivered and ignored. I fetched it. Dropped it banner-side up in her lap.

"What's this, Clare?"

Mother Nature Protests, said the headline, and beneath it a photo, curling birchbark nailed to a pole. There was writing on the silvery scroll, only the heading bold enough to be read. *Mercy.*

Skimming the article, she shrank down in her chair. You and your precious camp. Apparently the town's mayor was behind you one hundred percent. She was a real

318

powerhouse, the reporter felt bound to note, athletic, with striking green eyes.

The teacher let out a small, sick breath. Let the newspaper slip to the floor, drew her knees up and hugged them, hard.

OUR LADY OF MERCY

Mary had always known she'd have to return to Mercy sooner or later. In the last years before his death Castor had taught her the layout of the downtown, the basics of begging for money or a meal. "Don't let 'em look down their noses," he'd told her, "and don't you never shrink down in their sight."

Still, once he was dead and buried, she held out for as long as humanly possible, surviving on half-rations for over a month, exhausting even the emergency supplies.

When the day finally came, she took the same route she had as a girl. Only this time, instead of crawling into a hedge, she made her way straight to the southbound road. Faces came to windows, a few even ventured out front doors. By the time she reached the first shops, they were coming out of the cracks in the walls, lining up along Fourth Avenue as though she were some kind of one-woman parade.

It helped a little that she'd grown up hearing their darkest secrets. She had yet to put faces to names, but once she did, she'd know who among them had preyed upon friends and family, and who preferred to take things out on themselves.

A handful of them had been good to Castor, and those

were the ones she went looking for, though not with handouts in mind. A few odd jobs a month were all she needed to get by—cleaning out coops, digging weeds, washing storefronts, shovelling snow. Scrubbing the church steps turned out to be the best—just get one of them to go for it and the rest had to follow to save face. She'd be down on her knees in front of St. Andrew's Anglican and old Mrs. Stitchen from St. Mary's would come waddling by. "You come and see us when you're done with this *place.*" Then one of the Uniteds would spot her over at St. Mary's. By the end of the day she'd have one hell of a backache and a month's worth of kerosene and flour.

The butcher turned out to be the kindest of the lot. That initial bewildering day, his shop was the first one she braved.

"Are you Castor's girl?" he asked, and when she nodded, he knew better than to ask any more. There was no sign of a woman about the place, but the ring on his finger made Mary remember something Castor had seen.

"There's Tommy Rose," he'd muttered over a bottle one night. "Poor bugger. Big as he is, still keepin' to his side of the bed."

The butcher wrapped up four soup bones with more meat on them than Mary had seen in a week, and refused to hear of her working it off. "It'll only go to the dogs," he told her. "I've got more bones than I know what to do with. You take a few off my hands whenever you're in town."

AN INSTALLATION
(clare)

Every page is divided now, the floor a sea of colour, the teacher and I adrift. Squatting, I clear an island of rug, tip forward and select the initial shape. The teacher watches, her heart in her mouth. After a moment I stand, pick my way through the paper like a long-legged bird, stoop and choose the second fragment—its top a half-diamond, its bottom a scalloping skirt. I rotate it slowly in my hands, return to centre, lay it flat where it fits precisely along the first.

The teacher gasps.

SOUTHERN RED-BACKED VOLE
(clethrionomys gapperi)

"You got any pets, Reverend?" Mary asks.

"Me? No."

"How come?"

He shrugs. "I got my fill of animals growing up on a farm. If you're not feeding them, you're cleaning up their mess."

"Junior's cleaner than me."

"I'm sure she is."

"Cleaner than you too, smartass. They're great preeners, they do themselves all over every day. Mates preen each other, too. It's something to see, two big owls nibbling each other all over, sighing and grunting the whole time. Poor little Junior's stuck with me."

Carl frowns. "I beg your pardon?"

"You have to catch her in the right mood. It's best when she's kind of dopey, got her eyes half closed, face feathers pulled back. Then all you have to do is lower your head and nudge it at her beak."

"And she—preens you?"

"Yeah, she kind of nibbles along your scalp and tugs on the hair. Not so it hurts—well, except for the odd yank. Hey, we should see if she'll do you."

"Me?" He shakes his head. "No thanks."

"Come on, Reverend, you'll like it. It feels good."

"I'll take your word on it."

"They mate for life, you know." Her voice startles him, suddenly close.

"Oh?"

"Uh-huh. It's quite the courtship. Mid-winter the male spots the female he wants, and what's the first thing he does? Brings her a gift. A vole maybe. Dives into the snow for it, flies up with it hanging from his beak. He lands right in front of her and starts tilting his head side to side, showing it off. If she likes him, she makes herself little—starts bobbing her head, shifting on her claws, mewing at him— just like a chick. Then she tilts her head, too. Their faces are so flat it's like two halves of a single head when they meet. Once she takes food from him, that's it. That first offering makes the bond."

Carl's breath catches in his throat. He was standing at his office window the first time he laid eyes on Jenny. The rush was unprecedented, located for the first time ever in his chest rather than his groin. Banks of Morden Blush roses crowded the church doors. He tore his hand badly ripping several blooms free, his legs carrying him across the grounds to the bench where she sat waiting for her bus. She was twenty then, less than half his age. And yet she smiled at him, extended her delicate hand.

"He keeps it up, too," Mary adds. "Feeds her all through winter, all the time she's brooding. Once they're hatched, he brings food for the babies too. That one out there now's a hell of a hunter. You'll see. He'll be off at the crack of dawn."

LAVINIA'S HEART

Lavinia's bedclothes are downstairs in the washing machine now, twisted in a sodden ring. She lies spread-eagled on the naked duvet, having traded in the *apricot glow* for a white, knee-length number the catalogue called a spa wrap, though any idiot can see it's just a bathrobe.

How long could she lie like this before somebody came to cover her up? A few days? A week?

Mama was always kicking her covers off, sedated or no. Lavinia learned to check on her three, even four times a night. No matter how cold it was, the quilt would be back on the floor. It took vigilance, being the one in charge. That and hard work and a lot of planning—things like making shopping lists during recess, stopping off at Conklin's or Rose's on her way home from school.

Rose's Fine Meats. Lavinia can still picture the old hand-painted sign with its lacklustre, peeling rose.

Two nice pork chops, please.

She said it in her best grown-up voice, but Mr. Rose just stood there, looking past her with troubled eyes. She heard the bell jangle, turned in time to see a man in ragged clothing stumble through the door.

"Castor," said the butcher.

"Tommy," said the man.

Lavinia would have known who he was even if she hadn't seen him arguing with Mama on that terrible night. She'd have known because he had Daddy's hair. And Daddy's cheekbones. And Daddy's eyes.

"Tommy," he said again, "I seen this girl through your window, and I come in here to pay my respects."

"That's fine, Castor."

The man swayed a little on the spot. Lavinia could smell something like medicine coming off him in waves.

"Lavinia," Mr. Rose said gently, "this man is your uncle."

It had been two long, hard months, but Lavinia remembered well what she'd witnessed—Mama's dark, screaming mouth, the man crying like a baby as she backed him away from their house.

"Lavinia?" Mr. Rose tried again. "Honey, I know it's hard to lose somebody, but—"

She turned back to the counter. "Two nice pork chops," she said again. "You can put it on my mother's account." The butcher's face fell. Behind her she heard a sad shuffling, followed by the brassy tinkle of the door.

Lavinia feels a tear snake down her temple. He was a good man, that butcher. Far too good to go the way he did.

He could get away with feeding the dogs when it was only now and then, but the town got wise to him once he started tossing scraps out every night. Something else they picked up on—in less than a year the pack of strays had doubled in size, and they were cockier, too. No more slinking through the shadows, now they came marching down Train Street bold as brass.

Angry letters appeared in the *Mercy Herald*. Complaints were lodged with the RCMP, with the town council, but none of it made him stop. Then people started buying their meat at the new supermarket out on the highway. It wasn't long before the butcher pulled down the blinds, not much longer before he let the dogs in to clean the place out. He was getting on in years by then. People figured maybe his hip gave out, or else one of the big ones knocked him down.

Lavinia was part of the crowd when they carried him out. There was nothing to see, really, just a lump covered over with a sheet. It was the din that made it awful, the relentless baying that arose from inside the shop. She cringes, recalling how she added her voice to that of the mob. *Of course they have to be killed! What are we going to do, wait until they take a child?* She cheered along with the rest of them when the men shouldered their guns and went in.

Little pools well up in her ears. Can she really be crying for a pack of feral dogs, for the sad old man who invited them in? At least Mr. Rose went quickly. At least he didn't deteriorate year by year, hanging on for decades, spoon-fed and slobbering at the Mercy Retirement Lodge.

Lavinia sits up suddenly, as though responding to an alarm. How long has it been since she visited? Not since Carl showed up. Maybe even a couple of weeks before that. What if they're not treating her well? Oh God, what if she's *dying*?

She leaps to her feet, scarcely noticing the heel. Dropping the robe, she shoves the closet door away on its rail. So what if Mama won't know her—she can still sit beside the bed, still hold the poor woman's hand. Besides, who better to visit on your birthday than the woman who gave you life?

Lavinia pokes her head through the neck of a sweatshirt and shoots a glance at the clock. A quarter to five. Not visiting hours, certainly, but just let them try and stop her. She's the *mayor*, for Christ's sake. That's got to be good for something.

OUR LADY OF THE LAKE

The Reverend is showing signs of recovery. The swelling around his eyes has gone down considerably, but it's more than that—his colour is good, and there's a gentleness about his mouth and jaw. Mary plays with the idea of trusting him, of telling him what she's never breathed to a living soul.

She could start with how she knew about him and Lavinia, how she managed to witness their little excursion, the pair of them dogging their hired expert, plotting to take down the bog. Or she could go further back, to how she learned the bog's history—its evolution flashing before her eyes, compressed like the life story of something about to die. No, she'd have to go further still. How could he begin to believe her—to understand what she was saying, even—without knowing how it all began?

It was spring, perhaps a month before she would turn twenty. One step the moss was solid and the next she was sinking, up to her waist in a hole. She should've hauled herself out immediately—she knew how fast the bog could suck a body down—but for some reason she held perfectly still, letting the water creep coldly up her legs.

Castor had spoken of the bog water often, telling her how it preserved things like pickles while it tanned them like hides. "That's history down there, Mary. Whole moose and marten and lynx, animals we got no names for, ones we never even seen."

She didn't plan it, just cupped her hands and dipped them and drank. It was unlike any water she'd known, brown and gritty, with long slimy strings, and so acid it burned her tongue. In an instant her bearings were gone. A dark wave came crashing, forcing her to shut her eyes.

It was a simple vision, brief and still. The woman was curled on her side as though sleeping. She'd bloated up badly, turned all coppery from the tannin—her skin, her dress, her hair. Her eyes were closed, her mouth wedged open with peat. Even her teeth were red.

Mary had never owned a mirror, but she'd caught sight of herself in enough shop windows and little pools to know. She wasn't frightened. It was a comfort to be shown where she would one day rest.

Dragging herself out of the sinkhole took every ounce of strength she had. She had to lie face down on the moss for ages before she could manage the short walk home. Stepping into the empty house, she felt a flood of sadness, followed by an eddying sense of relief. She was glad not to have to tell Castor. It would have grieved him to learn he'd passed the gift along.

AN UNVEILING
(clare)

The teacher can see now how the frames deceive, how an arm sprouts in one panel and grows under the black border to the next. Mere roads across country, these lines, the land carrying on beneath.

It's impossible, she knows, for anyone to have done this, let alone a disturbed child of three. Each segment its own conception, drawn separately, yet somehow designed to be cut free and mated to make sense on all sides. *Savant*, she thinks. Human calculators, mnemonic miracles, a blind slave boy at the piano, separate songs in his cotton-flayed hands.

I lift up a finger and point. She understands me, touches several fragments until I signal by letting the gesture drop. She picks up the next piece, handling it carefully so as not to disturb its design.

PAPER BIRCH
(betula papyrifera)

When Mary approaches again to examine his eyes, Carl reaches up impulsively, instinctively—as an infant would. His fingers brush one of her breasts. She doesn't lean into him, doesn't pull away.

"You want to know why I made all those scrolls?" she says quietly.

He lets his hand drop. "Do I have a choice?"

"Have you thought about what it would look like, Reverend? What would actually happen if you were to tear out this bog?" He feels her settle beside him on the bed. "They're felling the trees, nests and all, the eggs and fledglings smashed. The parents are circling and screaming overhead—"

"All right." He folds his arms over his pounding heart. "I get the idea."

"But the birds are just the beginning. All kinds of animals go down with the forest—least weasels, fishers, martens. Moose and black bear stampede for the borders, only to find nothing but farmland or road or town. Then come the stumpers, ripping up dens as they go. Cutters slash up the peat, and a million trails through the litter get sliced to ribbons, the lifelines of the voles and the mice, the shrews and the wood frogs and the hares. Of course, they don't need those lifelines any more, because they fall under the cutter blades too, and get crushed or split nose to tail, and even the ones that somehow escape end up drowning when the bog water rises to fill the wounds. Next comes the giant vacuum, sucking up the centuries, all the old bodies—the birds and the beasts and, hell, a few people too. Not to mention the newly dead. Talk about your Apocalypse. Maybe not rivers of blood, but there'll be plenty of it flowing all the same."

He gives in to the picture, covering his face with his hands.

"Don't touch, Reverend."

"Could you please," he says weakly, "please stop calling me that."

"What, *Reverend*? Isn't that what you are?"

"My name is Carl."

"Okay." She lays a hand on his heaving shoulder. "Carl."

8

oo-hoo!" The time-bird gives the last of five big cheers as I ease the final fragment into place. Standing on the coffee table, the teacher looks down over the big picture on her floor. It's all there, Preacher—your story, and mine, and even a few pieces of her own. The medium may be opaque, but like me, she's acquired the knack of looking through.

She works quickly, holds up the roll of Scotch tape for my permission, then begins fixing strips along borders, reinforcing the whole. I hold out a splayed hand and she nods, tearing several short pieces on the tiny plastic teeth, sticking them to my fingers' blunt tips.

Every panel secure, the teacher lays a large white sheet over my work and proceeds to roll. "We'll take it to show Daddy, shall we, Clare? Show Daddy?" The narrative scrolls in on itself. Her hands nimble and strong, she ties it with one of your gifts, an unsuitably garish silk scarf.

It's too long for the car—she has to prop open the hatch and fasten it down. "Okay, Clare," she tells me. "Drawing safe." She scoops me up without thinking, and without thinking, I cling to her neck.

⁑

Carl drops into a deep sleep just before dawn, feels himself dragged up slowly on a line of soft, insistent cries. His eyes open stickily before he remembers they can't, swamping him in aqueous light.

"Mary!" he yells. "MARY!"

"I'm right here." A shadow separates itself and moves toward him, tall and sweeping as a walking tree. He scrambles to the edge of the bed, wincing as he blinks.

"Hey, can you see me?" She bends in close. Her face is watery. Light reaches down through her hair as if through a bed of shifting kelp.

"Yes." He swallows hard. "I can."

"Nice blue eyes you were hiding," she says, straightening. "Probably even nicer when the whites aren't red."

"Yes." He finds himself suddenly awkward. "Yes, I'm sure."

"I'm just feeding Junior." She moves away from him. "Want to watch?"

On the far wall the window is a square of gold. Beside it, something stirs—a smudge like a large grey cat.

"I can't," he mumbles. "I can't really see that far."

"So come closer."

Mary lifts a chunk of something dark from a lucent tin plate and brings it up to her mouth. She leans out tenderly, the smudge rising to meet her in a kind of kiss.

Carl looks down at his clenched hands, watches the fingers separate, become distinct.

331

"Shit, Carl," Mary says softly, "don't you trust me yet?"

He lifts his gaze. The house is a marvel. With all the churches he's toured, there's been nothing to rival this brilliance. He stands up, his legs wobbly, as though they, like his eyes, are brand new.

Up close, Mary is lovely. Her bare, lined face, the bruise at her jaw, the astonishing black mass of her hair. She steps aside to reveal Junior, bobbing like a wave in her nest.

She's bog-coloured—dead wood, live wood, lichen and moss—her plumage an illusive blur. At first Carl assumes it's due to his vision, only the rest of her is sharp now— olive-green bill, inner lids sweeping clear across bright yellow eyes. A slight breeze through the window lifts a few plumes and he realizes why focusing is so hard. Each feather is semi-transparent, the pattern shifting, layers deep.

"Here." Mary cuts a chunk of raw, powerful-smelling meat and holds it up to Carl's lips. He accepts without question. Sticks his neck out and gives it away.

ACKNOWLEDGEMENTS

My sincere thanks to the Canada Council and the
Manitoba Arts Council for allowing me the time to
write this book.

I'm grateful to the following people for sharing their
expertise: Monsignor Jaworski at Our Lady of Perpetual
Help; Dr. Robert Wrigley at the Assiniboine Park Zoo;
Jason Greenall and William Koonz at Conservation
Manitoba; Diane Boyd and Carole Boily at the Grey
Nun Archives, Saint Boniface; Doug Smith; the staff of
the St. Paul's College Library at the University of
Manitoba.

Thanks to Matthew and his family, as well as to Vicki
Hatt, for allowing me to observe and learn. And thanks
to George Plumb, who built the Glass Castle in the
Cowichan Valley.

Special thanks to my editor, Anne Collins, and to my
agents, Denise Bukowski and Janette Shipston.

To family and friends too numerous to name, I offer
my undying gratitude for your unflagging support.

Most of all, I'm thankful to—and for—my beloved
husband, Clive.

ALISSA YORK has lived all over Canada and now makes her home in Winnipeg with her husband. She is the winner of the 1999 Journey Prize and the Bronwen Wallace Award. Her first collection of stories, *Any Given Power,* won the Mary Scorer Award for Best Book by a Manitoba Publisher, and was shortlisted for the Danuta Gleed Award. Film rights to three connected stories from the collection have been optioned by Buffalo Gal Pictures. In 2001, Alissa won the John Hirsch Award for Most Promising Manitoba Writer.